Big Boys -The Legacy

Sidechick Blues Sequel

by Nikida Bellezza

Edited by Dan Owens

1

Big Boys -The Legacy   By Nikida Bellezza

First, and foremost I thank God for all that He has done, doing and going to do. I am far from perfect, but I am not far from His love. Thank you to my readers, those I know personally, those I've come to know, and those that I may never get to know. Thank you for giving me the chance to literally entertain you!

-Nikida

Big Boys -The Legacy   By Nikida Bellezza

This book is a work of fantasy fiction. In this book the reader will find frequent use of coarse language, sensitive subject matter, sexual content As well as other adult language and situations.

READER DISCRESTION IS ADVISED

Big Boys -The Legacy   By Nikida Bellezza

<u>**The Back Story**</u>

Georgetown, South Carolina, 1950

Cecil

As I stared at the Big Boy throne, I saw the three seats with three crowns sparkling against one another. Suddenly one seat is kicked away sending the crown sailing out into utter darkness.

"What is going on here? Who's there?!" I demanded to know.

That's when a hooded man walked out of a dark shadowy area and over to me. The man held out his hand, he was holding three acorns.

"What's going on?" I asked confused.

The hooded strangers cheeks as he knelt down and buried two of the acorns. The minute he stood back on his feet, two very tall oak trees sprout from the ground. I figured that the other acorn was still enclosed in his hand. Yet when he reopened his hand again, the acorn was gone.

"What happened to it?" I asked looking from his hand to his face.

The smile on the hooded strangers face faded and from nowhere he produced a gun that was aimed at my heart. Before I could protest, the trigger was pulled, blasting me into a black hole.

"Ahhh!" I shouted waking from my sleep.

"Cecil, baby, what's the matter?" my wife Tabitha asked awaking from her sleep as well.

"Nothing baby, go back to sleep." I said as I sat up and moved over to the edge of the bed. I buried my face into my hands trying to understand the dream. I knew that it was a warning, but from who, for what? I thought to myself.

"Baby, what is it?" Tabitha asked as she rubbed my back.

"Tabby, go to sleep sweetheart, everything is fine." I lied as I stood to my feet.

4

I left the room before she could say another word. I didn't want to get into a discussion with her over something that I could not explain. I didn't know if the dream were a warning, or the result of me eating greasy foods before bed. But it wasn't the first time I dreamed that I was killed, and more than likely wouldn't be the last.

I walked into the kitchen and put on a pot of water to make myself a cup of coffee. I grabbed a mug from the cabinet and sat at the table to wait for the water to boil.

A few minutes later I heard Ms. Elizabeth's heavy cane slowly stomping its way across the floor. Ms. Elizabeth was a woman who attended our church. She'd stay with us from time to time to help Tabitha with the children.

"Ms. Elizabeth?" I called out to her.

"Cee, what are you doing up at this hour?" She called out to me.

"What am I doing awake, what are you doing awake? Is everything okay?" I asked going out into the hallway to meet her. I lent her my arm as support and we made our way into the kitchen.

"Yes, yes, I'm fine. Just couldn't sleep is all. There's trouble in my soul, something big is coming." She said taking my arm.

"Big like what?" I asked as we entered the kitchen.

"I don't know, but seeing how you're awake at this hour, you must know it too." She said accusingly.

I helped her to her seat, and then I walked over to the stove to check the water.

"Have some coffee?" I asked.

"No, no, then I'll never get back to sleep." She declined waving her hand around.

"Okay, well I'm going to have some." I said as I started making myself a cup.

5

"A man can hide from many things, but sleep ain't one of them." Ms. Elizabeth said.

"You're right about that Ms. E, and that's what the coffee is for." I chuckled.

"Cee, come have a seat with me." She requested extending her arm out to me.

I grabbed my mug from the counter and walked over while stirring my coffee.

"Ma'am." I said encouraging her to speak what was on her mind.

"You and I both know that something troubling is in the air. Only I think you know more about what it is than I do." She spoke in a very serious tone.

"I don't know what's going on. I keep having these dreams where a crown is being stolen, a seed isn't being planted, and I'm killed." I said shaking my head as I felt my heart rate increase.

"What do you mean by a seed isn't being planted? What's happening?" Ms. Elizabeth asked.

"Well, in every dream someone is holding 3 seeds in their hands. In one dream, it was an apple seed, another dream a pear seeds, and in tonight's dream the seed was an acorn. The person would hold the seeds in their hand to show me that they exist, then they would either make a fist and the fruit would disappear, or the seed would be carried out of their hand floating away in a current of wind." I explained.

"Oh my." Ms. Elizabeth said now holding her chest.

"What is it?" I asked knowing that she was a very spiritual person which made her more in tune with signs and their meanings.

"Well first your crown is in danger, your seeds, your children, especially the boy child is in danger, and the seeds represent the children, and your legacy. Someone wants you and your offspring dead." Ms. Elizabeth said as her eyes became moist.

6

"I don't understand, why?" I asked as an eerie feeling fell around me like a cloak.

"Even upon being given the answer, you will never understand how the ones you trust could betray you." Ms. Elizabeth said.

"The ones I trust... Ms. E, I don't think I..." I started but was cut off.

"Send your family away at once! Tell no one where they are going. Don't even allow them to tell you. Tell Tabitha to take the children and flee." Ms. Elizabeth said as she grabbed my hand.

"Ms. E, with all due respect, it was only a dream." I argued.

"It was not a dream. It was a premonition of what's to come." Ms. E said sounding worried.

"So are the Big Boys at risk?" I asked wondering if I needed to call a meeting.

"No Cecil, the Big Boys *are* the risk." She said slowly as she shook her head.

I dropped back in my seat and stared at the elderly woman as though she had lost her mind completely.

"I don't know what it is that you have, that they want, but they plan to get it." Ms. E continued.

"This makes no sense at all." I said as I stood to my feet.

"Doesn't it? She asked.

"What if you're wrong?" I asked leaning down on the table.

"What if I'm right?" She asked back.

"Damnit Ms. Elizabeth! You don't just tell a man that he's going to be killed without being sure! You are a wise woman, but I'm afraid that you have no idea what you're talking about on this one. Arthur and Douglas are my brothers. They would not do what you say..." I shouted.

7

She went into the pocket of her housecoat and pulled out a small glass vessel filled with a clear liquid. She then went into her other pocket and pulled out a large wad of money and sat it next to the vessel.

I stared down at the contents in disbelief.

"What is this?" I asked looking from the contents to her.

"Cecil..." Ms. E began.

"Honey, why are you shouting, what's going on?" My wife said as she walked into the kitchen.

"Tabby, go back to bed honey this doesn't concern you! Ms. E, I've asked you a question. What the hell is all of this?!" I shouted.

"This has everything to do with her. She needs to know what is going on." Ms. E Said calmly.

"Were you sent here to kill me?" I asked in disbelief.

"Oh my gawd!" Tabitha whimpered as she covered her mouth.

"Yes, I was." Ms. E said somberly.

"No Ms. Elizabeth! This can't be true!" Tabitha cried out.

"Who sent you?" I demanded to know.

She lowered her head as tears began to fall from her eyes.

"Why Ms. Elizabeth? Why?!" Tabitha cried.

"*WHO SENT YOU*?!" I shouted waking the children.

"Ms. Tabby, please tend to the children while I speak with Cecil." Ms. E said. She obviously had some information that she didn't want to be revealed in front of Tabitha.

Tabitha stood frozen looking from me to Ms. E.

8

"Tabby, baby, it's okay. Go make sure the children are alright before they come in here." I said as I touched her arm.

Tabitha looked up at me with tear filled eyes. I gently touched her face before nodding towards the door gesturing for her to leave. She nodded her head and left the room.

"Talk." I said after hearing Tabitha opening the door to our daughter's bedroom.

"I was told that you are becoming a problem, and that you... must die." Ms. E said looking down as her words trailed off into a mumble.

"By who, and why did they get you involved?" I asked.

"Cecil, I can't tell you that." Ms. E said shaking her head.

"You'd better." I threatened.

"I'm a dead woman if I do." She said as more tears fell from her weak eyes.

"And I have nothing to lose" I replied.

"They threatened to kill my grandson, Ricardo." She said looking up at me accusingly.

I returned her stare, in a show of bluff that the mention of her grandson meant anything to me.

"Why would they do that?" I asked.

"Because they don't know, or they would've killed him themselves." She replied.

"Enough with the riddles. Talk old woman, I don't have time for these old adages and wives tales. Tell me what the fuck is going on!" I shouted.

"It's no adage, or wives tale Cecil. I know that Ricardo is your son! I know that you've been having an affair with Linda, my foolish daughter! But The Big Boys don't know. I thought it was why they wanted you dead, but no, apparently you pissed them off in a different way. Not only do they want you dead, they want your seeds wiped off the face of this earth! If I were you,

9

I'd play nice with me, because I am the bridge between your life and the afterlife." Ms. E sassed.

"If what you are saying is true, *Elizabeth,* then not only is my family in danger, but the life of your grandson as well." I said getting in her face.

"They don't know that Ricardo is yours." Ms. E said.

"And why would you ever tell them?" I asked.

"I wouldn't, his life, unlike yours, means more to me than anything in this world." Ms. E replied.

"So what is it that you want?" I asked realizing for the first time that she wanted to bargain.

"I will buy your family fleeing time, but in return, I want Tabitha to take Ricardo too. He must be as protected as your other children." Ms. E said.

"And what about Linda, she's supposed to just let go of her son without protest?" I asked

"She will have no choice. She either sends him away, or I tell Earl that Ricardo is not his son!" Ms. E exclaimed.

"And Earl?" I asked.

"You let me worry about Earl." She said.

I nodded my head as Tabitha came back into the room.

"Is everything alright?" She asked looking from me to Ms. E.

"No, it isn't. Come with me, I need to speak with you." I said reaching for her.

"Cecil, you don't have much time." Ms. E said.

'They're coming tonight?" I asked.

"No, but you will die tonight, you've already been given the poison. You won't last through the night. I'm sorry." She said as she stood from the table.

"You conniving bitch!" I exclaimed lunging towards her.

"Cecil! No!" Tabitha exclaimed grabbing my arm.

"Don't waste your time hurting me, spend your last few moments with your wife." She said before heading out of the kitchen.

I dropped to my knees and lowered my head into my hands.

"Cecil, baby, what is she talking about. Cecil, what does she mean by your last few moments?" Tabitha asked frantically.

I was too angry, and too hurt to answer my wife. But I knew that I didn't have much time and needed to snap out of my fog of anger and regret.

I looked up at Tabitha, my beautiful wife standing there cluelessly, and helplessly. Her tears pierced through my heart like tiny daggers.

As much as I hated to admit it, Elizabeth was right, this isn't the time to be overcome with anger, this is the time to spend with my family.

I stood to my feet and took my wife's hand and wiped the tears from her eyes.

"Cecil, what's going on?" She managed to ask through quivering lips.

"They want me dead baby." I simply said.

"Who wants you dead? And why?" She asked.

I looked into her sad brown eyes and wanted to die immediately.

"My brothers, I don't know why, but it is so. Whatever the reason, it doesn't matter now, I've already been given the poison. It's just a matter of time now." I said.

"Oh my Lord, oh god, oh my god!" Tabitha broke down crying.

"Tabby baby, if I'm about to die, don't waste this time that we have left crying. I need you to be strong. There is more that I need to tell you, and you are not going to like it. But I need you

11

sober for this, because as I've said, I don't know how much time I have left." I said.

"Go on." She sobbed into my chest.

"The Big Boys want me dead, but not just me, they want all of my seeds dead. I don't know why they want to wipe out the Powers bloodline, and I don't have time to figure it out. But what I need you to do is take the kids and leave tonight. Run away as far as you can go and keep going. Never come back here." I said.

"But, I thought they were a brotherhood of peace, I don't understand, why do they..." Tabitha started.

"IT DOESNT MATTER, don't you understand, we don't have time to make sense of any of this baby. I just need you to hop in that car, take the kids, a get the hell away from here! Go, don't look back, don't come back and trust no one." I said grabbing her shoulders to get her to focus.

"So just like that, my life is supposed to just go on without you? Me and the kids are supposed to just pick up like it's okay that you're being ripped away from us?" Tabitha asked sobbing.

I turned her face up to look at me as I felt a tear drain from my eyes.

"We don't have a choice." I said.

She put her arms around me and cried hard into my chest

A few moments later we heard the side door open and close. We turned our attention towards the door to see Elizabeth holding her grandson Ricardo in her arms.

"What's going on?" Tabitha asked.

"Couldn't even give us a moment." I said looking at Elizabeth.

"You have 3 and it seems that you've already wasted 2 and a half if she doesn't already know what this means." Elizabeth sassed.

"Ms. Elizabeth, what is happening to you? I've never heard you speak with such a tone." Tabitha said.

"Will you tell her, or should I?" Elizabeth said ignoring Tabitha.

"Tell me what?" Tabitha asked looking from Elizabeth to me.

"Tabby, Ricardo is my son. He too is in danger, and I need you to take him with you and the children." I said looking from Elizabeth to my wife.

"No, Ricardo is Linda and Earl's son. Tell him Ms. Elizabeth." Tabitha said.

"What he says is true; I am so sorry Ms. Tabitha." Elizabeth spoke softly.

"This is too much. I can't handle this right now." Tabitha said as she walked out of the kitchen.

I followed Tabitha into our bedroom and closed the door behind us.

"Tabby, I'm sorry." I said for a lack of anything else to say.

"Oh you're sorry? You're sorry for fathering a child and then leaving me to raise him alone?!" She screamed.

"I'm sorry for cheating, I'm sorry for putting you in a position where you have to feel all the worse pain of your life all at once. I'm sorry for not seeing the plan for my demise. I'm sorry that I won't grow older with you, and I won't see our kids grow older." I said.

"NO, YOU DON'T GET TO FEEL SORRY FOR YOURSELF GOTDAMNIT! YOU DON'T! YOU'RE WRONG HERE! YOU CREATED THIS WHOLE MESS, AND NOW YOU'RE LEAVING ME TO CLEAN IT UP! HOW DARE YOU TRY TO MAKE ME FEEL SORRY FOR YOU?!" Tabitha screamed with so much force it caused her to tremble.

"Tabitha, we don't have time for this. She's already given me the poison; I can die at any

13

minute. Yes, I'm an asshole, I am a jackass, I'm all the things you want to call me, but I will not let you makes those your last words to me. I will not allow you to live with that regret. I love you more than anything in this life and the next. I have no excuse for the pain I've laid on your heart, none. But now there is a baby out there who needs your help to stay alive. If they want me dead, they will kill him if they ever discover that he is my son. Please, please, you are the most compassionate person I know, and I need you to step into that right now." I begged.

Tabitha looked at me for a few seconds before letting out a deep sigh.

"This isn't fair." She said finally said as she put her arms around my neck.

"I know, and I'm sorry that I have to ask you to mother a child that I created with another woman." I said.

"Not the baby, I can love him because he is a part of you. What's not fair is that I have to lose you." She said as new tears wet her eyes.

I leaned in and gently kissed her lips just as I felt my heart ripple out three heavy thumps.

I fell forward grabbing my chest.

"Cecil?!" Tabitha asked concerned as she sat me down on the bed.

"I think it's... it's happening... oh god." I said trying to talk.

"Oh Cecil, baby, what should I do, what should I be doing?" Tabitha asked crying.

"Tabby, quickly, go... go into the closet. Top shelf, get the brown chest." I said as I lie back on the bed trying to ease the pressure in my chest and stomach.

"Okay." She said as she ran around to our closet. She returned a few moments later with the brown wooden chest.

"This chest?" She asked holding it up for me to see.

"Yes darling, that chest. In there... you'll find some vital information, and I think... I think

14

it's what they're really after. Tell no one of this chest... or....... its contents. Guard it... with your life." I said coughing through my statement.

"Yes baby, anything you want. I promise." Tabitha said as she sat next to me on the bed.

"Now Tabby, I need you to.... pack up all.... all of the kids... and... get out of here.... tonight. Please, don't look back... don't come back... trust no one... and tell no one where you're going. Leave... get out of here... and never look back..." I said.

"Okay my love, okay!" Tabitha said just as our door was opened.

"The poison should be taking affect now. You all had better get going." Elizabeth said.

"Elizabeth, my husband is dying?! How could you even *think* of asking me to leave his side?!" Tabitha shouted.

"She is ... she's right Tabby, go, now, please." I struggled to say.

"I won't, I can't leave you like this!" Tabitha cried.

"Look here, you don't have a choice. They will be here soon, and they will kill everyone in this damn house! Get them kids and get the hell out of here!" Elizabeth yelled as she yanked Tabitha's arm to pull her up.

"Get your filthy fucking hands off me you old psycho bitch! You did this to him! You killed him! You did this to him! After we trusted you! After we let you in our home! You did this!" Tabitha screamed as she punched the elderly woman in the face.

"Tabby!" I tried to shout but my voice was lost in my throat.

"You pretended to be someone that we could trust, but all along you were a snake! A snake! And you have the audacity to sit here and tell me that I can't love on my husband! How dare you!" Tabitha shouted.

My eyes began to spin around in my head and I could barely make out what they were

15

saying. I knew that with my last bit of strength I needed to get to Tabitha to stop her from beating Elizabeth to death.

I saw a shadow of what looked like the shape of Tabitha walk away, and when she returned I heard someone scream.

"Tabby.....Tabby...Tabby..." I tried to say but to no avail. Either I wasn't being heard, or I was being ignored. A few seconds later I heard a loud boom sound. I knew that Tabby had shot Elizabeth. I tried to sit up but I couldn't move, so with every ounce of energy I could muster I screamed out.

"GIVE ME THE GUN, GET OUT!"

I didn't know how long it took, but I eventually felt the gun being placed in my hand. The last thing I remembered feeling was a wet kiss against my cheek before I succumbed to the darkness.

~~~~

40 YEARS LATER

Monterrey, Mexico, 1990

"Your coffee sir." Said Ariana the chambermaid as she leaned forward with her tray of drinks.

"Thank you Ariana, please, leave us." Art son of Arthur Jones I, demanded as he waved her away.

Ariana curtsied and exited the room as instructed, closing the doors behind her.

"So, what do you have for me?" Arthur asked his son after taking a sip of his well brewed coffee.

"Father, I've found Tabitha. She's currently living in Louisiana. After he Cecil died, that's where she ran with the children..." Art said

"And she took the Will with her no doubt." Arthur said interrupting his son.

"Yes, it was never found in the house." Art confirmed.

"And what came of the boy?" Arthur asked before sipping his coffee again.

"He's dead, died of some sort of sickness a few years ago, but he has a 15 years old son who's still in Tabitha's care." Art said watching his father intently, waiting for the words he knew were coming next.

Arthur nodded his head and looked around as though he were thinking of a way to handle the situation at hand. He knew what he wanted to do, he just needed to be sure that it was being done to the right person. He needed more proof that this Tabitha was in fact the woman they were looking for.

"You're not convinced." Art said sounding disappointed.

"Are *you*?" Arthur asked.

17

"How about now?" Art asked back after sitting two 5x7's of Tabitha on the table in front of his father.

Arthur sat forward nearly missing the table as he sat his coffee down off to the side of him.

"I'll be damned." He said as he slowly lifted one of the pictures.

"She's made a nice little life for herself out there. She owns a clothing boutique, drives a Mercedes, and she lives in an affluent neighborhood. Grace Harbor." Art said.

"Big Boy money?" Arthur asked looking up from the picture.

"That I don't know, but if she is, it's hush-*hush*. She doesn't seem to be connected. I think she's doing this on her own." Art said.

"Nonsense, I know he's left her something. No man would be fool enough not to see to it that his family survives upon his death.

"Well, there's still the Will." Art said cracking his knuckles. He was ready to get down to business. He, like his father craved power and became possessed men when it came to the acquisition of more power.

"The Will is important, this is true, but what we need more than that is the boy." Arthur said as he sat back in his seat. He knew that his son was ready to pounce, he groomed him well. But he needed him to keep a clear head. There was no doubt in Arthur's mind that he would have all that he sought to get. To him, life was like a game of chess, each move requiring intricate thought and patience.

"She lives very freely, as though she is comfortable and not fearful for her life. So getting the boy will not be difficult" Art assured his father.

"Then I tell you what. You take the lead on this one, but only the lead. Keep your hands clean, do you understand me?" Arthur asked.

18

By Nikida Bellezza

"Okay, so I am to recover the Will, and take care of the boy?" Art asked.

"Tabitha is a smart woman, the Will isn't going to be easy to find. But where there's a Will, there's a way, of this I am sure. Simply take care of the boy, and *I* will worry about the Will." Arthur explained.

"So for now just kill the boy?" Art asked again to be certain.

"Yes, it is a must that he dies." Arthur replied.

"Then I'll get right on it." Art said as he stood to his feet.

"Keep your hands clean. " Arthur said as he grabbed his sons arm.

"Yes father." Art said before walking towards the door.

"You can run Tabitha, but you can't hide." Arthur said with a smile as he lift his mug to sip more of his coffee.

"Grandpa! Can Deytwon and I go to the park?! Lil Marcus shouted as he and Deytwon ran into Arthur's study.

"There are my favorite two men. Come here boys, let me look at you!" Arthur said with an all new glow, as he swept Marcus up and put him on his knee.

"You two boys are going to be powerful men one day? Do you know that?" Arthur asked looking from Marcus to Deytwon.

"Of course! You tell me every time you see me!" Marcus said with a shrug

"How about you young man, do you understand this?" Arthur asked looking down at Deytwon who always seemed so serious.

"Yes sir." Deytwon replied with a head nod.

"One day, you two will run this world, and no one will be able to stop you. Allow no one to come between you, because a house divided cannot stand, and it can easily be conquered." Arthur said, speaking wisdom to the four year old boys as though they were grown men.

"We're brother's grandpa, always!" Marcus said.

"Always." Deytwon added still wearing his serious scowl.

Arthur looked down at Deytwon but didn't speak. Most children, including Marcus were very easy going and carefree, but Deytwon always seemed reserved and calculated. Like he knew and understood things that were far beyond the understanding of a child, and maybe even many adults. Even as a child he seemed powerful and uncompromising. But Arthur wasn't worried, as long as they trained the boys to love one another and to work as a unit, he knew that Deytwon would be an asset to his role in the Big Boys Organization, and a severe problem for everyone else.

"So can we grandpa?" Marcus asked snapping Arthur out of his thoughts

"Yeah, sure, you guys go get ready. I'll have Luis go out with you." Arthur said as he pressed a button next to his chair to call the butler.

"Yes! Let's go! Let's play Gi Joe!" Marcus yelled as he ran out of the room with Deytwon running behind him.

"We're going to the park dad, don't wait up!" Marcus shouted running passed his father.

"Don't leave the property!" Big Marcus shouted behind the boys.

"Son, it's a 150 acre park connected to a 300 acre estate. There's no way that they can leave the property. Besides, Luis will be with them, and there are always the surveillance cameras." Arthur said.

"Of course. How are you Grandad." Big Marcus asked as he moved into hug his grandfather.

"Arthur Cletus Jones the First. Nice to meet you" Arthur said extending his hand for

Marcus to shake.

"Here comes the point." Big Marcus replied with a chuckle as he met his grandfather's hand.

"I own and run half the world, and what's not mine, belongs to my kin. How am I doing? Just fine young man, just fine. Now, how are *you*?" Arthur said as he pushed the button on a remote to retract the curtains. The sunshine slipped in and spilled all across the room, revealing a large beautiful garden with a mountainous landscape in the backdrop. The sun sat just above the mountain top as though it were relaxing for a few moments. Arthur was always big on scenery, he needed something to look at while he tried to settle his thoughts.

"I've been well. How do you like life outside of the states?" Big Marcus asked as he took a seat.

"There's no place outside of HELL that I can't get comfortable or make comfortable. So to answer your question, quite perfectly." Arthur answered.

"Good to hear. So who's the woman?" Big Marcus asked nodding his head towards the pictures on the table.

"Awww, this my boy, is the key to our infinite success." Arthur said as he took up Tabitha's picture.

"*That* woman?" Big Marcus asked confused.

"Oh, right, you don't know who this is, do you? The woman that you see here in this picture, is none other than Tabitha Powers. " Arthur said as he handed his grandson the picture.

"So we've found her." Big Marcus replied as a smile crept his face.

"*We've* found her." Arthur confirmed as he rubbed his hands together.

By Nikida Bellezza

One Month Later

"If it breaks to the right, this game is ours." Arthur whispered into his grandson Big Marcus' ear as he prepared to putt.

Big Marcus chuckled. He swung the club and struck the ball just enough to force it into the hole.

"Excellent." Arthur moaned in approval before he turned to nod his head at his opponents.

"Good game." said Jim Rouger, their opponent, as he handed his clubs to his caddy

"So it was. I'll be looking forward to the transfer by Friday." Arthur said as he and the older gentleman embraced.

"Of course." He replied, then he and his grandson walked off to their golf car.

"Your game is getting a lot better, you're almost as good as your grandfather's." Arthur said as he and Big Marcus walked towards their carts as well.

"Yeah, I've been getting in a lot of practice in, ever since I started that club." Big Marcus replied handing his club to the caddy before stepping into the golf cart

"You play amongst your membership?" Arthur asked with a raised eyebrow. He didn't condone his heirs acting as commoners. He set a tone and expected them to follow it to a T.

"Of course not. I play on my own course. It's just that when I opened the club I figured I'd better know what I'm doing, if I'm going to be doing it." Marcus explained.

"Touché'." Arthur said just as Art pulled up in a gold cart being driven by the a member of his security team.

"Dad?" Big Marcus asked confused as he stepped outside of his cart.

"Father, son, a word please." Art said once he exited the cart.

By Nikida Bellezza

The men walked out towards the middle of the golf course to be certain that no one was listening.

"What do you have for me son?" Arthur asked knowing that if Art were interrupting them, he must've had a hell of a reason.

"One down, the Will to go." Art said with a sinister grin.

"The boy is dead?" Arthur asked liking his answers straight forward free of riddles.

"The boy is dead." Art confirmed.

"Perfect." Marcus said.

'Who took care of it?" Arthur asked.

"Ghost." Art answered.

"Excellent." Arthur said as he pat his son on the back.

The three men discuss a few more things before parting ways.

~~~~~

...Meanwhile in Louisiana

"Tabitha, I am so sorry for the loss of Rico, we loved him like a son." Marilyn said as she tried to comfort the grieving woman.

"They shot my baby in cold blood!" Tabitha cried out. Her heart was writhing in immense pain. Pain that she hadn't experienced since the day her husband was killed.

"Ms. Tabitha, I can't sit in this house, I have to get out of here. I'm sorry." Ashley said as she touched Tabitha's arm.

Tabitha looked up at the young girl and nearly fell to pieces. Her eyes were maroon and puffy from all the crying. She looked weak, as though she were ready to pass out herself. The worse part of it was, Ashley was carrying the baby of her now dead son. The poor young girl who was still early on in her own life, now carrying one that she will be forced to raise alone.

Tabitha took Ashley into her arms and held her tightly. Even though she didn't like that Ashley and Rico had conceived a life together at such a young age, she still loved the young naive girl nonetheless.

"Ashley, baby, go on outside so that Ms. Tabitha and I can talk." Marilyn said with a soft touch to her grieving daughters arm.

Ashley let go of Ms. Tabitha and walked out of the house without saying a word.

"I hope she's going to be okay, this is going to be so hard for her." Tabitha said sobbing.

"Yes, it will, which is what I need to talk to you about Tabitha." Marilyn said with ease.

"What is it Marilyn?" Tabitha asked in a more sober tone as she prepped herself to hear the worse.

Big Boys -The Legacy   By Nikida Bellezza

"Henry and I have been thinking, this neighborhood is getting a little rough, and now with Rico gone, Ashley may not stand a chance here alone. What with everyone pointing their fingers at her for being 14 and pregnant. We think that we would all do better if our family just moved away." Marilyn said.

"Oh dear God!" Tabitha wailed as she fell back against Marilyn. Marilyn opened her arms and comforted her friend.

Tabitha didn't put up the fight that Marilyn had anticipated. Truth be told, because Tabitha wasn't sure if her son being killed was random, or orchestrated by the Big Boys, whom she feared would always be in pursuit of her for the boy, she knew that for the safety of the baby, that it was best that they did leave.

A month later Marilyn and her husband Henry moved their expecting daughter to a row-house in South East, Washington DC. Three months after the move, Henry passed away from a heart attack.

Young Ashley took the death of her grandfather very hard and subconsciously linked it to the death of Rico, her first love and father of her child.

In the midst of all her pain, Ashley found solace in the 90's drug scene that was popping heavily in the streets of Washington DC. She finally succumbed to the lure of the streets after giving birth to a baby girl whom she named Angel.

*****

CHAPTER 1

Present Day

ANGEL

    I stood in the bathroom mirror and stared at my reflection. The chocolate woman looking back at me looked a bit perplexed but happy at the same time. Every so often she'd smile nervously as she'd look up from the pregnancy test sitting on the edge of the sink, which read pregnant. She was going to be a mother, something she'd never dreamed of being in a million years. But neither did she ever dream that she would become Queen over a powerful Brotherhood.

    I smiled at my thoughts as I gently rubbed my stomach. The only other time I remember being happier is when I married Deytwon, and now I was having his baby. It just didn't get any better than this. I have a sexy, handsome, strong, intelligent man, all the money in the world and now I'm pregnant with our first child. I didn't know if I deserved any of this knowing that I only came into it after being a side chick, but I damn sure wasn't about to let it go.

    "Baby, you in here"! I heard Deytwon ask as he entered the bedroom.

    "Yeah, I'm in *here* Dey!" I called out to him as I grabbed the pregnancy test and held it behind my back.

    "Oh, I've been looking all over the house for you. I'm heading out to Chicago to attend a business meeting, wanna come?" He asked after kissing me.

    "Well, do you have to go today?" I asked as I walked by him turning around to avoid showing him the test.

    "Not really, not if you need me here." He said as he sat in a chair after following me out of the bathroom.

"Well, you know I need you, but that's not the reason." I said sitting in his lap and placing my arms around his neck.

"Oh, somebody is feelin' some kinda way, huh?" He asked as he kissed my neck.

"Always." I replied enjoying his lips on me. Then I felt him rub his way up my arms and onto my hands.

"What's this?" He asked pulling away from our kiss.

"Well baby, I've been feeling under the weather and so, I took a pregnancy test." I admitted.

Deytwon looked at me as he took the tester from my fingers before dropping his eyes down on the results.

"Baby" He said as a huge smile eased across his face.

"Yes, you're going to be a daddy." I replied.

He stood to his feet and swopped me up into his arms.

"Why does God keep blessing me, who *am* I?' he asked looking into my eyes.

"Why wouldn't *HE*?" I asked as I touched his face.

He looked at me lovingly before moving in to kiss my lips.

"I love you more than life itself." He said after pulling away.

"I love you, and I just want to say, thank you for rescuing me, thank you for bringing me into and helping me survive in this life. I wouldn't have imagined in a million years that I would be this woman, and loved so much by a man like you. It's like a dream that I'm so afraid to wake up from." I said as tears fell from my eyes.

"Everything about your life before *was* a dream, *this* is you awakening from that dream. This is the life you were always meant to live. Don't be afraid to go all in and live it to the fullest."

Deytwon said wiping my tears away.

"Can you believe that we're going to be parents? I'm going to be someone's mother!" I said as I turned around to look at myself in the full length mirror. I smoothed my hand down the front of my shirt, over my stomach and imagined feeling a baby moving around inside.

"You're going to be a great mother. I couldn't be happier that we're starting our family now. It's the norm for Big Boy Leaders to stop having children after the first boy is born. Actually Marcus and I were deemed to be *good luck*, because we were both born male, and born in the same year. But if you don't mind, I would love to have a whole church of kids with you." Deytwon said as he walked up behind me and put his arm around me.

"So you want a big family?" I asked looking at him in the mirror.

"As big as you allow. I would love to have a house full of children." Deytwon said.

"Okay, let's do it." I said turning around to face him. He leaned in to kiss my lips, then swung me around in his arms.

~~~~~

Chapter 2

MARCUS

Milan, Italy

"Excuse me, Mr. Jones?" Katrina, my stewardess said interrupting my call.

"Give me a sec Fi." I said before looking up at Katrina.

"I don't mean to interrupt, but we have arrived safely in Italy, and Prime Minister Ricci is standing just outside waiting." She said with a smile

"Thank you Katrina, as always you've made this the perfect flight." I said as I zipped my pants.

"My pleasure." She replied before walking away.

"Wow, you couldn't wait for me," Fina asked reminding me that she was still on the phone as I watched Katrina from the back.

"Cut that out, every main course needs an appetizer." I replied as I stood to my feet.

"*Amante*, I am a top *cucina*!" She moaned. I loved when she spoke Italian words, they made her accent sound even sexier."

"Indeed. Let me get off this plane. I will be by to see you around seven, be ready, and you know all of what that means." I said.

"I do, I know exactly what that means. Ahh yes, I must go now too. Mi papa has asked me to escort a Powerful Dignitary around." Fina sighed." She replied.

"Powerful?" I asked hearing my trigger word. I walked over to the door to my private plane just as it was opening.

"Yes, he's here now, I will speak with you later Papi." She said before ending the call.

I smiled as I adjusted my suit and tie, then I nodded at the pilot to open the door.

I slipped on my shades as I stepped out onto the staircase to exit my plane

"Welcome to Italy Mr. Jones." Said a woman who stood at the bottom of the stairs

I nodded at her, and then turned my attention to the back door of the black Lancia Thema parked a few feet away.

The chauffeur opened the door and out stepped PM Corrado Ricci. I watched as he declined the chauffeurs attempt to dust his suit, and instead pointed him in the direction of the car just behind his.

"Mr. Jones, it is a pleasure to have you here. If there is anything that you require at any time, please only ask." The woman said with a head bow as I stepped onto the ground.

"I will hold you to that madam." I smiled.

"Mr. Jones, welcome!" PM Corrado Ricci said as he walked over to me with his arms stretched out.

"Everywhere I go." I replied giving him a slight embrace.

"Indeed, indeed. I would like you to meet my beautiful daughter, Fina. Come Fina, I would like you to meet Mr. Jones. Mr. Jones will be visiting Italy for a few days to conduct some business." Ricci said thinking that he was introducing us.

I smile at her and stuck my hand out. Her eyes grew wide for a few seconds before she pulled on her game face.

"Nice to meet you Fina." I said as she met my hand.

"You as well Mr. Jones." She replied giving my hand a gentle caress.

"I'm trying to talk Mr. Jones into joining us for dinner tonight. Why don't you tell him

30

how delicious the cousine will be." Ricci said looking at his daughter.

"Unitevi a noi per la cena." She said smoothly. (*Join us for dinner)*

"Sarei onorato." I replied to the shock of Ricci and Fina. (*I would be honored*)

"Oh, so you speak Italian." Ricci asked amazed.

"Ottimo." I replied. (*very well*)

"Magnifico. So will you join us for dinner?" Ricci asked.

I raised my hand in the air signaling that I was ready for my car to come forward. Seconds later my Lambourgini Aventador pulled up.

"I tell you what, I'm going to get settled in at the Armani, grab a shower, some food and a little chill, and I'll let you know." I said as the chauffeur grabbed my bags and opened the door for me.

"That's fair. You get settled, I'll send Fina along so that she may give you a tour while you are here." Ricci said.

"Well, she can come now, maybe show the sights that are along the way to my hotel. Then I can send her back in my car." I suggested.

"Uh, okay, I suppose that will be alright. This way she can get to her party that she's been so anxious about a little earlier." Ricci said looking over at Fina.

"It is okay with me if it is okay with you Signore." Fina said speaking with a heavy Italian accent that she didn't use while on the phone with me a few minutes ago.

"Excellent, lets ride." I said holding my arm out for her to get into my car.

31

"Magnifico! If I do not see you before you part. Please, enjoy your stay in Milan Italy." Ricci said.

"I intend to." I said as I climbed in the car behind Fina. As soon as the chauffeur closed the door Fina jumped on my lap and started pulling at my clothes.

"Damn shawty, can we at least get away from your dad before we go all in?" I asked with a chuckle.

"Like you care." she mumbled between kissing my neck and pulling my dick out of my pants.

"I really don't." I said with a laugh as I gripped the back of her head pulling her off of me.

She looked up at me smiling; she loved it when I was rough with her. Her threshold for pain was insane.

"Get on your knees." I demanded.

"Only if you promise.." She said seductively.

"The only thing that I promise is if you fuck me over, you and everything you love, will die." I said.

"And that you'll spank me with this!" She sang unphased as she snapped my belt in the air.

"Crazy bitch, I didn't even know you had that. Now I *got* to beat you." I said as I shoved her onto the floor and yanked up her dress. She giggled and pulled her panties down and slapped her own ass.

"Right there papichulo!" She exclaimed.

I shook my head before whacking at her a couple times. S&M wasn't my type of shit, but it turned her sick ass on like a muthafucka.

"Fuck this shit, I'm horny, put this dick in your mouth." I said as I tossed the belt to the side.

"Awww papi, it was just getting good." She wined.

"Yeah, for you. But I'm not here to get you off, it's quite the opposite. Now, my dick ain't gonna suck itself. If it could, I wouldn't need you here at all, would I?" I asked quite frankly.

She pretended to pout as she got on her knees

"It would be my pleasure, to pleasure you, Misier Jones." She said seductively before taking me into her mouth. She sucked me off during the entire ride to the hotel, bringing me to orgasm twice and swallowing me whole both times.

When the driver stopped the car, she jumped up and cleaned her face.

"So are you ready for a few hours of the best sex of your life papi?" She asked rubbing my dick.

"Maybe later. For now I'm 'bout to go up in here, clean up, and chill." I said as the chauffeur opened the door for me.

"What? I'm not coming with you?" She asked shocked as she grabbed my arm to keep me in the car.

"*What*, you thought you *were*?" I asked curiously before stepping out of the car,

"But I thought we were going to have a sex session." She said after stepping out of the car behind me.

"But, I got *mine*. You didn't get yours?" I asked glancing at the chauffeur who headed towards the hotel entrance with my bags.

"You know I didn't get mine. You didn't fuck me!" She pouted folding her arms across her chest.

"Aww shit, well maybe next time.." I started before grabbing her throat with a death grip and shoving her against the car.

"You try to rob me, I will murder your ass. Don't get me fucked up with the rest of the lames whose dick you keep in your mouth." I said as I snatched my wallet out of her pocket with my free hand.

"You *dare* put your hands on me? Do you know who *I* am? Do you know who my *father* is? We can have you killed before you make it to your room, *nigger*." She said with a sick smirk.

"Oh yeah? I'm a nigger, and I don't know who you and your father are? Then why don't you show me right here, since I won't make it to my room." I said grabbing her by the back of her head forcing her back into the car face first. She was about to get a lesson on who the fuck Marcus Jones was, and a little bit on how this nigger got down.

~~~~~

DEYTWON

'Baby, I know that you're busy, I wanted to tell you that I love you and that I am so proud to be carrying your baby inside me. Have a great day sexy!' Read the text Angel had just sent.

"Mr. Richards, hello?" Priscilla called out to me. We were having a video conference when my mind had become sidetracked by Angel's text.

"Yes Priscilla, carry on." I said after clearing my throat.

"Is everything okay sir? There's nothing that I need to discuss that can't be turned into a report and faxed right over if you're preoccupied." Priscilla assured me.

"No, I'm good, carry on. Although I would like to see these facts in writing as well." I confirmed.

"Of course sir. Well, now that your properties in Manhattan are ready to be leased it seems you've caused a bidding war. On the list are Michael Vandt Co and George Whelin Co. Their bids did however scare off smaller companies like Franklyn Horace and Douglas Z." She said flipping through paperwork. Also, Michael Vandt, George Whelin and Nan Stewart are in a bidding war over your property in Brookville." She said.

"Excellent." I replied with a smile.

"So how long before you make a decision?" She asked knowing what my smile meant.

"Well, let me take a look at the numbers and I will get back to you on that. Meanwhile, it seems like you have New York on lock for me, once these two major deals close, you can expect a fifty percent raise." I said.

"Oh my, thank you so much Mr. Richards. That is very generous of you." She said.

"You work very hard for me, you deserve it." I replied as I jotted down a reminder about her raise.

"Sir, I can work a lot harder for you by covering more of your properties outside of New York." She said.

"I appreciate your eagerness to assist me further, however, I make it a point to never allow left hand know what the right hand is doing. I cover all of my properties, I don't need anyone else to." I replied.

"Understood sir.

"Well, in other news the congressional leader Allen Sparks has invited you to his leadership luncheon next month, and Governor Frederick Tillary is still waiting to know your position on backing his scholarship fund." She said.

"Would you consider going to the luncheon in my place?" I asked knowing that I would not attend. I like my power felt, not seen.

"I'd be honored sir." She replied.

"Great, if Tillary calls again let him know that I'll be in touch. Then message me right after." I said.

"Yes sir. Well, that's all I have for now, is there anything that you need assistance with at the moment?" She asked.

"No, that will be all." I replied.

"Okay, well talk to you soon, have a good one." She said with a wave.

"You also." I replied before flipping to my next conference.

"Hello Mr. Richards, you're looking well." Said Zachary the young man in charge of my properties in Northern Texas.

"Thank you, so what you got for me?" I asked.

"Well, Michael Vandt co has severely outbid Savannah Holtz for the lease in Frisco. They also outbid Kirk Schmire co for the property in Plano." He said sounding pleased.

"Excellent, get those numbers to me by the end of the day." I said.

"Not a problem. Also you've successfully acquired the properties in Allen and Mickinney. I have that information right here as well. Other than that, your Young Entrepreneurs Society, bka, *YES*, is booming. The sponsorships are pouring in and the list of potential recruits is growing fast from all across the country." Zachary announced.

"Perfect, this is in your jurisdiction, so I expect you to keep an eye on it and to keep me abreast." I said.

"Of course Mr. Richards. He replied.

"So when can I expect literature on these developments?" I asked.

"Within five minutes of the close of this conference, sir." He said.

"Well then, keep up the good work and I will talk to you soon." I said.

"Yes sir." He beamed before I flipped to my next conference.

"Good afternoon Mr. Richards, you're looking well." Said Sheila, manager of my properties in Michigan.

"One hundred points for Sheila. So, what you got for me?" I asked.

"Well, Michael Vandt Co is scheduled to sign their lease tomorrow for the properties in Bloomfield Hills. Now, Johnathan Riggly Co has joined the bid for the property in Novi, and has since outbid George Whelin co, so as of right now the race is tight between Michael Vandt co and Jonathan Riggly co. " Sheila said.

"Perfect, anything else?" I asked.

"Yes, Michael Vandt is fighting you neck and neck for that railroad property. They've just surpassed your bid by twenty percent." Sheila said looking worried.

What she didn't know was that my money is endless but I didn't want to raise eyebrows by putting up a sum that 'ol Michael Vandtussen couldn't compete with. Michael was a ruthless businessman, he enjoyed bullying and acquiring smaller businesses and flexing his muscles during bids. He grew up with a silver spoon in his mouth and used his inheritance to turn it platinum.

"That's fine, raise it by thirty percent. If Michael Vandt co surpasses that, bow out." I said.

"Yes sir Mr. Richards." Sheila replied.

After speaking with Sheila I decided to give my broker a call.

"Hey, Mr. Rich, how's it going?" He asked always excited to hear from me.

"You tell me Scotty." I replied.

"Well, your stocks are on the rise, all except Concept Viral, that new tech company you invested in." He said looking through my portfolio.

"Yeah? They're folding?" I asked.

"Not quite, but they're not rising either, and for a tech company that's a little weird." Scotty said

"It is, so what is this, a mom and pop business or some dweebs in their basement on the come up?" I asked.

"Looks more like dweebs. You wanna pull?" Scotty asked.

"Not yet, just keep an eye on them for me." I said

"You betcha." He said jotting down a note.

"Okay on to the next thing. I want to buy twenty more shares of Michael Vandt co." I said.

"Twenty more, that would put you at forty-eight shares. Do I detect a silent killer?" Scotty asked jokingly.

"Are you asking me for an explanation?" I asked seriously.

"No sir, I apologize, I was making a bad joke." Scotty said as he straightened up.

"There's no time to joke when there is money to be made. I monopolize money, I don't play with monopoly money, got it?"

"Understood, so I'll put you down for twenty more shares in Michael Vandt Co. " Scotty said.

"Yes, ASAP." I replied.

"On it right away Mr. Richards." He said

"Okay, fax me the info by days end." I said.

"You will have it before you leave that soon sir." Scotty assured me.

"Perfect, that's it for now. Talk to you soon" I said

Scotty saluted me before I flipped to my next conference.

An hour later I leaned back in my recliner and put my feet up on the table as Carole, my assistant collected all of my faxes and put them in their proper categories.

"Excuse me Mr. Richards, would you like me to place these documents in the file cabinet, or will you be taking them with you tonight?" Carole asked.

"I'll be taking them all with me. Please place them in the limo for me, let the chauffeur know that I'll be down in a few minutes, after that you can take off." I said.

"Thank you Mr. Richards, have a good evening." Carole said as she grabbed the files tucking them under her arms.

"Good evening." I replied as I reached for the remote control to turn the screen back on. I figured that this would be as good a time as any to tell my dad about the baby.

"Son, what a pleasure. How are you, how's the wife?" My father asked after he appeared on the screen.

"I'm good dad, Angel is wonderful. How are you and mom?" I asked.

"We are wonderful, we're thinking of moving again. Your mom says Hawaii, I'm thinking Brazil." My father said.

"Really? Italy isn't doing it for you guys anymore?" I asked surprised.

"It's a beautiful place, we own a nice massive chunk of land that we've built a village on. But we're ready for something else, something new." My father explained.

"I gotcha, well change is good." I said.

"It can be, however, I know that you didn't just call to hold a one sided conversation about your mother and I. What's going on son?" He asked.

"Well, dad, we just found out that Angel is pregnant." I said through the widest smile that I could muster.

"Son, that is magnificent news! Another branch on the Big Boy tree! Amber! Amber, come into the courtyard, quick!" My father said as he pushed a button next to his seat to call my mother on the intercom.

"Douglas, is everything okay?" I heard her voice boom in through the room.

"I am on the phone with Deytwon, come here woman!" My father demanded.

"Oh, my baby, I'm coming!" My mother said.

"*Women!*" My dad said as he shook his head.

I chuckled at him enjoying every minute of it. I loved their relationship, always have.

"So how far along is she?" He asked.

"We don't know yet, we've made an appointment with the doctor, so we'll find all of that out Saturday." I said.

"Son, if this child is born a male, he will be your successor. This will be the first full blood born in the Big Boys Brotherhood. This is a very special occasion." My father said.

"What's an occasion?" My mother asked as she rode her cart up to my dad.

"Deytwon." My father said nodding his head towards me to share the news

"Good evening, ma." I said.

"Good evening my love, how are you, how is Angel?" She asked.

"We've already done all of this, get to the good part!" My father urged.

"She is fine, in fact, she is expecting our first child." I said with a chuckle.

"Oh my! That is so wonderful! Douglas, did you hear that? Our son is going to be a father!" My mother shouted as she stood to her feet.

"Nooooo, you don't saaaaay." My father said looking at my mother.

"Oh quiet you! Son, we are so proud of you! How is Angel, is she excited?" My mother asked.

"Very, we are both very excited about becoming parents. We're going to find out how far along she is in a few days." I said.

"Okay, well we have to call a meeting soon to discuss the ceremony. The ceremony is normally at 4 months, just after the sex of the baby has been determined. That way we'll know if we're embrocating the next King." My father said.

"How about 3 month from Saturday, on Big Boy Island?" I suggested.

"Sounds perfect, you notify Marcus, I'll speak with the other Elders." My father said.

"Okay, well, it was nice speaking with you all but I must be on my way. I love you both, have a good evening." I said

"Good night, son." My father said.

"Good night, baby!" My mother shouted.

I smiled before ending the video call with my folks. It was always good to hear from them and know that they were well and in good spirits. I just had one more call to make, and that was to Marcus, but that would have to come later, I was anxious to get home to Angel, we decided to go out and celebrate the good news.

After making sure everything was secured, I gathered my things and headed down to my awaiting limo.

******

CHAPTER 3

MARCUS

After violating every part of her, I shoved Fina out leaving her sprawled on the ground next to the car. She didn't moved when I stepped over her body but I knew that she wasn't dead, I didn't do enough to her to kill her. Not of course unless she died of embarrassment, as I recorded the entire thing. I knew that this would turn into something serious, as Ricci had big pull in the underworld as well as the political world, but it didn't worry me any, because his pull, was nothing compared to my own.

I walked into the hotel and adjusted my tie before being approached by a man who looked as though he was the manager.

"Mr. Jones, may I presume?" He asked.

"You presume correct." I answered waiting for him to get to his point

"Welcome to The Bulgari. Thank you for gracing us with your presence. It is always a pleasure servicing a Big Boy, sir. I am Salvatore Marino, the manager, and I am at your service." Salvatore said.

"Thank you, I appreciate that." I replied.

"Here is your key, and the bell hop has already taken your things to your room. You are all set up in the Superior Suite. Please, if you need anything, don't hesitate to ask." Salvatore said.

"I never do." I replied removing the key from one hand and then shaking money into his other hand.

"Sir, you are most kind." He said after peaking down at the money. I chuckled before walking away.

I pushed the button on the elevator just as I heard the sound of a siren pull up to the hotel.

"Lei è ben!" A woman shouted as she and others rushed to the door.

"Oh no!" shouted someone else in the crowd.

"Lei è Fina Ricci! La figlia del primo ministro Ricci!" Shouted another woman as she bent down to get a good look at Fina. (*she is Fina Ricci, daughter of Prime Minister Ricci*)

Fina looked around at the spectators as pictures were being taken of her. She tried to scramble to her feet but fell on her butt. The ambulance crew ran to her side and hurried her inside the ambulance.

When the doors to the elevator opened I stepped inside and hit the button for the Superior suites.

~~~~~

ANGEL

"Hello?" Salisha asked answering the phone.

"Yes girl, are you sitting down?" I asked as I lay back on my bed.

"No, I'm walking towards L'Enfant Plaza on my way home from work. Why, what's going on?" She asked.

"Damn, I miss DC." I said more to myself.

"Chick please, you good. Plus, you ain't never got to work another day in your life, you're doing alright! Now what's going on?" She asked.

"Whatever, so anyway!" I said.

"*ANGEL!*" Salisha shouted.

"I'm pregnant." I blurted out.

"*OHHH MYYY GAAAAWD!* Girlah! I just knew it was a matter of time! Oh my gawd! I'm so happy for you! Congratulations!" Salisha screamed into my phone

"Thank you girl! I am so excited! I can't believe that I'm about to be somebody's mother though. Me, just six years ago I was damn near living on the streets, swearing to god that I would never push a baby out!" I said ready to cry thinking about my past.

"You are not that same girl, you are a grown woman who has come into her own. You are doing great, and you are going to be a great mama! Oh my gaaaaaaawd I can't believe my girl is pregnant! What you got going on this weekend, I'm coming up there!" Salisha said.

"Nothin just chillin, come on up, I'll send you a ticket." I said excited to hear that my girl wanted to come be with me to share my excitement. Before Deytwon came around Salisha was the only family that I had. She took me in and let me stay with her after my grandmother passed.

45

I don't know if Deytwon or Marcus for that matter, would've ever found me if I had been living on the streets.

"You're always trying to pay somebody's way. I ain't broke, I will get my ass on the greyhound and I'll be there. You just meet me at the station!" Salisha said.

"I'm not calling you broke. Stop being defensive, after all you've done for me, it's the least I can do." I said seriously.

"Angel, you are my girl, you needed a place to stay, and I had one. What was I supposed to do?" Salisha asked.

"Whatever, you can't just let me have a moment can you? Anyway, so what you been up to?" I asked.

"Shit, just my job and my husband. Anthony said he's ready to start a family, girl he's really been pushing." Salisha said.

"Why does he have to push, you ain't wit' it?" I asked confused.

"I mean, I am, but I'm not. I just don't see what the rush is. We're married today, we'll be married for the rest of our lives. Why do I have to just jump up and have a child right now?" She asked.

"I mean, you don't have to jump up and do it, but you do ji' wanna do it before you get to old to run around with them right? I mean, thirty is right around the corner, and you know it's all downhill after that." I teased.

"Chick please, thirty is still five years off for me, I'm good. Just 'cause you jumped out there don't mean everybody else have to." She said with a chuckle.

"Many men, many, many, many, many men, be hatin' on me, lawd I don't cry no mo', don't look to the sky no mo'. Have mercy on me, have mercy on my soul, don't let my heart turn

cold..." I sang.

"You so dumb! Oh by the way, before I forget, I'm throwing a birthday party for Anthony

at. I'll try to give you all the deets in advance so that you can come through. It should be real

nice." Salisha said.

"Cool, you know I'm there." I replied excited to have an excuse to revisit my old stomping

grounds. I loved our life in New York, we lived in a very upscale community, but I missed DC.

"Aright girl, well let me get up in this station, I'll call you after I make the arrangements

to let you know what's what for this weekend," She said.

"Okay, aright lady, talk to you later." I said.

"Later babe." She said before ending the call.

I tossed the phone on the bed and headed to the bathroom to take a shower. I knew that

Deytwon would be on his way home soon and I wanted to make sure I was ready. Otherwise he'd

get comfortable waiting for me and start moving sluggishly.

By the time I finished styling my hair, Deytwon was walking through our bedroom door.

"Uhm, excuse me Miss, you're beautiful and all, but where in the hell is my wife?"

Deytwon said as he pulled off his cufflinks.

"Oh, that chick? She said she had enough of you and decided to run off. Luckily I'm here

to replace her. You see, I know what she has in you, even if she doesn't." I replied as I walked

over to him and started undoing the buttons on his shirt.

"Damn, I'm sure gonna miss her." He said.

"No you won't, I promise." I whispered with a soft lick to his ear.

I felt him put his arms around me pulling me in close to him. The smell of his cologne

47

radiating off him made me want to rip his clothes off.

I let go of him and grabbed him by the collar pulling him into a deep kiss

He raised his hands to cup and fondled my breast as he kissed down my neck. Seconds later I heard my dress being pulled apart.

"Baby you're ripping the dress, this is a *Gabbana!*" I said panting.

"I'll buy you another one." He replied in a husky lust filled voice as he continued to rip the dress from of my body.

I yanked his shirt down and off his arms and pulled his tee shirt over his head. He unhooked my bra freeing the ladies and proceeded to devour them as he walked me towards the bed.

"Get on your knees." He said turning me around to face the bed once we were there. I stepped out of my panties and got up on the bed as he undid his pants. Once I was positioned on my knees I felt him slip a finger inside me. He moaned as he played in my wetness.

"Damn baby, damn." He moaned to himself. Then he pushed himself inside and grabbed my hands holding them behind my back pulling me into a binding position.

"Uhhh... punish me daddie!" I demanded.

"Damn right!" He said as he began to pump in his long, deep strokes.

~~~~~

MARCUS

After I took my shower and got in some rest. I got dressed to head to my business meeting. I hadn't heard from Fina or Ricci since the incident, but I knew that eventually they would test me. Some people were born to learn shit the hard way, and I was the best teacher in the business.

After dressing, I looked at myself in the mirror from every angle that I could possibly be seen from. Once I was satisfied that all eyes on me would be satisfied, I grabbed my cell and left out of the suite.

"Good evening Mr. Jones, shall I call the elevator for you?" The bell hop who was assigned to my room asked.

"You know, that'd be great." I replied as I followed him over to the elevator where he pushed the button. The elevator arrived within seconds.

"That was quick." I said looking at the bellhop.

"Yes sir, this is your elevator, it is only to service you while you are here." He replied.

"It's like, it knows." I replied as I stepped on. The bellhop stepped on behind me and pressed the button for the lobby.

When we got to the lobby I shook a couple hundred into his hand and walked off towards the entrance where my car sat waiting for me.

"Good evening Mr. Jones." The chauffeur said as he opened the door for me.

I looked around and took a deep breath.

"Yes, it is." I said before getting into the car.

It didn't take long for us to arrive at my conference center, a building I had built to conduct business in, when visiting Milan. Very few people knew that I owned the building or the property that it was on, but I found it pertinent to always conduct business in my house, no matter where I was, because that would always make it on my terms.

The chauffeur parked the car in front of the building and walked around to open the door for me.

"Senoj's Conferenza, sir." The chauffeur said as he opened my door. (*Conference*)

"Thank you sir, your service has been immaculate." I said as I stepped out of the Lamborghini. I shook a couple hundred into his hand and walked over to the building where the doorman opened the door for me.

"Welcome to Senoj's Conferenza Centro. Are you here for the meeting with PM Ricci?" The doorman asked once I was inside. (*Conference Center*)

"Come again? Uh, mi scusi?" I asked. (*excuse me*)

"Yes, PM Ricci has called an emergency meeting commandeering the Conferenza. He is in the room now." The doorman said.

"Oh yeah. Okay, grazie!" I said with a wide grin. (*thanks*)

"So Ricci commandeers *my* building, and takes over *my* meeting, fucking up *my* business? This nigga really don't know about me, but he's damn sure about to find out." I said as I made a quick phone call.

"Sir Jones, it is an honor to hear from you. How may I service you today?" Asked Leonardo, head of my demolition team in Northern Italy.

"Yes, I'm thinking of rebuilding, and I need my Senoj's Conferenza building destroyed today in about 45 minutes. Can your men handle that?" I asked as though they had a choice.

"Yes Sir, anything for you sir. I'll get the team together now." Leonardo assured me.

"Excellent." I replied before ending the call.

I turned towards the doorman who looked frightened.

I pulled out two one hundred dollar bills and threw them at him.

"Get the fuck outta here." I said to him before walking off.

"Thank you sir, I promise to keep quiet sir!" He said after bending down to pick up the money.

"Why? I never asked you to." I said as I stepped onto the elevator and pressed the button.

~~~~~

DEYTWON

"Baby, I love when you come home and take it." Angel said with her lips brushing against my neck. She had collapsed on top of me after riding us both into a powerful orgasm.

"Do ya now?" I asked as I rubbed my hands along her body.

"Mmhmmm, yes yes, yesss!" She said as she sat up on me.

"Seconds?" I asked watching her dance on me.

"No, we gotta go eat!" She said as she slipped her fingers through mine.

"Awww baby, you still trying to do that?" I asked.

"Yes baby! We haven't had a night out in a while. Now that I'm pregnant we need to get in as much *us* time as possible. We'll never have these moments again." Angel said.

"Yeah, you're right. Let's go get in the shower." I said as I sat up.

"No, uh uh, we'll get in there, and start up all over again. We'd never get out of here. No, I'll get in the shower first, then you." She said with a chuckle as she eased off of me and headed towards the bathroom.

I admired her thick chocolate body as she sashayed towards the bathroom. The bounce of her ass was so hypnotic it took everything I had in me to keep from chasing her down. Shaking it off, I stood up to stretch, then I headed for the shower in my office.

I stood inside and allowed the hot water to beat down on me for a few moments as the steam started lifting Angel's scent from my body and into the air. I breathed in deeply as I lowered my head letting the water beat my neck and upper back.

I began to think of Angel and how she quickly became my weakness from the moment I first laid eyes on her in the library. She has no idea the power that she has over me, from her eyes, to her lips, her touch, her voice, her scent. It all drives me crazy. I would die and kill for her, easily and without second thought. Now that she was pregnant with my child, it made her all the more precious to me, while making me a more dangerous man.

After my shower I wrapped a towel around myself and walked back to the bedroom where Angel was still in the bathroom.

I walked over to the closet and used the remote hanging on the side of the wall to open the door. Then I pressed the button to start the rotation of the conveyer belt of my suits. I planned to take Angel on a helicopter ride to an exclusive restaurant on Catskill Mountains. The weather was perfect but even if there was snow everywhere, the outdoor restaurant was well heated and didn't even require jackets. I swear, the things they do for the wealthy.

It took me all of fifteen minutes to choose my suit and tie and to be completely dressed. Angel of course was just starting to put the finishing touches on her hair. I knew from experience that this meant she needed another forty-five minutes to an hour.

I decided to take this time to give Marcus a call to share the news of Angel's pregnancy. He and I haven't spent very much time together since the wedding, but we haven't had any issues either. Besides that, Marcus was and always will be my brother, through thick and thin.

I sat at my desk and called Marcus from my desk phone.

"Yo.." He replied answering the phone.

*****

CHAPTER 4

MARCUS

"Look gentlemen, it is our guest of honor, please welcome Mr. Jones." Ricci said as I entered the conference room where I heard the voices coming from.

"Now *that's* an introduction. You know what, I'm going to start having folks do that every time I walk into any room." I said as I took a seat at the head of the table.

"If you get another chance to, *eh.*" Ricci said pointing a finger at me.

"And that welcome. You know you've arrived when a muthafucka can make you feel welcome in your *own* place!" I said as I slapped my hand against the table in an exaggerated show of gratitude. I let my hands linger on the table for a few extra seconds to expose the Big Boy ring on my finger.

"He's in a good mood? I like this, I like this a lot. Well this is good, now let's get to the point of this little meeting, shall we?" Ricci asked.

I waved my hand at him to continue.

"Tell me Marcus, have you seen Fina lately? Last I saw her she seemed to be fucked up and disoriented, how was she when *you* left her?" Ricci asked as he walked closer to me and had a seat on the table.

"Marcus huh? Ricci, I understand that you're upset about your daughter, but that gives you no right to call me Marcus. Let's not get beside ourselves, my name is Mr. Jones." I said as I popped a grape in my mouth from the bowl sitting on the table. My original meeting was catered, which explained why the conference room was full of food.

"Listen here you little prick! I don't give a fuck what your name is! You put your hands on my family, I put my hands on you! Got it? Now, did you fuck over my daughter, or not?!" Ricci

54

Big Boys -The Legacy   By Nikida Bellezza

shouted shoving the bowl of grapes to the floor.

I looked down at the bowl of grapes that Ricci knocked to the floor, then back up at him.

"Is this supposed to evoke some kind of fear in me?" I asked arching my fingers.

"You see, the problem with you fucking Americans is that you're so fucking arrogant! You think you can shit all over everything and everyone, even in their own land. And the problem with you monkey Americans is, you think you deserve to live like the rest of us. Fucking Big Boys. I know who you really are! You savages started as slaves who came into some money. Your mamas probably sucked good dick. No, your fathers probably sucked the dick." Ricci declared before he and his men broke out in hearty laughter. So I laughed with them.

"Oh, the monkey finds it funny too." Ricci said looking between me and his men.

"Monkey huh?" I asked chuckling more.

"Yes, monkey, oooh ooh ahh. Or do you like the term nigger better?" He asked as the laughter stopped.

I went into my coat pocket and pulled out my cigar case. I opened it, retrieved a cigar, smelled it then closed the case.

"You know Ricci, Fina too had me fucked up and called me nigger once." I said pausing to light my cigar.

"So I made her say it again, and again, yeah, and again, while gargling with my seeds in her mouth." I said before taking a pull.

"Funny though, I guess she didn't like her reward because I never heard her say it again." I continued while blowing smoke from my mouth.

"You motherfucking cocksucker!" Ricci shouted as he stormed towards me.

"No, no, she's the cock sucker, I'm the cock suckeree... it was my dick, her mouth." I replied correcting him.

"Son of a bitch. Do you know who I am? I'm Carrado Ricci. I..." He started but I cut him short.

"Yeah, yeah, but do you know who *I* am? No? *Show him.*" I said. His guards all turned their weapons on him.

"What the fuck is this?" He asked shocked.

"According to you, some dick sucking slave shit." I replied..

"Che cosa sta succedendo qui?" Ricci asked turning to face his guards. (*what is going on here?*)

"Io sono più potente di te ." I answered him, speaking Italian as well. (*I am more powerful than you*)

"You won't get away with this you son of a bitch!" Ricci shouted.

"Get away with it? You really don't know me, do ya boy? I'm Marcus Jones, head of the Big Boys. Who gonna check me, and live? Besides, how will others like you learn if I don't send them this message?" I said as I put out my cigar against the table before standing to leave.

"Slaves, you monkeys were and will always be seen as slaves! My men were obviously weak, but one day you will meet your match, and he will murder you slowly! You will beg for death!" Ricci shouted.

"My *match*? Shiiit, I meet that fool every day. Oh, look, there he go right now. You plan on killin me homie? I asked myself looking in the mirror .

"Kill you, nigga please, you all I aspire to be in life. Fuck that nigga Ricci talking 'bout?" I said answering myself like a lunatic. Then I adjusted my tie and turned my attention back to Ricci who had turned beet red.

56

I smiled and winked at him before heading for the door.

"YOU'RE CRAZY! You're a crazy looney muthafucker! You belong locked up eating shit off the floor!! You monkey mother fucker!" Ricci shouted.

"Hmmm, I think after they make your body whistle, I'll have them mince you, and force feed you to your mother." I said as though it sounded like a great idea. Then I reached for the door knob.

"WAIT!" Ricci shouted behind me.

"You're in no position to bargain Ricci. You have nothing that I want, or couldn't have if I did." I said.

"Then why are you doing this?" He asked.

"Because no one kills a Big Boy, and yet, you tried to. You see, contrary to popular belief, I'm not an American, I don't belong to any place on this planet, because this world, is mine. And its inhabitants will do well to know it." I explained.

"I was only protecting my daughter." Ricci said in tears.

"If you really wanted to protect her, you should have taught her to be a lady, and not a tramp. Not that it would've mattered much, because if she was destined to cross my path, she would've become a tramp regardless." I said.

"Please, leave my family out of this. This dies here, with me." He said in a calmer tone. The mention of his mother sobered his ass the fuck up real quick.

"We'll see." I replied then I nodded at the gun men and left the room.

As soon as the door closed behind me Ricci went in on his once disciples.

"Mutiny, for a cold hearted dirty monkey nigger!" He exclaimed.

"Sorry sir, it's just business." One person spoke up.

"See you all in hell!" Ricci screamed as my elevator door opened and the gunshots rang.

Once outside I nodded towards my demolition team as I headed to my awaiting car.

"Mr. Jones." The chauffeur said as he held the door open for me.

"Take me to my plane, this place is through." I said to the chauffeur before stepping inside the Lamborghini

"Of course sir." The chauffeur replied closing the door behind me.

A few seconds later I felt my phone buzz.

"What do you want Tiff?" I asked aloud assuming that it was my wife. I took out my phone to see that it was actually Deytwon calling.

"Yo." I said answering the phone.

"What's good with that elusive man named Marcus?" He asked jokingly

"Oh you know he always out here fuckin something up." I said just as the building I had just walked out of exploded giving the car a jolt.

"Hey man, it wouldn't be you if you weren't." Deytwon said with a chuckle. He was in an unusually good mood.

"Who knows me better than you?" So what's good man, why you smiling so hard?" I asked.

"Just got some good news, man, Angels pregnant." Deytwon said.

'*What the fuck?*' I thought to myself.

"Yeah?" I asked trying to summons the sound of excitement.

"Yeah, we just found out. It's a little too soon to know if it's a boy or a girl yet, but man, the legacy continues." Deytwon said.

I shook my head. I loved Deytwon probably more than anybody in my life. He was the most real, most loyal and most fair person I knew. When our fathers bowed out and had us take over, the only advice my folks gave me was instructions on how to be ruthless. But Deytwon showed me what family was. I learned through him that someone can be trusted, and that there are loyal people out here that would have your back no matter what. I would do anything for him except, lessen my greatness.

Angel had more power than both Deytwon and me. Now that she was his wife, and about to give birth to a hybrid baby, the child will assume lordship over me and mine, I couldn't let that happen. I thought to myself.

"Hello, you still there?" Deytwon's voice snapped me out of my thoughts.

"Yeah man, my bad, just got to thinking about me and Tiffani. Congrats on that." I said changing my tone to sound happy for him.

"Thanks man. So we're gonna have the announcement ceremony in a couple months. I'll let you know all the details when I get them together." Deytwon said. I looked at the phone puzzled before answering.

"Right, well that's what's up man. I'm happy for y'all." I lied.

"Bet, thanks man that means a lot to me. Look Angel and I are about to have dinner so I'll get talk to you later." Deytwon said.

"Peace." I replied before ending the call.

"Ain't this about a bitch! Should've killed that bitch when I had a chance." I said to myself as we pulled into the field where my plane sat waiting for me.

The chauffeur opened my door and I walked over to board my plane. It was good that this was going to be a long flight, I needed to strategize my next move.

CHAPTER 5

ANGEL

"Heeeeeey girl!" Salisha said as she stepped off the bus.

"Hey!" I exclaimed as we embraced and spin around.

"Ohh, wait, don't wanna squish the baby!" She said as she let go and rubbed my stomach.

"You are crazy girl, come on let's get your stuff." I said as we walked over to where the driver was taking the suitcases off the bus.

"Excuse me, the blue one. No, the navy blue one. Yes, thank ya kindly!" Salisha said to the bus driver.

"Later country mama!" Said some guy as he walked by us.

"Aright Ked!" Salisha replied with a chuckle.

"Country mama?" I asked as we walked towards the awaiting Bentley

"Girl, I'm on a bus filled with New Jersey and New York people, so every time I talk they just gotta know where I'm from because I sound so country to them." She said dragging her bag along. I burst out laughing.

"I'm like, I know y'all seen me get on this bus in DC at Union Station, come on. So every time one of them hit me with that country shit, I started talkin' that up north slang they famous for." She continued.

"Oh nooooo." I said laughing.

"So you were the only one from DC or Maryland on the bus?" I asked as the chauffeur got out of the car and opened the trunk for Salisha's bag.

"Nah, there were a couple others, but they were older, they weren't paying us no mind. But all in all it was a cool bus ride, we basically laughed the whole ride up here." She said.

"That's good." I said after the chauffeur opened the door for us to get in.

"Girl, I can get used to this here, you don't have to drive or open your own doors? That's what I'm talking about!" She said once we were in the car and the door was closed.

"It's a helluva come up for a chick from the ghetto." I added.

"No doubt. So where we 'bout to go? I need a lil sip of something." She said.

"I know a place. Manny, can you take us to Roseo's." I said.

"Yes, ma'am." He said as he started up the car.

"So what's new, mommy to be? I know Deytwon's excited, he already know what school the baby going to, don't he?" Salisha asked.

"He's very excited, we find out how far along I am tomorrow." I said.

"Tomorrow? What am I supposed to do while y'all off doing that?" I don't know nothin' about New York, especially that uppity ass town y'all live in." She said.

"Chick please, you coming with us. And there ain't nothing wrong with Brookville!" I replied.

"Coming with y'all? How you work that one out? Deytwon cool with that?" She asked.

"He will be, when he finds out." I said.

"Oh nah, uh uh, you ain't about to pit me against him. Deytwon does not strike me as someone who likes things to be sprung on him. You won't be getting me carried." She exclaimed.

"You say that like he's abusive or something." I said.

"No, but he is a very serious dude, he be about his business and I'm not about to be the one who finds out what happens when you get in the way of his business. Nope, try again." She said.

"Whatever, then I guess you can just chill at the house until we get back, or we'll have a car take you on a tour." I suggested.

"Girl, I guess. So anyway, I told Anthony that you're pregnant, now his ass is really pressing me to have a baby. Girl I don't know what I'm going to do. He really wants to start this family, like right now?" She said.

"I still don't get what the problem is. Y'all both working good jobs. Y'all about to get a house. Got money in the bank, y'all doing good. What you waitin' for?" I asked.

She sighed and shook her head.

"What is it Salisha, what's going on?" I asked.

"I don't know. Once upon a time, I wanted to be a mother more than anything. I wanted to carry and have Anthony's baby as much as I wanted to be his wife." Salisha said looking out of the window.

"So what happened? I asked

"That's just it, nothing happened. I never got pregnant. At first I figured it was because we never really did it while I was ovulating. So I started paying attention and trying to do it mostly then. But months went by, hell, a year went by and nothing." She said as she shook her head.

"Have you been to see your doctor?" I asked. She looked at me as though I were stupid.

"Angel what kind of question is that? Of course I've been to see the doctor. They don't know what it is. They say I'm perfectly healthy." She replied

"Then maybe its him." I said for a lack of anything else to say.

"How, he has two kids already from two chicks he messed with before we even met. He's fertile, I just think its me." She said

"And what does he have to say about this?" I asked.

62

By Nikida Bellezza

"Nothing, because he doesn't know. No one knows." She replied.

"So why are you sharing this info with me, instead of your husband?" I asked confused.

"Because, I don't want to break his heart. He really, *really* wants us to have children."

Salisha replied

"So, you'd rather he just thought his wife didn't want to have children with him, rather than telling him the truth?" I asked.

"You know Angel, I wouldn't expect you to understand. Life always works out in your favor. No matter what you do, you never have to suffer any real consequences, and then, shit like this happens for you." She said pointing at the car, and holding my arm up.

"Okay, first of all, you won't be doing that. Don't turn this around on me just to avoid the bigger issue." I said.

"And what's that?" She asked with an attitude.

"You're hurt, disappointed and afraid." I said.

"What, how would you know how I feel?" She asked visibly upset.

"Because its exactly how I would feel. And I probably wouldn't want to tell you either." I replied calmly. She shook her head and looked out of the window bringing her hand up to her mouth before the tears started flowing. I pulled her towards me and held her in my arms.

"What kind of woman am I, if I can't even give my husband a child?" She asked crying.

"You're no less of a woman, it just may not be time right now. It's better to do things when its time, than before its time." I said.

"I just feel like a failure as his wife." She said.

"You wouldn't feel that way if you talked to him about all of this. Anthony loves you, and he will understand." I assured her.

"You're right." She said as she sat up and wiped her eyes.

"Of course I am, all my good advice came from you. Now let's get in here and get a drink up in ya!" I said as the chauffeur pulled up in front of the little restaurant.

~~~

Big Boys -The Legacy   By Nikida Bellezza

MARCUS

"So how did you enjoy your stint in Italy?" My father asked as I pulled my suspenders over my shoulder. He hit me on the video chat while I was getting dressed to visit a gentlemen club.

"Wonderful actually, it was all I dreamed it would be." I replied sarcastically.

"You've been before, Marcus." My father said sounding annoyed.

"Oh, then it was better than any visit I've had thus far." I said with the same tone as I put on my suit jacket.

"Okay, let me get to the point of this call. What was that all about with Ricci?" He asked.

"*Ricci*?" I asked pretending to be confused.

"One of the Prime Ministers. I got a report that he was shot to death and then the men who killed him were killed in an explosion at the Senoj's Conference Center." My father said.

"Say what now? That was on the news?" I asked.

"Because of the caliber of the hit, they wouldn't broadcast it on the news. The news simply reported that he died in his sleep." My father said sounding frustrated.

"You got a point here, I really have something I need to do tonight." I said stepping into my shoes.

"Marcus, it's important that our allies outweigh our enemies. Now, Ricci wasn't a very important ally, but Italy is. We don't want them to deem this move to be an act of disrespect." My Father explained.

"I have a question, what exactly makes Italy, an ally of the Big Boys?" I asked.

"The fact that The Big Boys have a seat on the board of The Italites, the group who runs Italy. They elect the ministers to position. Ricci was put in place, by them." My father said.

65

Big Boys -The Legacy   By Nikida Bellezza

"Well, I guess they'd better look for another pawn to play." I said as I started adjusting my tie.

"Son, you are in charge now, and you run things the way you see fit. But please don't carelessly sever the ties the Big Boys have established to keep us in strict power. We are amongst the few who control the world. But this is so, because of the ties that we have with the Brotherhoods that trust us to uphold the secrets of the old ways. When they've had enough, they get together and they vote. If they vote your Brotherhood out, they not only kick you out, they wipe you out. We have been involved in several votes and the demise of several once powerful Brotherhoods. Please be mindful that you do not cause us to be one of them." My Father said.

"I get you." I replied to shut him up. It became clear to me a long time ago that my father didn't know me very well. He offered advice to me as though he were giving advice to someone foolish. He either had little knowledge, or little regard for my insatiable craving for power. Because of this, I'd skip over him and seek advice from my Great-grandfather, the only one who seemed to share my power hunger mentality.

"Very well. In other news, Deytwon and Angel are expecting their first child, are you aware?" My father asked.

"I am, he called to let me know." I answered ready to be done with this call.

"It is customary for the next leadership to grow together. Are you and Tiffani considering children at this time?" My father asked.

"Pop, this is a can of worms that I'm not interested in opening right now. As always I enjoy our conversations, however I do have a rather pressing matter to attend to at the moment. So until the next time, give my love to mom, and have a good evening." I said as I walked over to my glass casing and chose a watch to wear.

"Very well son, have a good evening. Talk to you soon." He said before disappearing from the screen.

I walked to my cologne center and chose the brand that I wanted to wear, then I pressed the button to activate the spray mist. Dressing was probably my second favorite thing tied with fuckin. My closet is one of the largest rooms in my house. Inside there were separate sections for the different categories that I put my clothes, shoes and accessories in. It was equipped with a built in Travelator, as Andrew the decorator called it, which moved me around the room.

"I love my life." I said as I stepped out of the room. I then touched the nob to locked the door behind myself.

"Hey baby, I thought I'd catch you up here. You have a second?" Tiffani asked as she walked down the hall.

"For you, I got life without parole, what's good babygirl?" I asked taking her into my arms.

"Well, I just got off the phone with your mom, and she said that Deytwon and Angel are expecting their first child." She started then paused.

In my mind I rolled my eyes., but didn't do it in front of her. I knew that this was a touchy subject for her. But at the same time, I didn't appreciate my parents trying to tag team us to reproduce. We will have kids when I say so, and not a second before.

"*And*, baby, what's up?" I asked hurrying her along with her statement.

"So, don't you think it's time for us to start trying?" She asked.

I took her hands into mine and looked her in the eyes.

"No one rushes the Jones' to do shit. We will do this on our time, and our time only. Not every set of leaders need to be born within minutes of each other." I assured her.

"Yeah, but baby, I think I'm ready." She said.

"So let me ask you this, were you ready before you talked to my mother?" I asked testing her.

"Yes, actually I was." She replied.

"But you didn't think to say anything til now?" I asked.

"I just wanted..." She stuttered.

"Tiff, you know I hate when people stutter. It means they're lying, and I don't deal too well with folks who lie to me, least of all my wife." I said walking away from her.

"Marcus, you're not always the easiest person to talk to. I mean, we've been married for six years and not once did you bring up the idea of kids. I barely know that you want any, outside of the fact that you need them for the Jones bloodline." She said.

"When have I ever denied you anything you wanted?" I asked.

"Never, but this isn't just about what I want, it's about us, what we want for us." She said.

"A baby is a lot of work Tiff." I said.

"When its love, it doesn't feel like work." She said as she slid her arms around me.

"But I won't be able to be self-centered anymore." I said looking down at her. She started laughing.

"See, you don't get me, I thought you of all people understood me, but you don't." I teased.

"Baby, I get you, I got you and I have you." She said cupping my face in her soft hands.

"Aright babygirl, we can do this, but one thing, let's go all out. Let's away for a week. Just me and you, locked in a room that overlooks the entire Island." I said.

"That sounds great." She said.

"Bet, we'll leave next week." I said.

"Next week? That's not enough time for me to get everything I need together." She exclaimed.

"I don't know about you, but everything I need is up under these clothes. " I said tugging her shirt and sweatpants.

"You are crazy! Okay baby, next week." She said before kissing my lips.

"I love you woman." I said after pulling away.

"I love you." She replied.

"Aright baby, I'm 'bout to leave. See you after while." I said with a slap to her ass before walking away.

"Okay baby." She replied heading in the opposite direction.

I took the elevator down to the first floor of my home and went outside to meet the limo.

The driver took me around to the field on my property where I kept my private jet.

"Welcome aboard, Mr. Jones." Said Lisa, my private stewardess.

"Indeed, let the pilot know that I am ready to roll, then do me a favor and lose the shirt. I feel like flying topless tonight." I said.

"Excellent choice." She replied with a wide grin before disappearing to tell the pilot to take off.

"Would you like a warm blanket for your ride sir?" Lisa asked coming back almost as quickly as she left.

"Yes, but fix me a drink first." I said as my phone began ringing.

"Your usual?" She asked as she started unbuttoning her blouse.

"Yo?" I asked answering the phone as I nodded my head at Lisa.

"King Jomar, I received your alert." Said Dexter Alfini, my lower chair in the Italites Brotherhood. Being in an elite leadership position made me a King, Jomar was simply my Jones Marcus, which is something many didn't know.

"Sir Dexter." I replied.

"The mess is cleaned, King Jomar" He replied.

"Good, enjoy your evening." I replied before ending the call.

"Your drink, Mr. Jones." Lisa said.

"Why thank you beautiful." I said taking it from her. She then got down on her knees and started unbuttoning my suit jacket.

"And your warm blanket." She said.

"Why thank you beautiful." I said as I loosened my belt for her.

She undid my pants and pulled my dick out, then she made most of it disappear in her mouth.

By the time we arrived in Boston she had just finished riding me.

I loved being the man.

*****

CHAPTER 6

DEYTWON

"Yeah, Dr. Madison, how are you?" I asked as I took a seat on the balcony just outside the living room.

"Hello, Mr. Richards, I'm well, how are you and Angel?" She asked back.

"We are wonderful. I was calling to confirm the time you'll be coming by tomorrow." I said.

"Coming by tomorrow?" She asked confused.

"Yeah, for Angels' appointment." I said to jog her memory.

"I'm sorry Mr. Jones, I don't have you down here on my schedule for tomorrow. In fact I had planned to be away from my office all day." She said.

"Hmm, I thought Angel called you to let you know. We just found out that she's pregnant, and we wanted an appointment to let us know how far along she is." I said.

"Okay, we'll first, congratulations to the both of you. And second, I can be there tomorrow around, three in the afternoon?" She said.

"That works fine. I appreciate that, I really thought Angel made the appointment." I said.

"No worries, it's my pleasure." Dr. Madison assured me.

"Okay, see you tomorrow at three." I replied.

"Tah-tah." She said.

"That woman, I need to get her an assistant or something." I said as I tossed the phone into the chair next to me and sat back in my own.

"That's exactly what she need." I said as I reached over to grab my phone again.

"Hello, Mr. Richards." Emily one of my assistance asked answering the phone.

"Em, I need you to work something out for me ASAP. My wife needs an assistant. I need you to find about ten of the best assistants, with qualifying skills, and good references. I need them here Sunday at 1pm for an interview. Can you work that out for me?" I asked.

"Of course Mr. Richards, it would be my pleasure, sir." She replied eagerly.

"I appreciate that, have them meet me at my office on Richards Way, got it?" I asked.

"I most certainly do, I am going to get on it right now sir." She said.

"Cool, see you then, take care." I said then I hung up the phone just as I heard Angel walk into the living room.

I stood up and walked back into the house to see her and Salisha plopping down on the couches.

"Hey baby, how was your day?" I asked walking over to give her a kiss.

"Hey, it was cool. It's always good hanging out with my girl." She said pointing at Salisha.

"Hey Deytwon." Salisha said with a wave.

"Hey lady, how you been?" I asked leaning in to give her a slight hug.

"I been cool, and you?" She asked.

"Oh, I'm always good. So babe, I need to do a couple pop ups, but before I forget, I made the appointment with the Doctor for tomorrow at three." I said.

"You're just now making that appointment? I thought you been made it." She said looking at me surprised.

"No, I thought you were going to make it. Luckily, I called to verify the time, or we wouldn't have an appointment at all. But anyway, I figured that meant you got too much going on, so Sunday we're going to be interviewing assistants." I said.

"Baby, I don't need an assistant." She said.

"Baby, trust me, an assistant will make your life much easier. Just go with me on this." I said.

"Okay baby, I'll try it." She said shaking her head.

"My girl. Aright baby, y'all go 'head and enjoy y'all ladies night. I'm about to go shower and change. Don't wait up." I said before kissing her.

"Aright baby." She replied after pulling back from the kiss.

"Later, Lish." I said dapping her up.

"Airght." She replied

~~~~~

MARCUS

"Welcome to the Badd Boyz Club Mr. Jones" sang two scantily clad chocolate twins as they opened the doors for me.

"Shiiit, I feel welcome now." I said looking them both over.

"If you need anything, please, do not hesitate to let me know." Said the twin on the left before slipping her finger deep into her throat and sucked it out.

"Her, me, or us." The other twin said licking her lips.

"Bet." I replied with a smile as I watched them try to entice me.

"Mr. Jones, the man of the century! How are ya?" Asked Winston, as he walked over to shake my hand. Winston is the proprietor of the gentleman's club. It was an exclusive club that was invite only. One had to be at least a billionaire to be considered for membership It wasn't for the rich, it was for the wealthy. Only the baddest women between the ages of 18 and 24 were allowed to work there, and they were required to take a pill called Noxlent which keeps them from getting pregnant for six month stretches. They only needed to take it twice a year, and it was only available to the extremely wealthy.

Wealthy men would came to the club for business and pleasure. It was one of the hottest Gentlemen clubs on the East coast.

"At least somebody knows it. What's good man?" I asked slapping hands with him.

"Business as always. Well sir, the penthouse is ready for you, we got the baddest of the baddest up there waiting for you to keep you entertained until your meeting starts. Anything else you need, please, holla at me." Winston said.

"Bet that, so which one of these fine ladies gonna escort me tonight?" I asked looking around.

"Oh, my man, you know I worked everything out. IS-SIS it's showtime!" Winston said clapping his hands twice.

A set of doors opened and out walked a tall, thickass number eight. She was wearing a white mask with a feather sprouting from the side of it. Her honey glazed skin was smooth and flawless from her enormous round breast, down to her round hips, on to her sexy ass feet. She was dressed in black feathers that were fashioned around her in the shape of a short toga.

"Nice." I said looking at her.

"Only the best for you Mr. Jones. Now Isis here is barely touched. She is the legend of the Badd Boyz Club, only a select few have seen her, and even less than that have touched her. She is the newest addition, and a cold freak." Winston said looking at her with lust in his eyes.

"You know this?" I asked looking over at him.

"Not the way you're about to, but it *was* in her resume." Winston replied catching my drift.

"I'll let you know." I said looking back at Isis.

"Yes sir." Winston said as he opened the door that lead to the elevator. Isis walked through and I followed behind.

~~~~

DEYTWON

"Mr. Rich, I didn't know you were coming tonight." Said Eddie, the manager at my New York branch of Sides resturant.

"You weren't supposed to, I come and go as I please, and your job is to always be ready for me." I said as I walked further into the restaurant.

"Yes sir." He replied.

"So how is business tonight? We're looking pretty full, is anybody spending money?" I asked.

"Yes sir, we have all the money men in here, they're just tossing it. Ever since the hustlers found out about it, they've been frequenting the place." Eddie boasted.

"Hustlers, or The Hustlers?" I asked knowing that I taught him the difference. The Hustlers were a syndicate of Hustlers who live by a certain hustling creed. While they weren't on Big Boy status, they still operated with a since of dignity which placed them above the average hustler. I preferred them to regular street hustlers. Street hustles didn't believe in honor, except towards themselves. To me they tended to be sloppier and had no real love for the hustle, only for the intake.

"Well, both really." He answered sheepishly.

"Hmmm, have there been any problems?" I asked.

"No sir, everyone seems to be operating accordingly." Eddie assured me.

"Very good, I need you to do me a favor." I said.

"Name it." Eddie said.

"If anyone steps out of line, make a cruel example out of them. And from now on, if you're going to be allowing anythings in my restaurant. I want pat-downs of anyone not flashing

76

a Big Boy Ring. Got it?" I asked.

"Yes sir, on both." Eddie replied.

I nodded my head at him before stepping off. I decided to take a tour around the place to make sure that everything and everyone was up to my standards. I was pleased to see that the restaurant was as much a hit in New York as it was in Maryland. Everyone seemed to be enjoying mature casual conversations with their company. They were all eating and drinking, which let me know that they were spending money and this pleased me. I went up into my office and looked through some numbers. I made sure payroll and everything else was in perfect order before I took my leave. I had 4 other restaurants to hit before my meeting with Marcus in Boston. My next stop was the Sides in Maryland.

~~~~~

Big Boys -The Legacy   By Nikida Bellezza

ANGEL

"Why you so quiet over there?" I asked Salisha who was lying on her back with her feet straight up in the air. She seemed to be gazing at her toes or something on her feet. We decided to chill in our relaxing room. This is where all of our softest couches, and loveseats were. Deytwon and I would come in here to read and lounge around all day. We made the room soundproof because when we were in there, we didn't want to be bothered. We called this room heaven.

"Just thinking." She replied wiggling her feet around.

"About?" I asked as I put my magazine down.

"Well, you know how Anthony's birthday is coming up. It would be nice if my big gift to him were me telling him that I'm pregnant." She said turning over on the couch to face me.

"That's it, we need some fun in our lives, 'cause I know you ain't come out here to depress me!" I said swinging my legs around to stand to my feet.

"Oh, I'm sorry, I thought I was talking to my best friend. My name is Salisha, and you are?" She asked sarcastically.

"Let's go, I know a fun karaoke bar. It will have you cracking up, these people really think they can sing!" I said with a chuckle as I sat up.

"Fine, but this ain't some fancy smancy place where I have to wear a ball gown is it? I mean you are the lifestyles of the rich and famous now." She said as she sat up as well.

"No, you can wear jeans and a tee for all I care, and get it right hunny, it's the lifestyles of the wealthy and infamous!" I laughed as I stood to leave the room.

"Trick!" Salisha called behind me.

When we go to the Karaoke bar we took seats in the center to get a great view of the stage. I knew that Deytwon wouldn't approve, if he were going to go to a Karaoke bar at all, he would

78

expect VIP treatment there, which usually included some sort of box seats with a great view and a personal waiter. While I appreciated being a part of the wealthiest 1%, I was still that girl from the hood living off of $12 an hour, at heart.

After watching three acts, I told Salisha that I was going to the bathroom, but I really went to sneak and sign Salisha and I up as a duet act to sing Destiny Child's song *Bills Bills Bills*.

"Girl, your were right, these people are terrible!" Salisha said laughing when I got back to the table.

"I told you, but they don't care, it's all about having fun." I said

"No doubt, but I wish I would get my ass up there and embarrass myself like that. Nah, I'm good!" She said taking up her drink.

"Excuse me lady, where you from?" Asked a guy sitting at the table next to us. He was with two other guys who were equally as fine as he was.

"DC, why?" Salisha asked.

"Thought so, you don't sound like everybody else up here. I'm from DC too, Marquette." He said reaching his hand out towards Salisha.

"Nice to meet you, Salisha…and this is my girl Angel." Salisha said introducing me.

"Nice to meet y'all, this my man Pete and Jason. They just came up here to visit me, I go to Syracuse." Marquette said.

"Yeah, I'm up here visiting my girl, but I do have a husband at home." Salisha said.

"He not cool with your girl, or did you leave him home for a reason?" Marquette asked.

"Nah, this weekend is all about the ladies." Salisha said.

"Bet, so what part of the city you from?" Marquette asked.

"Southeast." The one named Jason said speaking up.

79

"Uhm you know *me*?" Salisha asked with an attitude.

"Yeah, and you know me too, Jay, Wally's cousin." Jason said pointing at himself.

"Oh my fuckin gawd! Jay I ain't seen you in a minute. How you been? How's Wally?" Salisha asked.

"I been good doing my thing. Wally cool, he just got out so he trying to walk the line now. How 'bout you, you still wit' cuz?" Jason asked.

"Yeah, we're married now." Salisha said showing off her ring.

"Oh, that's what's up. How 'bout you Angel, sittin' over there all quiet and shit. What you been up to?" Jay asked me.

"Life, just chillin' really." I replied not wanting to give them the details of who I was now. Jay and Wally were a part of the stick up kids back in Southeast, and Marquette looked very familiar to me, just couldn't place him.

"That's what's up, so you married too?" He asked.

"Yup, sure am." I replied casually.

"Small world." Marquette said as he raised his glass.

The one who had been quiet the whole time leaned over and whispered something to Marquette and then to Jay. They all turned to look at me for a second and chuckled.

"Next up, Salisha and Angel singing, *Bills, Bills, Bills*, by Destiny's Child!" Said the MC.

"What the hell? No you didn't!" Salisha exclaimed.

"Yes I did, come on girl!" I said grabbing her hand and dragging her up to the stage.

"Break a leg ladies!" Jay shouted towards us.

"I'm gonna kill you!" Salisha said with a chuckle as the music started.

We sang the song, doing our little dance. We entertained the crowd so much that we did two more songs. Then I was ready to go.

"Girl, thank you for dragging me out, I had a ball!" Salisha said as we walked out of the bar.

"I knew that this was all you needed. To sing and dance in front of a bunch of people that you will never see again." I said with a laugh.

"Hey, you ladies leaving so soon?" Marquette asked as he followed us out of the bar.

"Yup, got an early morning tomorrow." I said as I raised my hand for the car to come over to pick us up.

"On a *Saturday*? Pete asked in disbelief. This was the first time we heard his voice all night.

"Believe it or not." I replied.

"Aye, let me ask you a question, you ever heard of a restaurant called Sides?" Pete asked.

"No." Salisha answered.

"I was talkin to your girl. I think I saw her up there about a year or so ago. I could be wrong." Pete said sounding as though he had a point to make.

"I may have, what's it to you?" I asked.

"Nah, I just was wondering if that was you, as a side chick on Mr. Marcus Jones arm." Pete said trying to be a smart ass.

Salisha and I looked at one another.

"What's it to you?" I asked as the Mercedes limo pulled up.

"I'm just sayin ma', you seem a lil stuck up, for a side chick." He said with a chuckle.

"Hey, hold up slim, you need to chill that shit the fuck out. You don't be talking to my girl

81

like that." Salisha said ready to jump in his face.

"Nah, don't worry about it Lish. Let me ask you a question. What are you, a Hustler or something,?" I asked figuring that he was too classless to be a Lifestyle and damn sure couldn't be a Big Boy.

"Damn right." He said standing with his arms folded.

"So then that means you recognize this ring, am I right?" I asked showing him my Big Boy Leadership ring.

His eyes grew wide and his jaw dropped as he got a good look at the ring.

"You're the 3rd heir." He said sounding astonished.

"I *am*." I confirmed.

"I am so sorry ma'am. Please forgive my ignorance and disrespect." He said lowering his head.

"What the *fuck*?!" Marquette squawked

"It happens, but only *once*." I replied before turning to walk over to the limo.

"Yes ma'am, understood, I am deeply sorry." Pete replied with an all knew level of respect.

"Mmhmm!" Salisha said with a finger snap before joining me at the limo.

"Angel, *who are you*?" Jay asked as I got into the limo.

"A very powerful woman." Pete said as I winked at Jay.

~~~~~

Big Boys -The Legacy   By Nikida Bellezza

MARCUS

I watched Isis seductively dance around the room. Her moves were hypnotic, it was like she didn't have any bones in her body. No matter the movement of her hands, arms and legs, she kept her hips winding, round and round, up and down, bouncing, circles. She kept the rhythm up through three songs. Eventually I turned the music off as my dick was ready to jump off and up into her.

"You can dance, I get that, but what can you do for me?" I asked.

She smiled behind her mask as she stalked her way over to me. With each step she dropped a feather until she was standing directly in front of me, wearing three feathers.

"What is it that you require Mr. Jones?" She asked speaking in a deep Jamaican accent.

"Are you any good at fucking?" I asked.

"I'm the best." She replied.

"Would you bet your life on that?" I asked to make things interesting.

"My life against what?" She asked.

"You're not afraid to die?" I asked intrigued by her lack of hesitation.

"I live to die, but if I'm betting my life, I want the deal to be worth my while." She said.

" I don't pay for pussy." I said with a chuckle.

"You only make bets on it?" She asked.

"Something like that. Really, you have nothing that I want or can't get. So technically, there's nothing that I can win." I explained.

"But if it's not the best, you're willing to kill me?" She asked.

"*That's* what I win." I said.

"And my life is what I win if I am the best, as I say?" She asked.

83

I tapped my nose.

"But my life is already my own." She said.

"Then make this shit interesting, put it up." I said.

"How will I know, that I've won?" She asked as she sat on my lap with her knees on both sides of me.

"When I put my hands around your neck to choke you, I'll stop short of taking your life." I said as I ripped the rest of the feather off and grabbed her breasts giving them a squeeze before licking all over them.

"Deal." She moaned throwing her head back.

~~~~~

DEYTWON

"Mr. Richards, there is someone here to see you." Said Eric the manager of my Miami branch of Sides.

"See me?" I asked to be sure that I heard him correctly.

"Yes sir." Eric replied.

"Eric, I was under the impression that you understood that I don't do surprises." I said.

"I understand sir, but these gentlemen were insistent. They saw you walk in and you weren't being escorted so they inquired about you. When I told them that you were the owner they insisted on meeting you." Eric explained.

"In nothing you said did I hear a good reason for you to be disturbing me now." I said.

"I'm sorry sir, I will send them away." Eric said lowering his head.

"If they didn't listen to you before, they know not to listen to you now. Give me five minutes. I will buzz when I'm ready for them to come in." I said angry that I was being disrespected in such a way. Apparently Eric was a little fearful of these men, or they wouldn't have been able to out talk him. Eric was certainly not the man I needed running my establishment.

"Yes sir. The older one name is Gumpy, he's a well-known..." Eric began.

"I'm well aware of who he is. I profile everyone who comes in every one of my establishments. As I've told you before, I do not like surprises. I will buzz when I am ready." I said interrupting him as I pointed towards the door.

"Yes sir." Eric said before turning to leave.

"Eric, starting immediately, you are now an escort. Send Garvin up on your way down." I said.

"Yes sir." Eric said sounding defeated.

I pushed the third button on the side of my watch to alert my assassination team nearest Miami. Then I pulled up the surveillance video of all the folks who entered my restaurant. From there I typed in the name gumpy, which pulled up his profile, and his fingerprint which is taken the moment any table or wall in my restaurant is touched. I faxed over the photo of him and his two men to my assassin team.

Although I wasn't worried about a street nigga, I've heard stories of the arrogance of Gumpy, and I knew that he would be coming to me with a 'deal' that would undoubtedly have us linking up. He will soon learn that I don't tolerate disrespect on any level, and I don't give second chances.

A few minutes later I buzzed to let them know that I was ready for them to come in. A few seconds after that, Eric walked through the door with three goon looking men behind him.

"Mr. Richards... Mr. Gumpy, Moon and Q." Eric said introducing the men who all wore what were supposed to be intimidating mugs.

"Nice to meet you Richards." Gumpy said as he walked closer to my desk and took a seat. The other two walked over and plopped down on my couch.

I chuckled to myself thinking, '*these niggas really don't know.*'

"First of all, Eric told you what my name is. It's Mr. Richards, second, I didn't invite any of you to have a seat, so I'm gonna need you back up on your feet. I'll decide if what you have to say is worth having a seat for. Now, after you've stood to your feet do me a favor, fuck the casualties, and get to the point." I said.

"Whoa, whoa, hold dog, what's all the hostility for. We're businessmen just like you, no bad blood." Gumpy said as he stood to his feet. His boys stood to theirs and one slipped his hand

By Nikida Bellezza

into his jacket.

"Did Eric tell you that I don't do unscheduled visits?" I asked.

"He did, but this is about business, and you're a businessman. What man about his business turn down money?" Gumpy asked.

"Man, fuck this shit Gump, this square ass nigga ain't even about to have us begging for shit. We run these mufuckin streets out here!" The one named Moon said.

"Nigga shut that shit the fuck up! You ruining the whole reason we came up here to meet him. Calm that shit the fuck down. I'm the boss!" Gumpy exclaimed.

I smiled and plucked the first ball on my Newton's Cradle display that set on the edge of my desk.

"What is it that you fellas do, anyway?" I asked as I sat back in my seat.

"I run these streets feel me. I traffic everything from drugs to women. Whatever happens here, goes through me, or it don't go down at all." Gumpy proclaimed as he slapped hands with Q.

"So this business of yours, it's *lucrative*?" I asked.

"Man, I wipe my ass with money." Gumpy said.

"Sounds good. I want in." I said sitting forward in my seat.

"See man, that's what I'm talking about! I knew you were a man about his business. See, I figure I usher in some business for you. I know all the money baggers and they would love a place like this. And you let us set up shop in here..." Gumpy started explaining.

"No, I'm afraid you've miss understood. No, this is mine, and I don't share, I grew up as an only child. I never learned how to share. I'm in on *your* business, I figure you'll give me thirty percent of your monthly gross profit." I said interrupting Gumpy.

87

'*The fuck*?" The three men said all at once.

"And what I'm supposed to be get getting out this bullshit deal?" Gumpy asked holding his hand out to his men.

"Your life." I replied as though he just asked the stupidest question in history.

"This bitchass nigga, I should smoke yo bitchass right now! You come to our house talkin that bullshit bitch?!" Moon said pointing his gun in my face.

I looked up at him unphased.

"Cool it nigga, he got all these fuckin cameras in here. You'll be locked up before you get to your car! Chill the fuck out. We'll see him again." Gumpy said holding Moons arm down.

"True shit. We will see you again my nigga." Moon said as he put his gun back in his pants.

"You in *my* city, let's see if you make it out of *my* city. Let's roll." Gumpy said looking at me hard.

I took out a piece of stationary and wrote the number to my casual line on it.

"Gumps." I called behind him. He turned around and mugged me but didn't speak.

"My number, in case you change your mind." I said

He looked at me for a second, and then seemed to have an epiphany that moved his legs towards me. I dropped the paper on my desk.

"Yeah, I'll take this, in case *you* change *your* mind." He said snatching the paper up.

They walked out of my office mumbling something that I couldn't make out.

A few moments later my phone rang, I looked down to see that it was Marcus.

"What's good?" I asked answering the phone.

"Yo, where you at my nigga? You still coming to Boston for this meeting?" He asked.

"Yeah, it ain't shit but eleven, you ready to call it a night already?" I asked.

"Shiiit, I'm ready to leave Boston, there's always something else I could be doing." Marcus said.

"True, I'm in Miami checking up on Sides. Soon as I handle this lil bit of business, I'm on my plane out that way. Should be there no later than two-thirty." I said.

"Stayin out all night? What the wife gon' say my nigga, what they wife gon' say." Marcus teased.

"You let that be my worry. Who's there now anyway?" I asked changing the subject.

"The entire Myth body, with the exception of you." Marcus replied.

"Why are you even there on time, oh, Winston got a new Geisha?" I asked knowing Marcus too well.

"*Had* a new Geisha." Marcus replied with a chuckle.

"I don't even want to know." I said as my casual line began to ring.

"Look, let me get that line, I'll be on my way in a minute." I said.

"Bet." Marcus replied before ending the call.

"Richards." I said answering the phone.

"Mr. Richards, this is Gumpy, I'm ready to talk sir." Gumpy said humbly.

"I'm glad you see it my way." I said.

"I had no choice, you took out my men. They were good soldiers." Gumpy said sounding as though he were crying.

"Your tears speak volumes. So here is how it's going to work. I will send someone to collect my money on the same day, at the same time every month. No matter how your business is going, my money will never be short. You got me?" I asked.

89

"How you muscling in on me man? How you feel good, getting something for nothin' on the backs of the niggas whose fingers bleed to get what they got?" Gumpy asked.

"Gump, nothin about you or your organization interests me. Not that chump change y'all call money, or that poison you sell. You wipe your ass with money, I wipe my ass with property deeds. I really have no time nor the desire to fuck around with you. However, your basking in niggerish ignorance had you come at me in what I felt to be the most disrespectful of ways. You left me no choice but to muscle you. Now, your arrogance got your boys killed. Come on man, do better, be better. You don't know shit about me, or who I am, but I know all about you. That's the difference between you and I" I explained.

"So I'm just supposed to suck your dick and let you fuck me in the ass?" Gump asked.

"You got a fam Gump?" I asked.

"Yeah, I got a fam, that's who I do what I do for." He said,

"Can they make it without you?" I asked.

"What nigga?" He shot back.

"How long before you get to Plumber Drive?" I asked.

"How the fuck you know where I stay?" Gumpy demanded to know.

"Gump, it would behoove you to check yourself when you're talking to the man who has your life in his hands. I understand that I'm causing you a bit of stress, but watch yourself homeboy, I'm not a second chance type of cat, and I've already given you four." I said.

"What the *FUCK, BABY, WHAT'S GOING ON, WHO ARE THESE PEOPLE*?!" I heard Gumpy shout. He must've just arrived at his home where I had a few surprises waiting for him.

'Baby, what's going on, why are they holding us like this, what is this about?' I heard a woman's voice shout in Gumpy's background.

Big Boys -The Legacy   By Nikida Bellezza

"You did this!" Gumpy said now speaking to me.

"We got a deal Gump, or do you watch your family die before I have them kill you and *still* take over?" I asked.

"What's the deal?" He asked after giving up a surrendering sigh.

"You keep my neighborhood clean of all your drug and gang life bullshit. I don't want no problems for my patrons or their guest. Although quite frankly, the bulk of my patrons are connected and I really don't have to defend them at all. My place is a sanctuary, a safe haven for men of a certain standard to come through and live and be treated as such with the women of their choice, and I will keep it as such. Finally, for the level of disrespect that I've been shown by your and your folks, I'm going to need three million from each of you, and an extra mill on top because, well, I like round numbers. Since the other two are dead, their debt is on your head. So starting next week, I will send someone to collect my taxes. They will come for you once a month, on the same day, at the same time, every month. If you give the entire ten mill in one swoop, you will never have to worry about me again. If it seems to be taking you a lil long to pay that, I will add interest at fifty percent. Understand?" I asked changing my mind about the thirty percent. I didn't want to be in long term business with drug money.

"Yeah, I understand, you robbing me." Gump said

"I don't give a fuck how you process the shit, just get it done. So go 'head and let me know what it's gonna be, my men and I don't like to be kept waiting. We do have lives." I said.

"Deal." Gumpy said through clinched teeth.

"Solid." I replied before hanging up the phone. I pushed the button to call my assassins off. Then I packed up my things, locked up and took the elevator down.

"Mr. Richards, I want to apologize for earlier, I'm sorry for not stepping up. It's just that I know Gumpy and his boys, I know what they're capable of. I didn't want them to shoot up the place." Eric said after running up to me.

"Eric, look out there, what do you see?" I asked holding my hand out towards the patrons in the restaurant.

"Men eating with their Side chicks." He said stating the obvious.

"Hmm, okay, well with the exception of the folks that you know from the streets, the rest of these men are the bosses of men like Gumpy and his boys. There are men in this room right now that can shoot a uniformed police officer in front of an FBI Agent who's standing next to a judge and the Pope, and will never see a day in jail. Niggas making noise in the streets don't have any real power. It's the men behind the scenes, pulling the strings that you never hear from, that have the real power. And even they *know* to never force their way into a meeting with a man like me." I said.

"I understand sir." Eric replied.

"Enjoy your new position, my patrons are excellent tippers." I said with a pat to his back.

"Thank you, sir." Eric said.

I left the restaurant and got into my limo which took me to my plane. Once I boarded the plane I kicked my feet up and lay my head back to rest my eyes and saw my Angel.

~~~~~

ANGEL

"Girl this night was so crazy, but fun. I'm glad I came." Salisha sad as we got ready for bed. We were in one of the guest rooms that had two beds. I know that Deytwon didn't like sleeping separately from me, but with all the meetings he had lined up tonight, I knew that he wouldn't be home anytime soon.

"Yeah it was I'm glad you came too. I wish you lived closer, I haven't really made any friends out here yet." I admitted.

"Well hell, how can you? All this damn land y'all got, the next closes house is in damn near in another county." Salisha said.

"Yeah, Deytwon was saying that maybe I should sign up for some charities or something so that I can mingle with other socialites." I said.

"That's because Deytwon don't know you're hood bred." Salisha said with a yawn.

"What's that supposed to mean?" I asked offended.

"Chick please, what you going do, a girl from the hood, rubbing elbows with woman who's been living this life, their whole lives. They gonna be able to tell right off that you're not really from their world." She explained.

"So you're sayin' I can't make it out here?" I asked.

"No, I'm sayin, this socialite shit ain't you, but that's not a bad thing. Don't try to conform, just make who you are work for you." She said sounding as though she were seconds away from falling asleep.

"I guess." I replied.

"Don't guess, do it." She said.

"Night." I said turning out the light.

93

MARCUS

Deytwon finally walked in the door nearly two hours after I spoke with him on the phone. It didn't matter, every member of The Myth was thoroughly entertained by the women of the Badd Boyz Club. Plus that, they knew not to complain as Deytwon was in the leadership on the board along with myself, and then too, fucking with him was not an option I gave people. The Myth were a brotherhood that Deytwon and I joined and raised to the top of at early ages. We teamed up in many brotherhoods together that none of the Big Boy elders were aware of, but the Big Boys were amongst the most powerful.

"Good evening gentlemen, shall we began? What is the most pressing order of business, I'd like to wrap this up early tonight?" Deytwon said taking his seat at the opposite end of the table from me.

"We need to elect a new ambassador to represent the Myth's in the United Nations. Alrey Manz has passed away." Said Henry our vice chairman said speaking up.

"Who are our options?" Deytwon asked.

"Bronson and Willis." I said.

"Bronson is good. Shoot that alert to the United Nations, have Janice Charles announce it on Monday. Send Bronson the certificate no later than tomorrow evening." Deytwon said then he banged the gavel.

"Next?" I asked.

"China wants to know what we will do with the land that we've purchased and cleared. Now that the space is cleared there are buyers from around the world interested in it." Patrick said.

"Anyone willing to move to China to oversee the building on this land. This is to be a private business Conference Center where we will host meetings of the Elite." I asked.

"I will." Paul said raising his hand.

"Very well, you have one month to move." Deytwon replied banging the gavel.

While they continued with the confirmation I looked down at my phone to see that I had a message from Trina, my Boston pussy. I forgot I told her that I would be in town today, and I also didn't plan on Isis living up to her word. She left a nigga satisfied, I didn't even want no more tonight after cumming over and over again with her. So I gave Trina some lines and blocked her so that I wouldn't have to see messages of her begging me to come over.

It took about an hour but when the meeting finally ended I stayed behind with Deytwon while everyone else filed out.

"Good meeting." I said as I sat on the edge of the table.

"It was cool, so what you about to get into?" Deytwon asked as I closed up my briefcase.

"Shit, probably head on home. You know now that y'all are expecting a baby Tiff stalking my life about having one too." I replied.

"I mean, six years though, the hell were you waiting for?" He asked.

"You man. Ours gotta grow up together, like we did." I said.

"No doubt, well then y'all get on it. We need some successors for all the shit we got going." Deytwon said as he headed towards the door.

"You ever tell your father or grandfathers that you're at the head of other Elites?" I asked following him out of the room.

"Nah, you?" He asked back.

"Nah. It never came up." I replied.

"I bet it didn't." Deytwon chuckled.

95

"I mean, how would it go? A, yo dad, you really ain't got to worry about the other Brotherhoods, I run a couple of them? I mean, how do you fit that in a convo?" I asked as the elevator opened and we stepped in.

"True, there's just never a good time, right?" Deytwon replied jokingly.

"Exactly." I said.

*****

CHAPTER 7

DEYTWON

"Baaaaaby! Wake up, the doctor is driving up to the house now. I just opened the gate for her!" I heard Angel say. She was sitting on my stomach say as she moved my face from side to side in order to wake me up.

"Damn babygirl, what time is it?" I asked as I sat up and looked over at the alarm clock.

"Its three in the afternoon *Mr. Not getting in until three in the morning*!" She said climbing off of me.

"Business baby, I was handling business." I said swinging my legs over the edge of the bed.

"Mmmhmm. Well hurry and take a shower so that you can be with me while she examines me." Angel pulled on my arm to get me to stand up.

"Aright baby, but let me get up. I need to get myself together first. Trust me, when it's time for her to go down under, I'll be there. Just talk to her for a few and get some info until I come in the room." I said as I stood to my feet.

"Okay." She sighed before leaving the room.

I walked into our master bathroom and splashed water against my face. Then I brushed my teeth. Afterwards I turned on the shower and walked out to the closet to find some short shit to wear. This was going to be my chill day and I planned to be chillin in some chill clothes.

I had the conveyer belt bring my relaxing clothing forward. Then I picked out a pair of jeans and a black tee.

Once I was showered, dressed and fresh, I head down to the dining room where my place at the table was already set. It took a seat seconds before my food was brought out to me.

"Your bacon, eggs and toast Mr. Richards." Said Rosa the house maid.

"Thank you Rosa. Smells good." I said as I took up my fork.

"You're welcome sir, and here is your orange juice." She said sitting the juice next to my plate.

"Wonderful, as always." I replied.

"Is there anything else that you require sir?" She asked.

"No, thank you." I answered with a smile.

"Okay, well, bon appetite!" she said before walking away.

I said grace then proceeded to eat my breakfast.

After breakfast I joined Angel and the doctor in our lounge area. They were sitting on the sofas having a discussion. The doctor had a portable exam table set up next to a monitor in the middle of the open space.

"Hello ladies." I said as I walked in and sat next to Angel who was sitting on her feet.

Dr. Madison's eyebrows raise and lowered as she noticed my tattoos.

"Welcome Mr. Richards, I didn't know that you were a biker." She said sounding impressed.

"Yes, once upon a time. So what's going on, have you examined my wife yet? What do we know?" I asked looking from Angel to the Dr. Madison

"Ahem, well, I did draw some blood that I'll be taking back to the lab with me today. I was just explaining Pregnancy to Angel so that she'll understand all the changes her mind and body will go through, and how important it is to have a healthy pregnancy. We were actually waiting for you to begin the examination." The Dr. said.

"Okay, so baby you ready?" I asked rubbing her thigh. She looked up at me and shrugged.

"Yeah, I guess." She said with a giggle.

"Great, well, go change into this robe in the bathroom, and when you come out, just have a seat on the table." Dr. Madison said handing Angel a hospital robe to put on.

"Okay, be right back." Angel said as she took the robe and walked over to the bathroom in our lounge.

"So are you guys excited about having your first child?" Dr. Madison asked me.

"Pretty much, it's an exciting thing when the person you love the most gives you something so big and so powerful to look forward to." I answered.

"Wow, of all the couples I service, you two do seem to be the most in love." Dr. Madison said.

"Yeah. So you service several people?" I asked.

"A fair few." She replied.

"Hmm, so if my wife needs you, and you're tied up with someone else, what's the next move?" I asked.

"Well, then I would have my assistant come out." She said.

"See, that's not going to work for me. I'm not taking away from anyone else's significance, but I'm going to need my wife to be top priority. I only deal with Doctors, never their assistant, and the moment I am downgraded to an assistant, I leave the situation alone." I explained.

Dr. Madison looked shocked by my statement, and seemed to hesitate before replying.

"Mr. Richards, I do understand what you're saying, and where you're coming from, however, I took an oath to help all people equally. I don't foresee anything coming in between the service I provide for your wife and her immediate need, but, this is not something that I can promise." She said with ease.

"I respect that, believe me I do, and we'll use your services for now. Though I should let you know, you're about to become the backup Doctor." I said just as my cell rang.

"Richards." I said answering the phone.

"Yes, Mr. Richards, its Greg, man, I don't know what happened last night, but my man Pete is down here begging me to call you to apologize." Greg my manager at the Maryland Restaurant Sides said.

"Pete who, and apologize for what?" I asked not in the mood for no dumb shit.

"Apparently he was at the Karaoke Bar up in New York with your wife last night and he came at her a lil loose. That's when she let him know that she was a Big Boy. He said he apologized, he just wanted to be sure that you were cool. He said she gave him a pass, but he wanted to be sure. He came to me early this morning asking if I knew of her. When he said she was wearing a leadership ring, I knew it had to be your wife, no other woman wears a Big Boy ring, let alone one of leadership." Greg explained as Angel came out of the bathroom.

"Hey are we ready?" Angel asked.

"You were at a Karaoke Bar last night?" I asked looking up at her.

~~~~~~

MARCUS

"Which one do you like baby, the black or the white?" Tiffani asked holding up some lingerie for me to look at.

I was lying on bed watching my ceiling television when she walked into our bedroom talking to herself about them.

"I mean, it don't matter do it? I'm just goin' snatch it off anyway." I said looking over at her.

"Baby, it does matter. I want this trip to be special, and memorable." She said as she got up on the bed and sat next to me.

"It will be, because we're going as two, and coming back as three." I replied as I slipped my hand up her shirt and rubbed on her stomach.

"You really think I'll get pregnant?" She asked excited.

"I'm sure you will." I replied looking back up at the TV.

" What do you want, a boy or a girl?" She asked.

"It don't matter to me, but a boy would be dope." I replied still looking at the TV.

"I want a girl. I mean, I know you need a boy for the bloodline, but I would love to have a lil girl." Tiffani said as she lay beside me.

"Yeah, that would be dope." I replied not really hearing her.

"You aren't even listening to me!" She said turning over on her side to look at me.

"What? Girl, go 'head with that, if you're in the room, you're all I hear... *'cause you won't stop talking.*" I said mumbling that last part to myself.

"I heard that!" She laughed as she shoved me.

"My bad baby, but I notice that when you're worried about something you tend to babble.

101

So what's up, what's on your mind?" I asked as I sat up.

"Nothing. I don't want to babble your attention away from the all-important game you're watching." She said folding her arms like she was pouting.

I put my arms around her and pulled her back onto the bed and got on top of her.

"You know I hate when you do that shit right? So tell me what's up before I tickle it out of you." I said.

"No please baby, you know I hate to be tickled!" She said squirming already.

"Then tell me what's up?" I said.

"Okay, I basically just have a concern." She said.

"Which is" I asked.

"What if I can't get pregnant?" She asked seriously.

I looked down at her for what felt like the first time in years. Her beauty was enchanting and it sent shocks to my heart. I remembered what it felt like the first time I laid eyes on her. I remembered what I felt the moment I realized that I was in love with her.

"Baby, what is it?" She asked as she touched my face.

"Nothing, I don't want you to worry about getting pregnant. All I want you to do, is be happy and enjoy this next week. If it happens, it happens, and if it doesn't.." I said but I could no longer contain myself. I leaned in and kissed her.

~~~~~

Big Boys -The Legacy   By Nikida Bellezza

ANGEL

"Uhm, is this a bad time?" Dr. Madison asked interrupting the stare down that Deytwon and I were giving one another.

"Do you have another patient that you must get to or else?" Deytwon asked looking over at Dr. Madison.

"Deytwon!" I yelled.

He looked back over at me and shook his head.

"Thanks for the call man, let me speak to my wife... No doubt." Deytwon said as he got off the phone.

"Dr. Madison, can you please give us a second?" I asked.

"Sure." She said as she stood to her feet and left the room.

I closed the door behind her and turned around to see Deytwon looking over at me.

"Why are you looking at me like that? Is this where you become Ike Turner?" I asked with my arms folded.

"Angel, this ain't the time for sarcasm babygirl. You know that I would die before I ever put my hands on you in a harmful way. I just need you to explain to me what happened yesterday." He said calmly.

"Okay, well Salisha and I went to Karaoke. We sang a couple songs and we ran into a guy we knew from DC, who was with two other guys. One of the other guys remembered seeing me at Sides with Marcus, and he asked was it me." I said recalling the situation.

"And when he started coming at you sideways, what happened?" Deytwon asked.

"I showed him my ring, and he fell back." I said.

"So he didn't touch you, he didn't hurt you or anything like that?" Deytwon asked.

"No baby, I'm good." I said.

"Angel, I know that you're a grown woman, and you've been good all your life before you met me. But you are my wife now, and the third heir of a very Elite Brotherhood. It's important that you recognize this at all times. Know your position and play it accordingly. We are powerful, but we do have enemies. There are people who would kidnap you for ransom. I don't want you traveling without security from here on out." Deytwon said.

"So you're saying I need a babysitter?" I asked offended.

"For the sake of argument, yes. You need someone to look out for you like their life depended on it, because it will" He said.

"That's ridiculous!" I exclaimed.

"I have guards too. They aren't always seen, but they're felt when necessary. Yours can be the same way. I would feel better if I knew you were safe when I'm not with you." Deytwon said.

"Okay baby, okay." I said giving in. I knew that he was right, and there was so much to this world that I had no idea about. So arguing a point that I barely understood would be stupid.

He walked over and put his arms around me.

"I love you Angel, and I just need you to be safe. My life would lose all meaning if I lost you." He said.

"I know baby, I understand, and I love you too." I replied kissing him.

We brought the nurse back in and Deytwon apologized to her. She who confirmed that I was 12 weeks pregnant, and said we had to wait another few weeks to know the sex of the baby. All and all I was healthy and everything looked good, which is all we really cared about.

CHAPTER 8

DEYTWON

"Send the next one in." I said regretting the words after spitting them out. We had been at my Conference center interviewing personal assistants for Angel and so far all the ones we've interviewed were so bad I had thoughts of firing my assistant for booking them.

"Girl, oh my gawd, look at him?" I could hear Salisha mumble under her breath as she leaned into Angel.

"How you doin' my name is Brad Morris, assistant to the stars. Here is my resume', just ask me anything you'd like. I'm not shy and I don't scare easy." He said as he took time to shake each of our hands before sitting his blue folder down in front of me.

"Have a seat please, Mr. Morris." I said trying to figure out which land of make believe did become from. Between his black muscle shirt that he wore under a jean vest and blue jeans with slashes down each leg, I didn't know if he came for a job interview as an assistant for Angel, or to become rock star.

"So, let me tell you a little bit about the job. You will be my wife, Angel's assistant, making sure she knows about important appointments, and other little reminders. You'll be accompanying her shopping and any place she requires. She is not to hold or carry more than one package at any time. She is not to be coerced into doing anything that she feels uncomfortable doing. You two will always be accompanied by her personal security team who will not get in the way, but will be there just in case. Your hours will be between 8am and 7pm, Monday through Friday. Can you handle this?" I asked.

"Sounds perfect to me, where do I sign up?" He asked wiggling around in his chair.

"Well, let me look over this resume. Baby, you got a question for him?" I asked as I opened the folder that he sat in front of me.

"Where are you from?" I asked.

"San Francisco California hunny, can't you tell?" He asked with a snap.

"But you have like a New York accent, you must've been here for a minute." Salisha said.

"Girl, I was just playin' wit' you. It was a joke. I'm from Jersey City baby! I was born in Jersey, but I was made for New York." He said as he crossed his legs.

"So you moved to New York in 2011 when you worked in Queens for Frederick Quaker, the real estate mogul?" I asked.

"That's right. I worked for Freddie for three years before he moved to Cali. Then I worked for Gerard Clayton, as in Clayton Construction. I worked there for almost two years before I decided to move out here." Brad said.

"You do know that I can check these references out, right. I know both of these men personally." I said.

"Please do, you need my phone? I mean, don't threaten me with a good time, 'cause I'll take it!" He said.

Salisha and Angel fell out laughing.

"Baby, I like him." Angel said after catching her breath.

"Bet, let me make sure these references check out, and if they do, you're hired." I said as I stood to my feet to leave the room to make the call.

"Clayton." Gerard said answering the phone.

"Clayton, this is Richards, how are you?" I asked.

"Oh wow Deytwon, it's been a long time, how are you my friend?" Clayton asked

"You know me, I'm always good, but look, I don't want to keep you. I'm calling to get some info on a young dude I want to hire to be my wife's assistant. He said he worked for you so I'm giving you a call to check him out." I said.

"Aright, shoot." Gerard replied.

"Does the name Brad Morris ring a bell?" I asked.

"Oh yeah, Brady? He's a cool lil cat, but he's flaming like a muthafucka." Gerard said with a laugh.

"Yeah, that he is. So he's cool, he's about his business?" I asked.

"Oh yeah, he's good to go." Gerard replied

"Bet, thanks man. Aright, it was good talking to you too man." I said.

"'No doubt, we gotta get up sometime, let me know when." He said.

"For sure, aright then." I said before ending the call.

I didn't need to call the other reference, I trusted Gerard's word because he was one of the few men out there that I knew lived by their word. So I walked back into the room to let Brad know that he had the job.

When I got back inside, I saw that they turned the music on and Brad was teaching them some dance that neither of them was getting. I leaned against the doorway and watched them while shaking my head.

~~~~~

ANGEL

It had been a week since we chose Brad to be my new assistant, but Deytwon didn't want him to start until his background check came back. This was cool with me, the safer I was, the more secure Deytwon felt when his business meetings would take him away from home, like the one he had today.

It was a gorgeous day, so instead of spending it in the house, I figured I'd do a little shopping for the nursery.

We decided to move Deytwon's office downstairs and build a connecting door between our bedroom and his old office to use the space as a nursery. It was too early to detect the sex, so I was only shopping for neutral things.

"Welcome to Goo Goo's Nursery. I'm Ellen, is there anything in particular that you're looking for?" Ellen asked as soon as I stepped inside the store.

"Well I'm just looking for basic things. It's too early to know if it's a boy or girl yet." I replied.

"Yeah, I hear ya, and baby's things can be quite expensive. You don't want to break the bank and then can't afford the necessities." Ellen said talking in a child's voice.

"Right." I said pointing a finger at her.

"So let's see, are you a responsible mommy, do you have a budget missy?" Ellen asked now in a goofy voice as she waved a finger at me.

"Ellen, why don't you just show me around?" I asked fighting the urge to hold back my temper.

"Absolutely, let's just make sure we only touch what we're gonna purchase, alright" Ellen said.

"ENOUGH!" Shouted an elderly woman from the opposite end of the store. She stood there shaking against her walker as though standing was too much for her.

"What, grandma, what are you doing standing?" Ellen cried out as she ran towards her grandmother.

"Never you mind that. I have heard enough of you antagonizing this woman. You were raised better than that." Her grandmother scolded.

"Grandma, you don't know what you're talking about. If you knew anything, you'd know that her kind rarely has any money, and they steal." Ellen half whispered.

"You fool girl, if you knew anything you'd know you were standing before royalty!" Her grandmother exclaimed. I looked up at her in shock.

"*Royalty*? Her?" Ellen asked disgusted.

"She could buy and sell your ass for the rest of your days, and all you can do is try to insult her." She said before turning her attention to me.

"Dear heart, please forgive my fool grandchild for her ignorance." The grandmother said with a slight bow.

"But, how did you know?" I asked.

"Why, your ring, of course. There are only three of its kind, and they are only worn by the Leaders of the Big Boy Dynasty. You are the missing heir. You are Queen Angel." She said.

"Oh my gawd, I think I'm going to be sick!" Ellen said as she belted over holding her stomach."

"Remove yourself then" The woman said in disgust.

"Please, if you have time, sit with me a moment." The woman said offering me a seat in a sitting area just behind the register.

"OK." I complied.

"For starters, my name is Tabitha . I knew your great great grandfather, sir Cecil. He and the others started the Big Boys Brotherhood during slave times. Of course, I'm not telling you anything that you don't already know. With the money bequeathed to sir Cecil, the men went off and did great things, and now they are an elite entity known and respected throughout the elite world." Tabitha said.

"Money bequeathed to Cecil?" I asked as I understood that the money was left to the three leaders.

"Yes, it is in the original will. All property and lands were left to Cecil. Cecil wasn't a selfish man, and so he shared everything equally amongst the three of them. But to this day it is Cecil's name on the original properties, and money wells. His and his alone." Tabitha said as though she were confessing.

"But how do you know all of this?" I asked skeptical.

"Please, wait here." She said before wobbling to her feet. She grabbed hold of her walker and trembled her way out of the little room. She returned a few minutes later holding very old worn wooden box.

"Please, open it." She said. I looked down at the box and then back at her. She smiled and nodded at the box.

I blew dust from the top off the box before unlatching a little hatch that kept the box closed. I flipped the top open to see an old document with my great grandfather's name at the top.   *"Will and Testament, I hereby bequeath of my 8 mines, my diamond mind and a gold mine in Africa to Cecil Powers Philips, upon my death. He is also to receive my land on which he did serve and my stocks in cotton..."*

I looked up at Tabitha who watched me closely.

"Where did you get this?" I asked.

"The night Cecil's grandson, Cecil, was killed, he brought this to me to keep. He asked me to keep his family safe and to protect this document with my life, and I have." She said.

"Wait a minute, what do you mean the night he was killed? He voluntarily walked away from the Big Boys, he wanted no parts after seeing the direction they were heading in." I said reciting what I'd been told.

"Is that what they've told you? My dear, if Cecil had really walked away and forfeited his leadership that means he would've forfeited the entire Powers bloodlines involvement, including yours." She said.

"Yeah?" I asked encouraging her to go on.

"Why would they need to search for you, if your leadership was no more?" She asked looking at me hard as though she were waiting for me to connect the dots.

"I don't know." I said shaking my head.

Tabitha finally sighed as she sat back in her seat.

"Cecil was survived by a wife, a son and two daughters. The son was born to him and his mistress. That boy married and conceived your father, and later died from sickness. Then your father conceived you at a young age, he then was killed. After the death of your father, your grandparents moved your mother to Washington DC, where you were later born. They had no idea who the Big Boys were, or that they're daughter had been impregnated by one." Tabitha said.

"This is crazy! First of all, who are you, and how do you know about *my* life?! I exclaimed.

"I know that this is all hard to believe Angel. But you're going to have to trust me. The bottom line is, you are in eminent danger. That seed inside you is in great danger, especially if it is a boy. I implore you to not announce the sex if it is a boy. And stay away from doctors who especially service the Big Boys, please!" Tabitha begged.

"Who in the hell are *you*?!" I asked terrified by what she was telling me.

"I cannot tell you that. Just trust what I am saying, and do as I've told you." She replied.

"Lady, I came in here to get baby things and you start telling me all this conspiracy theory shit. I don't know what kind of looney bin I stumbled into, but you can save it for the next customer." I said as I stood to my feet and handed her back the box.

"Keep it. My time to protect it has come to an end." She said.

"Yeah, sure." I said before turning to leave.

"Have you been to the Big Boy Museum yet?" She called out behind me as I reached the door.

"No, I haven't." I replied turning around to face her.

"Go, I promise, all of the answers are there. But go alone, and stay until you find them. May the Grace of God be with you." Tabitha said as she stood to leave the room.

I looked down at the old wooden box in my hand and noticed the faint carving of the initials N T Philips. I remember that being told that this was the slave owner's name.

I looked back towards where Tabitha once stood and wondered if all that she had told me could be true. If it were, it would surely turn my entire world upside down.

******

CHAPTER 9

MARCUS

I walked in the house and tossed my bag onto the couch before heading into the kitchen to get myself something to drink.

"Mr. Jones, I think something is bothering Mrs. Jones, she is in your room crying." Said Edna our head maid.

"Thanks Edna." I said sitting my drink down. I took the elevator up to our floor and walked to the bedroom. Tiffani was lying on the bed crying on her pillow.

"Babygirl, what's going on?" I asked as I sat on the bed next to her.

"I failed us." She said.

"What you mean? Why you think that boo?" I asked lying next to her.

She handed me a pregnancy test stick that read 'not pregnant'.

"Tiff, babygirl. You didn't fail us just because your body isn't ready to conceive. And for real, how do you know it's *you* and not *me*?" I said wiping her tears away. I knew that she wanted to have children but It wasn't until now that I realized how badly.

"Why would it be you?" She asked looking up at me.

'Probably because I buss more nuts in one day than the average nigga do in a week.' I thought to myself.

"I mean, I don't know, I'm just sayin baby. I don't let you carry shit but a purse, you think I'm gonna let you carry a burden? I tell you what, if you want, we'll make an appointment to see Dr. Langly. She'll check us both out and see what's good. Cool?" I asked.

"Okay." Tiffani said as she put her arms around me.

I lay next to her on the bed and held her in my arms. She cried a little longer while I listened to her sob, but eventually I got cabin fever. I loved my house but the world was so big and I always had a need to be in it.

"Baby, let's go for a walk." I said barely believing that phrase came out of my mouth.

'Walk, fuck I mean walk?' my alter ego seemed to say.

"Walk where?" She asked.

"Our property, I mean, I've driven around it, but I've never walked it before." I said.

"Our entire property line? That's like over 100 acres!" She said.

"Not our entire property line, but just until we get tired." I suggested.

"Okay." She replied with a smile.

"Aright, let me take a shower and throw on some sweatpants. I said as I got out of bed and headed to the bathroom.

<><><><><>

"Damn." I said looking out over our property once we cleared the house.

"I know right, just seems to go on forever." She said looking around.

"Just like me." I said.

"How are you going to go on forever, if I can't even give you a baby?" She asked.

I took her hand and stopped us from walking.

"Tiff, can I be honest with you for a second?" I asked.

"Always." She replied.

"I mean, I do want a baby and all. But I'm not really tripping about that right now. I don't function well when I'm on another person's clock. Just because Deytwon is having a baby now, doesn't mean we need to hop up and do it. *I am* the Jones', I don't keep up with nobody." I

114

said.

"I know baby, but you know tradition..." Tiffany began.

"Fuck tradition, I don't live to make ghosts happy, I live to make sure we are happy. Do you not have everything you could possibly need?" I asked.

"I do." She said as she hugged up on my arm.

"Then please, let's let nature take its course. And if after some time I don't slide one up in you, we'll look at other options. Okay?" I asked.

"Okay baby." She replied.

I knew that she wasn't done with it, her desire to have a child seemed to come from somewhere within rather than having an external influence. I wanted to give her one, and I really thought she would've been pregnant by now after our week long sex fest, but she still wasn't. I hated not being able to provide her everything she desired, and couldn't help but feel like it was my fault that she wasn't getting pregnant. But at the same time, fatherhood wasn't at the top of my list at the moment. I still had some things I wanted to do before putting all of my focus on a child.

"Baby, where do you see us in thirty years?" Tiffani asked breaking my train of thought.

"Probably living on one of the islands that I own, chillin." I answered.

"We'll be old." She said.

"Nah, we'll just be in our fifties. We'll still be in good shape." I said.

"I hope the torch will be passed by then." She said.

"The Big Boy torch?" I asked looking over at her. She was looking away from me trying to hide the bothered expression on her face.

"Yeah." She replied looking down.

"Why?" I asked.

"Remember when we first met?" She asked.

"Yeah, you were Deytwon's date at the wedding ceremony when those two Nations united in marriage, Prince Albert and Princess Gineva." I said thinking back to that day.

"Yes, my dad really wanted me to marry Deytwon, but Deytwon introduced me to you. He told me that he thought I was a wonderful person but he felt that I would make a better match for you." Tiffani said.

"He *did*?" I asked surprised, I never knew that.

"Yes, so when you arrived, he sent that Princess that you came with off, and introduced me to you." She continued.

"I remember that." I replied. It was the first time I had ever met or even seen Tiffani.

"When I first saw you, I knew that you were the one for me. I knew it instantly." She said.

"I did too." I admitted. The first time I laid eyes on her, I knew that I had to have her. I had been with the world's most beautiful women, but Tiffani was the only one my heart ever recognized. There was something about her, and I still to this day don't know what it is. I just know that she belongs with me.

"And here we are, six years later." She said.

"Yeah, time flies when you're having fun." I said with a chuckle as we came to a pond. I had a bridge built to cross over the pond. I never imaged that I'd ever visit it, but I figured the bridge would give it some appeal.

"We have had some good times, but lately it's like, we barely have time for one another. Your businesses keep you away a lot." She said.

"I know, but I'm trying to lay down a solid foundation for our future. I have to make sure

116

that we're always straight, no matter what." I said half telling the truth.

"What's the *what*?" She asked taking a seat on the steps of the bridge.

"You never know Tiff, you can never be too prepared for the unexpected." I said.

"Are you telling me that if we retired now, from CEO of every business that you have, there's a possibility that we would sink?" She asked.

"Hello no, Big Boy funds alone will last for at least ten more generations if our predecessors live lavishly and another maybe thirty if they live responsibly. I simply enjoy being a mogul in my own right." I replied. Aside from Big Boy assets, my own personal net worth was well over 800 billion, *legally*.

"So then slowing down some, won't hurt you." She said taking my hand pulling me down to sit beside her.

"Slowing down? That's what happens just before you die, right? I asked.

"Not quite. It's that thing you do when you stop to smell the roses, and realize that there is so much more to life, than making money." She said turning my face to look at her.

"Shut your mouth." I said leaning back on the steps.

"There is, believe me." She said with a chuckle.

"How would you know? You came from money, your dad's an Oil Tycoon." I said.

"Yes and he's had two heart-attacks, a stroke and bypass surgery. I watched my mom cry herself to sleep worrying about my dad. I don't want that for me and I certainly don't want those problems for my husband." Tiffani said touching my face.

"Tiff, I can dig it, but the difference between me, and many other business moguls is, I have fun and I don't stress. If someone working for me is fuckin up, they don't get another chance, they're out. My business meetings are like one big party and everybody in attendance knows that they better bring me better news than they had at the last meeting. I'm all about progression." I said.

"And money." Tiffani added.

"You say that like it's a bad thing." I said now sitting forward looking over at her.

"You love money more than anything." She said.

"Except you." I replied.

"Maybe, but we're certainly in stiff competition." She said standing to her feet.

"As far back as I can remember, my family has always put the highest emphasis on money. Making it, keeping it and controlling it. It's in my blood, it's what I know, and it's what I'm good at." I said.

"It's not the only thing you're good at." She said with a smile and she knelt down on the step just below the one I was sitting on. She put her arms around me and sat her forehead against mine.

"I love you, woman." I said at which she smiled.

"I love you, man." She replied before kissing me.

~~~~~

DEYTWON

"Thank you Mr. Richards, I look forward to working with you in Dubai." Celsia said as we shook hands. I just hired her and a whole team of others to monitor the building of my new resort which was being constructed on some property that I owned in Dubai. I named it The Richland Resort, a place for the wealthy to come relax while vacationing in Dubai. It was expected to be up and running within two years.

"Thank you all for coming, may you each enjoy your stint in Dubai, and the rest of your day." I said after packing up the paperwork in my briefcase.

"Thank you." Came their replies.

I nodded my head before walking towards the door. I was anxious to get back home to meet James Lynn, my tailor. I had an appointment with him to be fitted for the suit I was having made to wear to our Baby Announcement Ceremony.

"Mr. Richards?" I heard one of the guys call behind me as I walked out of the conference room.

"Yes, uh, Michael?" I asked trying to remember his name.

"Yes sir, Michael Lundy." He replied blushing.

"Turn your flashers off, how can I help you?" I asked.

"Oh, sorry sir. Well, I was wondering, if you have time..." He began.

"Michael, the worst thing you can do when speaking with a businessman is to stutter and beat around the bush. We are always pressed for time. If there is something you want and do, either believe in it, or don't do it. Your job is to make me believe in what you're selling, not seem confused and unsure." I said.

"Yes, I see, that's what I'd like to speak with you about. I was wondering if you'd consider taking me under your wing. Help me learn the CEO business better, you're the head of countless businesses and organizations, some of which I thought were operating on their own." Michael said.

"You've been doing your research I see." I replied.

"Yes sir, I feel that I can learn a lot from you." He said.

"What gives you the desire to become a CEO?" I asked.

"It's in my blood, my dad is one, his dad was one and his father was one before that." Michael replied honestly.

"Family business?" I inquired already knowing as I do research on all applicants from their work history to the ties that their family have.

"Yes, Lundy Construction Parts." Michael said proudly.

"So your father is Charles Lundy?" I asked pretending to be intrigued.

"Yes, you *know* my father?" He asked.

"Very we'll. So now my question becomes, why don't you learn from him, and why are you working with me on this project?" I asked.

"We'll, I can use the experience, and as far as my dad goes, he's a better dictator than he is teacher, and he wants me to be the same way, except..." Michael began.

"You have to learn first." I interrupted nodding my head.

"Exactly." He said.

"We'll, I can certainly appreciate your stance in this situation, however I won't take you under my wing. My skills and expertise will be passed on to *my* son, to continue *my* legacy. I suggest that you go learn as much as you can from your father, and the rest through school and trial and error. It is far better to be a self-made man, than a man who has to get on the podium and thank a long list of contributors. Your father is the diving board, all you have to do is learn how to swim, then be brave enough to jump." I said.

"You think I can?" he asked.

"What difference does that make? Do *you* think you can? Because that's all that matters." I said pressing the button for the elevator.

"I *know* I can." He said with a boast of confidence.

"Bet." I said as the elevator arrived.

"Thank you Mr. Richards." Michael said as he and I stepped on the elevator.

"What did I do exactly?" I asked pressing L for lobby.

"You helped me realize that I have what it takes." He replied.

"Okay." I replied with a shrug. This boy had a lot to learn and so did his father if he thought he was going to use his kid as an inside track. I had a mind to purchase Lundy Construction and have them *all* working for me. Fuck with me if you want to.

~~~~~

Big Boys -The Legacy   By Nikida Bellezza

ANGEL

When I got home I went into my office and locked the door behind myself. I sat he box that Tabitha had given me on my chase and took a seat on my daybed. I wasn't sure that I was ready to open up this box of skeletons about my family. I had become okay with simply believing that I was abandoned. The information in this box was about to change everything.

My grandmother told me that my dad had been killed in a bad robbery back when they lived in South Carolina, and then she and my grandfather moved my mom to DC. She didn't talk much about my mother, other than to say that the streets took her. I never knew if she were dead or alive, and eventually I stopped caring. But now, I meet this strange woman who gives me a box of my history and I didn't know what to do with it. There could be things, truths in this box that could change my whole life.

I loved my life as wife to Deytwon, mother of his coming child and a leader of the Big Boys. I was finally in a place where I was completely happy. I felt safe, I felt secure, and I felt loved. I've done plenty of wrong in my life, and probably didn't deserve to be this happy, but if this were all a dream, I just wanted to stay asleep for as long as I could.

Eventually I took the box and stuffed it on the top shelf in the back of my closet. My life was going too well right now to stir the pot. If fate wants me to know what's in the box, it will give me a reason to look inside. Until then I'm just going to continue living my life as I knew it.

A few of weeks later Deytwon and I learned that we were having twin boys. The news was a shock to both of us. I didn't know what that would mean for the next set of leaders. Would they both lead, or would the one born first lead. Would one lead as a Richards and the other as a Powers. I didn't want to wrack my brain on it, but I knew eventually this would pose an issue.

******

CHAPTER 10

Two Months Later

DEYTWON

Today was the day of the announcement ceremony. It was being held at the MGM banquet hall in California. When it got out that the Big Boys were looking to host a ceremony of this caliber, all of the largest establishments went into a bidding war. They knew that we'd be bringing in the kind of money that could pay off the deficit and everybody wanted a piece of the action.

Whenever the Big Boys made public movements, we made sure to make the public move. We paid to have specific lanes between the airport and the hotel, shut down, as well as additional space for private planes and jets to land and the roads between them and the hotel shut down as well. We also paid for the full fleet services of 12 of the top limousine companies in the area to transport our guests from their planes or yachts to the hotel.

Everything was worked out down to the security. We used air patrol and street patrol, nothing was left to chance because the people in attendance were powerful enough to incite a terrorist attack. This was a very big deal.

"Your shoes Mr. Richards." Said Elton, my butler for the day, as he presented my shoes on a silk pillow.

"Thank you Elton." I replied as he sat them on the floor in front of my feet. I was in the Presidential suite getting dressed while Angel was in the Penthouse suite with the ladies.

"So we're doing all of this just to announce that I'm having a baby, what are we doing when the baby is born?" I asked as my butler dusted off my suit.

"No doubt." Marcus said as he watched himself in the mirror from different angles.

Big Boys -The Legacy   By Nikida Bellezza

Naturally Marcus and I had never been to an Announcement Ceremony as we were the last two successors born in the Big Boys Leadership.

"When the child is born we will have a inunction ceremony on Big Boy Island, where only a few select people will be allowed in attendance." My Grandfather said.

"It's not every day a leader is born, we must cherish and celebrate it." Marcus' father said.

I glanced over at Marcus who seemed to be staring out of the window at something. I could tell that his father's words bothered him some because he and Tiffani hadn't conceived yet, but he wasn't the type to show emotions that were anything less than happy.

"Gentlemen, I would like a word with Marcus." I announced once I was completely dressed.

He looked over at me confused.

"Yes, well, the ceremony will be starting soon, we should go take our places." My father said as they came and wished me well one by one before leaving the room.

"What's good?" Marcus asked once we were alone.

"How's everything with you and Tiff?" I asked walking over to sit on the couch.

"Awesome." He replied sarcastically.

"Come on man, its me." I said.

"What you lookin' for me to say dog? We good." He replied with a shrug.

"Look, I just know that they've been putting pressure on you to have a baby, because tradition is that the leaders are born together. I just wanted to know how's that going." I said.

"I've never been one to care too much about tradition. I do shit to make *me* happy." He replied.

124

"I feel you." I replied.

"What's my pressure to you anyway?" He asked.

"You're my brother, man. I mean, to be honest, I'd rather us be doing this shit together, like we've always done everything else this big. Just feels a little off." I admitted.

"Welcome to this shit called life." He said as he sat in the recliner.

"Airght man, you win, next subject. I want you to be the godfather of our baby." I said.

Marcus looked at me for a second, then he stood up and walked over to the bar.

"You know, Tiffani told me what you told her." He said reaching for a glass.

"Yeah, and what's that?" I asked sitting back.

"That you thought I was a better fit for her. She said you brought her to the wedding to hook us up." He continued as he poured himself a glass, then he grabbed another glass and filled it to the middle.

"*Yeah*." I replied waiting for the punchline.

He waved me over to the bar where the drinks sat. I stood and walked over and took a seat on a stool. He raised his drink towards me.

"I have never felt more complete than I did the day I met her. *You* did that for me." He said handing me my drink.

"We're brother's man." I said taking the glass from him.

"So it would be my honor, to be the godfather of your child. Cheers my nigga" He said before taping my glass.

"Cheers." I replied before taking the drink down.

"Come on, let's get down here and do this thing so we can get this party started." Marcus said after slamming his glass back down on the bar.

"Bet." I replied standing to my feet.

We looked at each other for a second before I stuck my hand out for him to shake. Which he took and turned it into a slight hug.

When we got down to the lobby our fathers and grandfathers were waiting by the door accompanied by Angel and the ladies. They were all gathered around looking at their watches and chatting about something that I couldn't quite make out.

"There they are!" My mother exclaimed.

"Great, are you guys ready?" My grandfather asked as they all walked towards us.

"Yes." I answered as my eyes fell upon Angel. She was even more beautiful than she had been on our wedding day. She wore a long silk gown with a diamond choker that matched her diamond crown perfectly.

She walked over to me with the biggest sexiest smile on her face and my heart began to pound to the beat of her walk.

"You look so handsome." She said to me.

"And you look gorgeous." I replied taking her hand.

"Okay, so we will go in and be seated. Then when the doors are opened, Mr. Jones will be escorted to his seat. Then Mr. and Mrs. Richards will step out and be escorted to their seats." Tiera the coordinator said.

"How about, since we three are the leadership, we are all either escorted at the same time, or all separately." I said. Marcus smirked and shook his head.

"Okay, okay, that actually works better." Tiera said.

"Okay, see you in there son, you two look so beautiful." My mother said as she took out her tissue.

"Alright, alright lets go so that we can get this show started." Marcus' grandfather said as he guided his wife into the hall.

"Baby, look at this place. I looked outside, there are limo's everywhere. You guys really do everything big." Angel said.

"Or why do it at all? And it's not you guys, it's *we*. You are a Big Boy, this isn't just about me, this is about us." I said.

"I know, it's just going to take some getting used to. We've been married for nearly a year and I'm still begging myself not to wake up." She said.

"Dreams are cool for a time, but eventually you have to allow yourself to wake up to live. Even if this were all limited to being just a dream, bask in it, jump in and be a part of it, so that when you finally do wake up, you'll have no regrets." I said.

"Well now that I have an assistant, I'm ready to step forward and do something's myself." She said.

"That's what I like to hear, the world is yours. Do with it what you will." I said.

"Excuse me Mr. and Mr. Richards, Mr. Jones, they're ready for you. " Tiera said as she stepped out of the banquette hall.

"Shall we?" I asked holding my arm out for her to take.

"We shall." She replied .

~~~~~

Big Boys -The Legacy   By Nikida Bellezza

ANGEL

When the three of us walked into the banquette hall, everyone stood to their feet and applauded. Tiera escorted us to our three chairs lined together on the platform.

The Richards and Jones Elders sat on their respective sides of us on a lower platform and also in Kingly chairs. Once Deytwon and I took our seats the room quieted and The Eldest Elders stepped forward to the microphone.

"Good Afternoon and welcome, I have never been one to sit through prolonged ceremonies, as many of you know, so I will get to the point quickly. This is a day of true significance, as it is the day that confirms that the Big Boys Legacy will continue on into the next generation. We've called you all here to witness and celebrate this paramount occasion, with us. It has been 64 years that Cecil Powers came to myself and Douglas, and said that he was stepping down. He said that the responsibility was too great and he could not handle it. Then, by some divine intervention…" Marcus' great-grandfathers words sent up a red flag in my mind.

"I thought they said it's been fifty years since a Powers was in Power." I whispered to Deytwon.

"That's what I've always been told. Maybe he's mistaken." Deytwon whispered back.

"Hmm." I replied as it was odd that he would confuse sixty-four with fifty. I also noted that the story I was told was Cecil didn't like the direction the Big Boys were headed in, so he stepped down, not that he couldn't handle it. This wasn't adding up and I was starting to wonder if Tabitha was really on to something with the things that she was saying.

'Maybe I will take a look in that box that she gave me after all.' I thought to myself just as Deytwon took my hand to stand me up. That's when I noticed the guests standing to their feet clapping their hands. I had missed the last of Marcus' grandfather's speech, and all of

128

Big Boys -The Legacy   By Nikida Bellezza

Deytwon's grandfathers speech by being occupied with my thoughts.

Deytwon and I walked over to the podium hand in hand. He put his arm around my waist and looked at me as though to ask if I were ready. I really didn't know what to say so I gestured for him to speak.

"Good afternoon to our Brother Marcus, the Big Boy elders, the Big Boy brotherhood in attendance, and our esteemed guests. Thank you for joining us today. Without further ado, it is with extreme merriment that we announce, we are expecting twin boys." Deytwon said.

The guests stood and applauded us as well as the elders. I looked around the room and smiled as Marcus and the Elders walked up to us.

"Thank you all for coming, now eat, drink, mingle, then get the fuck out!" Marcus' great-grandfather said at which everyone laughed.

"They always laugh, no one ever thinks I'm serious." he said looking at us before he and his wife walked away.

"Twins huh?" Marcus said as he stuck his hand out for Deytwon to shake.

"Yeah, we wanted to save that little surprise for this announcement." Deytwon said as he met Marcus' hand.

"Congratulations man, I guess now you got a Powers and a Richards." Marcus said.

"Powers-Richards." Deytwon said correcting him.

"That's what's up." He replied with a head nod before walking away.

"He feels slighted." I said watching him walk away.

"I hope not, but knowing my man, he just might. No worries, I'll talk to him later." Deytwon said before taking my hand and walking me back over to the table.

"Rich, congrats to you and your beautiful wife." Said some guy as he walked up to us and slapped hands with Deytwon.

"Thanks Kev, thanks for coming out" Deytwon replied.

"Wouldn't miss it, not *this*." He said.

"No doubt, how you doin' Sue, my wife and Big Boy leader Angel." Deytwon said introducing me to Kev's wife.

"Nice to meet you, you're so beautiful." Sue said.

"Thank you, nice to meet you too." I said as I raised my hand but Deytwon blocked me before I could initiate a handshake with her. I looked up at him and he shook his head at me.

"Well, let us get out of the way, I'm sure others would like to wish you well also." Kev said.

Deytwon nodded his head at him and he escorted his wife away, then the next couple stepped forward.

"Congratulations Mr. and Mrs. Richards, may God continue to bless you forever." Said some guy who extended his hand to Deytwon.

"Thanks Quintin, thanks for coming." Deytwon said as he met his hand.

"This is a big moment in Big Boy history, it was an honor to be invited." Quintin said.

Deytwon nodded his head at him just before he and his wife moved on.

"So, I'm not allowed to speak to anyone?" I asked still wondering why he wouldn't let me shake the woman's hand.

"You are the Queen, you can speak to anyone you want. But being that you are with child, no one must touch you. It's believed that spirits are transferred this way, and with you being pregnant those spirits can be transferred to the child. So you are not to be touched." He explained.

Big Boys -The Legacy   By Nikida Bellezza

"I hope she knew that because it looked like I was trying to carry her." I said turning back towards the people waiting to speak with us.

"Even if she didn't know, her husband knew, and if he is a good man, he will explain it to her." Deytwon said.

"Rich, congratulations to you and your beautiful wife, Queen Angel. God bless you." Said a man as he and his wife stepped forward.

"Gordon, thank you man, thank you guys for coming." Deytwon said as he and Gordon shook hands.

"Thank you." I said with a smile.

After greeting twenty more people I needed a break. I found Salisha who was sitting at a table sipping a drink with Anthony.

"Baby, I need a break, I'm going to go speak with Salisha." I said.

"Cool, but don't forget, no one touches you. If they do, let me know." He said.

"Okay daddy." I replied being smart.

"*I am* your daddy." He said as he pat my butt.

"No, you're they're daddy." I said rubbing my stomach.

He leaned in and kissed my stomach, I touched his face before turning to leave.

"Girl!" I said as I took a seat next to her.

"Hey girl what's wrong?" She asked concerned.

"Nothing I just needed a break, hey Anthony." I said.

"Hey Queen, how are you? You're looking lovely." He said.

"Thank you Anthony, I'm good." I replied.

"Cool, well, you ladies go 'head and have your girl talk, I'll find something to get into." He said as he stood up.

"Okay baby." Salisha said as Anthony kissed her.

"Girl, I've been dying to tell you something that I found out, but I didn't want to talk about it over the phone." I said grabbing her arm.

"I need to tell you something too, but that look on your face tells me that you should go first." She said.

"What, what do you have to tell me? You're pregnant?" I asked surprised.

"Girl hell no! You sound like Anthony. What I tell you about that?" She asked.

"Whatever, get to it then!" I exclaimed.

"Okay, well, you remember when we went to that Karaoke bar, and ran into them dudes, and one of them knew us from around the way?" She asked.

"Yeah, I nearly got my damn head chopped off by Deytwon, the guy with all the mouth made some calls and asked about me. Some guy called Dey and told him." I said rolling my eyes.

"You didn't tell Dey that you were going out?" She asked like it didn't make sense.

"I wasn't keeping it from him. I mean, it was a last minute decision, you know that, you were there when I made it." I said.

"Yeah, okay. But anyway, the nigga Jay went around tell telling everybody about you being big time." Salisha said.

"*What the fuck*?" I asked.

"Girl, people been calling me, inboxing me. I went to get my hair done, Karen and Tasha cold rushed me asking me questions. I was like what the hell?! Girl, it's all over the city about you being a part of some big gangsta shit. It's crazy!" Salisha said.

"That's, that bullshit! Why would he go spread some shit about me that he don't even

132

know nothing about?!" I said upset.

"Tell me about it." She agreed.

"Now I got to go tell Deytwon, I don't need to hear this lecture again." I said.

"You sure you want to tell him? Deytwon don't strike me as the man to fuck with. You just said Pete was calling all around trying to make sure it's understood that he was sorry for a mistake. Don't no niggas make moves like that unless they scared, and don't no nigga be scared of a nigga like that for no reason." Salisha reasoned.

"Salisha, I don't like keeping things from him. There is still so much that I don't understand about being a Big Boy. I have to let him handle the situations until I know and understand my position. It's not like he beats me, he just likes to make sure I'm okay. It's like he goes crazy when he thinks I'm in danger, or being disrespected. But he don't go crazy on me." I said.

"He really loves you." She said.

"I love him too." I replied.

"So what was it that you wanted to tell me?" She asked.

I forgot that I wanted to tell her about my conversation with Tabitha but the mood for that had been broken and I didn't feel like talking about it anymore.

Besides that, with Marcus' grandfather saying sixty-four years instead of fifty, I had to try to figure that out. Sixty-four don't sound nothing like fifty. It had more syllables, it wasn't a solid number, and it was a fourteen year difference. I needed to have a look at those papers Tabitha gave me.

"It wasn't important, I'll tell you later." I said waving it off.

"Okay, well look, my friendly ass man is over there talking to that creep ass Marcus, so let

133

me go over here and get him. You straight girl?" Salisha said still looking towards Anthony and Marcus.

"Yeah, go 'head, I need to get back to Deytwon." I said as I stood to my feet.

"Okay, talk to you in a lil bit." She said before she headed towards Anthony.

I walked back to the front with Deytwon who was still speaking to people.

"Hey babygirl, how's it going?" He asked putting his arm around me.

"I'm good, just a little tired." I said hugging on him.

"You ready to leave, because we can, or do you just want to go up to a room and take a nap?" He asked.

"No baby, I can wait." I said as I sat down in my chair.

"Earl, thank you for coming. Can you guys give my wife and I minute?" Deytwon said to the people in line.

"Of course." Earl said before leading his wife away. The line began to disperse.

"What's going on lady?" Deytwon said as he sat next to me.

"Nothing baby, just a little fatigued I guess. " I said laying my head on his shoulder.

"That conversation you were having with Salisha looked a lil intense. You wanna tell me about it?" He asked.

"Not right now baby, it's a long story." I said not feeling like getting into it.

"Okay, when you're ready." He said as he slid his fingers in between mine.

"I love you Dey." I said.

"I love you more." He replied.

Big Boys -The Legacy   By Nikida Bellezza

MARCUS

'This nigga is having twins? Get the fuck outta here.' I thought to myself as I made my way to the bar. I already knew what my great-grandfather was going to say, no need in bumping into him today. Now that Deytwon has two children on the way, two super hybrids, we were sure to be relinquishing some power to them.

"You know that we'll bring your drinks to you, Mr. Jones. You didn't have to waste a walk over." Said the woman behind the bar as I took a seat.

"No move I make is ever wasted. I do as I please, and I please all I do." I said flirting. She started blushing all over herself. I shook my head thinking about how easy she must be to fall for one of my weaker lines.

"I hear you, so what will it be Mr. Jones?" She asked.

"What are you offering?" I asked.

"Anything behind this counter." She replied.

"Is that right?" I asked.

"I wouldn't lie to you." She said.

"Like you know already. I tell you what, for now, just let me get some Ace of Spades, and the rest, we'll play by ear." I said losing interest in her quickly.

"Coming right up." She said turning around to grab the bottler and a glass. After she filled the glass she slid it over to me.

"Your drink Mr. Jones." She said sliding a finger across my hand.

"I appreciate you." I said sliding her fifty.

"No, it's free." She said.

"Nah, that's for you to pocket." I said before walking away.

135

"Marcus, my man, how's it going?" Asked Adonis a Big Boy who went to school with Deytwon and I. I hadn't seen him since he moved away to live in Tokyo.

"What's good man, how's it going?" I asked slapping hands with him.

"Pretty good, *pretty good*. Man, I haven't seen you guys in a long time. How's it been going?" He asked.

"Come on, when have you ever known things to go bad for me?" I asked.

"Right, right, almost forgot who I was talking to." Adonis said with a laugh.

"Oh nah, don't ever do that." I replied with a chuckle.

"True, so what's the plan for tonight?" He asked changing the subject.

"I mean, they may have a lil something but I ain't fuckin' wit' it. I'm just gonna scoop the Mrs. and get lost for a lil bit. You gotta do that every now and then, feel me." I said.

"True, Dena's been begging me to get her the hell out of Tokyo for a while." Adonis said.

"So do it." I said growing bored with his conversation.

"Soon as I can." He replied.

"Bet, we'll aright man, let me make my way around here. Be easy." I said slapping hands with him.

"Okay, you too, it was good seeing you." He said as I was walking away.

"Damn, why do I get bored with people so easily?" I asked myself before taking a sip of my drink.

I leaned against the wall and looked over at Deytwon and Angel. They were sitting on the throne accepting the well wishes of everyone who came forward to speak. They had been holding hands down between the seat the entire time. It always amazed me how much he seemed to love her, even after having pulled her straight out of the gutter. To me, she still seemed out of place in

136

our world, but that's probably because I knew where she came from, and that she could get down with the best prostitutes in the league. But I couldn't lie, she did clean up well, she was still a badd bitch for sure. If Deytwon was anybody else, I'd have her in the back somewhere sliding my dick in and out of her mouth. *'Who am I kidding, I'd be ramming my shit down her throat.'* I thought to myself as a smile crept upon my face.

"You're smiling, this must really be touching you, huh?" Tiffani asked as she wrapped her arms around me.

"Nah, actually I'm smiling about touching you." I said as I put an arm around her.

"That can always be arranged." She said smiling.

"Don't I know it." I replied before kissing her lips.

"So twins huh?" She asked as I pulled her into my embrace.

"Looks like." I replied with a careless shrug.

"Well, good for them." She said to my surprise.

"That's how I feel about it." I said.

"Yes, it will happen for us, when its time." She continued.

"When you talk like that, you make me want to buy you diamonds or something." I said.

"Yeah baby, because when things happen when they're supposed to, everything works out for the better." She said laughing through her speech.

"I'm going to buy you the house of diamonds." I said laughing with her.

"Sorry to interrupt, but Mrs. Jones, are you able to come with me, they want a picture with all of the ladies." Tiera, the coordinator said.

"Okay, be back baby." Tiffani said before following Tiera over to where Angel and the other ladies stood.

137

"What's up man, Marcus right?" Asked some tall linky guy as he approached me with his arm extended.

"Yeah, and *you*?" I asked shaking his hand.

"Oh yeah I'm Anthony, Salisha's husband. We met a few years ago at the girl's apartment back in DC. You and Angel was going to some big event or something. I ain't get a chance to rap with you at the wedding." He said.

'Damn nigga, the fuck am I, your hero? Fuck you remember all that shit for' I thought to myself.

"Oh Okay, yeah I got you. I knew your face, just couldn't place you til now." I said gassing him.

"Yeah, so you still stay out DC?" He asked.

'This nigga missed the 'no new' friends memo or what?' I thought to myself.

"Nah, that was just for the moment, I stay out Connecticut now." I lied.

"I feel you, tired of that city life. Me and Salisha talkin 'bout buying a house out Waldorf. Tryna make that move to Chuck County real soon." He said.

"That's a bet." I replied trying to remember if I had any land out there.

"So you still be on the Station, I haven't seen your ID in a minute." He asked.

"Every now and then, just been trying to tame this shit called life, ya feel me?" I asked glad to see Salisha walking over to us. Hopefully she was coming to get him.

"Baby, come to the limo with me, I need to change my shoes." Salisha said to Anthony after rolling her eyes at me.

"Baby don't be rude, you remember Marcus?" He asked pointing at me.

"What's up." I asked with a head nod and a devious smile. I knew she used to hate me for dogging Angel.

"Yeah, uhuh. Baby come on." She said dismissing me.

"Baby, I know you see me talkin'." Anthony said.

"Nah dog, don't let me get you in no trouble. I ain't one to break up happy homes. We'll get up later." I said sneaking a wink at Salisha. She rolled her eyes and grabbed Anthony's hand to pull him away.

"You must know women. Aye, but you got a number I can call, maybe we can get up some time" Anthony asked.

I reluctantly pulled out my card and gave it to him.

"Aright, my phone off right now, but I'll hit you up soon." He said rolling his eyes up to the sky as he was being pulled away.

I sipped my drink as I watched Salisha throw her big ass from side to side making her way across the room. Right then and there I made up my mind that she'd be next, for no reason other than for the hell of it.

After taking three dozen pictures with Deytwon and Angel, and a few dozen of my own, I decided to go out into the lobby area to get some air. When I got out there I saw Salisha leaning against the wall smoking a cigarette. When she noticed me she rolled her eyes and put the cigarette out against the wall.

"Don't stop on my account." I said as I leaned against the wall facing her.

"Don't flatter yourself, I was done." She said shaking her head trying to walk away. I grabbed hold of her hand and pulled her back towards me until she was standing against the wall again.

"You act like you hate me, but truth is, I don't think you hate me at all. In fact, I bet you want me..." I said once we were face to face.

"Ha! *Never* that!" She retorted. I licked my lips and moved in closer to her.

"Is that a challenge?" I asked in a lower tone. She blinked her eyes and swallowed hard before transfiguring her face to defy her emotions.

"Nigga please, Angel may have fallen for your bullshit but I'm not Angel. You wasn't shit then and you ain't shit now" she replied looking more convincing than she sounded

I smiled and nodded.

"Did she tell you?" I asked.

"Tell me what?" Salisha asked after folding her arms and cocking her head to the side.

"How I used to grab her by the back of her neck, snatch her panties off her body, and drive my dick in and out of her until her body would tremble and submit to me." I said.

"She never talked about sex with you, I figured it must've been some shit." She sassed.

"Yeah?" I asked laughing at her.

"Yeah!" She snapped.

"We'll see. In the meantime, go change your panties. I holla." I said before walking away.

"You wish you had an effect on my panties." She called behind me. I smiled knowing that I had her.

"You ain't got to admit it right now, but you will eventually. As for right now, if they're wet, just don't say anything at all." I said after turning around to face her.

She put her middle finger up at me.

"Soon, I promise." I said then I blew a kiss at her and turned to leave.

I walked back into the hall and took a seat in my chair. Deytwon and Angel had

140

abandoned their seats and were now on display in the crowd.

It was a serious catch 22 for me, while I was happy for Deytwon, at the same time I despised Angel. It wasn't her per se that I hated, it was her representation. She represented a family that I've been trained to hate. Aside from her affiliation with the Powers, Angel was a cool chick, not wifey material, but definitely someone you could chill with and fuck.

"A word sir." I heard my Grandfather say from behind.

"What's going on old man?" I asked standing to my feet.

"Old man he calls me." My grandfather said mocking me.

"You're the one confusing years, he stepped down sixty-four years ago? I could've sworn it was fifty." I said.

"It, was a lapse in my mental stability." He said.

I raised an eyebrow at him to encourage him to continue with his flimsy explanation.

"The doctor said I'm at the early stages of Alzheimer's disease. Soon I'll forget everything but my name." He said.

"Is that so?" I asked only half believing him, but not sure what his angle could be in lying to me.

"It is indeed so. Now, you caught what I said, but did you hear what they announced?" He asked.

"Twins." I replied.

"Twins, that means two babies. Both boys, born at the same time." He said.

"That's usually the way these things happen." I said urging him to make his point.

"Aright funny man, so his two little boys grow up and take the throne as Powers-Richards, and Richards, they will outnumber you. Still think it's funny?" My grandfather asked.

"I think it's funny that you won't leave it up to me." I said.

"I just told you, I am about to succumb to Alzheimer's, in a minute I won't be here to push you or to know what's going on enough to advise. I'm trying to help you! You can't keep dragging your feet on this, she was supposed to be dead by now! This ceremony was never supposed to happen. Jones' are men of their word. What the hell are you?!" He exclaimed though only loud enough for me to hear.

I turned to look at him like he was crazy. If he were anyone else talking to me this way he'd be dead where he stood, I'd see to it myself.

"Look, all I'm saying is, handle this before it goes any further. It's already gone far enough. End this bitch, before she brings your demise into this world." He said calming himself.

"Are you finished?" I asked.

"Yes, but one more question. Who do you answer to now?" He asked.

"Myself." I replied.

"A wise man, would keep it that way." He said.

"Take care of yourself old timer." I said holding my hand out for him to shake.

"Likewise." He said as he took my hand.

I looked out to the middle of the floor where Deytwon and Angel were standing. She rubbed her stomach as she smiled and spoke with the guests who flocked her into a circle.

"Anything to eat or drink Mr. Jones?" A waitress asked as she approached my table.

"Yeah another cup, nah, fuck that, bring me a bottle of Ace of Spades and a glass." I said not really in the mood to eat.

"Yes sir, I will be right back with it." She said before walking away.

"Kill the bitch." I said chuckling to myself as my grandfather's words replayed in my

142

head.

Killing her wasn't going to be a problem, I just didn't want to be sloppy with it.

Killing a Big Boy leader was big time shit. I needed a fall guy to take the heat because no doubt Deytwon would do his own investigation. That pussy already had him on stuck, I couldn't imagine how hard he'd go if she and his children were killed. Yeah, I definitely needed an in, and a fall guy.

A few seconds later Salisha walked back into the hall and over to Angel, where she pushed through the crowd until they were standing side by side.

"Hmm, and I think I just found both." I said to myself as the waitress returned with my bottle.

******

CHAPTER 11

DEYTWON

Angel was unusually quiet on the plane ride home, she mostly stared out of the window and slept. I knew that what she had been discussing with Salisha was rocking her mind because before the conversation she was good. I hated that she was still on civilian time, not realizing how powerful she really was. No matter the problem, there's no such thing as a problem without a solution for a Big Boy. Nothing a person can say or do should be of any consequence to us because in retrospect, we are larger than life. I needed her to understand that now more than ever because she would soon be giving birth to our children, whom I planned to train accordingly.

I watched her sleep for a few minutes before resting my head back against the seat. I began to organize the meetings that I had coming up within the next few weeks by distance and level of importance. I had a meeting coming up in London to confirm the land that I wanted to purchase for Richland Resort. I wanted to make it a worldwide resort. At the moment I was working on London and Dubai at the same time. I had six more countries that were going to follow suit in the coming years. Richland Resorts would be the last major deal that I would work on before falling back for a little while, although it would be at least five years before all eight Resorts would be up and running.

With Richland Resorts added to my empire, I'd have enough money to take care of everybody on the east coast if I so desired. I didn't see myself as greedy, I just wanted to be sure that my blood would be straight until the end of time.

After five and a half hours in the sky, the plane landed in our back field and we took a limo around to the front of the house. Angel was still tired so I carried her into the house and up to our room where I lay her across the bed and undressed her and pulled the cover up over her body

Then I took a shower, afterwards, I threw on some sweatpants and a tee-shirt and checked my messages. When I didn't hear anything that required my immediate attention, I got in bed next to my wife and went to sleep.

The next morning I woke up to kisses being planted all over my face. I opened my eyes to see her lips coming in on top of my right eye.

"Good morning baby." She said climbing on top of me.

"Morning, somebody in a good mood." I said looking up at her.

"Waking up next to you, how could I not be?" She asked.

"The pleasure is all mine. You eat yet?" I asked.

"No, I was waiting for you. Rosa just told me that breakfast was ready. You ready to go down and eat?" She asked.

"Yeah, come on." I replied with a slap to her ass.

She moved off of me and got off the bed. I sat up and stretched then I got out of bed to head downstairs with her.

When we got into the dining room area we took seats and our food was brought out immediately.

"Smells good." I said as Rosa sat my orange juice on the table.

"Yeah it does, I am so hungry." Angel said diving right into her food.

"Will you be needing anything else?" Rosa asked looking from me to Angel.

"No thank you." I replied. Angel simply shook her head no.

Rosa nodded her head and left the room.

"So, what do you have planned today?" Angel asked.

"Couple meetings, but nothing big, you got something planned for me?" I asked.

"No, just asking. It seems like it's going to be a nice day." She said.

"Yeah, it does, you wanna take a ride or a flight or something?" I asked.

"Where?" She asked back.

"Anywhere, doesn't matter." I replied.

"Well, I tell you what, go to your meetings, and then when you come back, andlet's go on a picnic." She said.

"That might not be until tonight baby." I said.

"That's okay, that's what tiki posts are for, remember?" She asked with a big smile.

"I do, and okay, we can do that." I replied with a chuckle.

"Cool." She said.

"So I have a question." I said thinking back to last night.

"What's that?" She asked.

"What was going on between you and Salisha that had you so vexed?" I asked.

Angel looked over at me for a second and sighed.

"Okay, so you know Salisha and I went to the karaoke bar a while ago, right?" She began.

"Right." I said replied.

"Along with the guy Pete, there were two other guys with him. One we knew, and the other was trying to holla at Salisha." She said with a pause.

"Get to the interesting stuff." I said as I started eating.

"Well, I guess after the way Pete kept apologizing, it kind of made the other two guys wonder who I was. So according to Salisha, the one named Jay went back to DC and told everybody that I became *'big time'*. So Salisha's been getting approached by a lot of people who knew both of us, asking about me and what I was into. I guess they figured he was telling the truth because no one's really seen me in a minute." Angel explained.

"Mmhmm." I replied.

"You mad?" She asked.

"Nah, I'm cool. How do you feel about this?" I asked.

"I'm good, I mean, I was blown, well I am still jive blown because rumors are so unnecessary. I don't understand why he felt the need to spread me across the city like that." Angel said.

"No worries. Weak niggas do weak shit. You can't expect more from them, because they live for less." I said touching her hand. She looked up at me and smiled.

"You always know what to say." She said.

"Shouldn't I?" I asked.

She smiled at me before looking down at her plate. She poked around at her food for a few moments then looked back up at me.

"Baby, you once said something about there being a Big Boy Museum." She asked.

"Yes, it's in a volcano on Big Boy Island." I answered.

"A volcano?" She chuckled.

"It's inactive, at least it has been for at least a century. If you'd like we can take a trip there. I haven't been since childhood." I said.

"I'm sorry, I still can't get passed the volcano part." she said shaking her head.

"It sounds odd, but it's unlike anything you've ever seen. You actually forget that you're in a volcano." I assured her.

147

"Who built it?" she inquired.

"The idea came from your great great-great-grandfather. It was constructed a few years before he died. Legend is he had a secret compartment where he kept his memoirs" I said.

"Legend?" She asked.

"Yeah, it's never been confirmed." I said.

"Well, yeah I'd like to visit it one of these days." She said.

"We can do that, no problem." I said.

"Cool. So okay baby, do your meetings today, then tonight, is all about us. A nice picnic under the stars." She said.

"Sounds good, I know just the place." I said.

After breakfast Angel went to take a shower and I went up to my closet to grab a suit. Then I made a quick call about the incident she had during Karaoke.

"Mr. Rich, how's it going?" Greg asked as he answered the phone.

"I'm good, look, I got a question. Remember that nigga Pete that came to you asking about me?" I asked.

"Yeah, Pete Sully, you need me to handle him?" Greg asked.

"Nah, I just needed his name. I need to find his homie, some nigga named Jay." I said.

"Is Jay in, or is he just some nigga?" Greg asked,

"Far as I know, he's just some nigga. I need to get in touch with him. Do this for me, have Pete meet me up Sides in two hours. Can you work that out for me?" I asked.

"Of course, it's done." Greg assured me.

"Bet, tell him it'd be good for him if he can have his homie Jay with him when I get there too." I added.

"Bet, I'm on it." Greg said.

"Aright." I said before ending the call.

I made one more call to my pilot to let him know that I'd be ready to take off soon. Then I picked out my suit and accessories and got dressed. I found Angel in the bedroom just coming out of the shower.

"Aright mama' I'm about to head out. You need anything before I go?" I asked walking up and putting my arms around her.

"Just you coming back home to me." She said turning around in my arms to face me.

"That's a given." I said then I leaned in to kiss her.

"I love you." She said when we pulled apart.

"I love you more." I replied.

We kissed again before I headed out. I took a limo around to my plane and boarded for my flight to Maryland.

Even though Pete had nothing to do with this Jay nigga's mouth, as a Hustler, it was his job to school his boy on the matter. He didn't have to tell him that Angel was a Big Boy, but he should've let him know that she was off limits and not to be disrespected. Respect was high on my list, running neck and neck with loyalty. I didn't take it lightly, nor did I offer light punishments for it.

I took out my phone and called Craig, head of the Hustlers to let him know that I was about to handle one of his men.

"Mr. Rich, how are ya?" Craig asked.

"I've been better. I'm calling because I'm having an issue with one of your folks." I said.

"Wow, if you're calling me, I know it's bad." Craig said.

"Yes, he fucked up twice. First, he disrespected my wife, which he apologized for after realizing who she was. Then he allowed one of his boys, who is not hooked up, to spread shit about my wife all over town." I explained.

"The *Queen*? He spoke on the Queen? Please Rich, accept my apologies on that. My boys know better. I don't know what he was thinking, but he is stripped as of this moment. Just tell me who the bitch nigga is and it's a wrap." Craig assured me.

"Actually Craig, I'm on my way to Maryland now. I've set up a meeting with him and the nigga who can't seem to keep my wife's name out his mouth. I've asked them to meet me at Sides. You're welcome to come be a spectator if you want. But this, I will be handling." I said.

"Understood, I'll meet you guys there." Craig said.

"Good, see you soon." I replied then I ended the call.

When I arrived in Maryland the plane landed in the back land of my restaurant. Then I was driven around to the front.

"Mr. Rich, hey I didn't know you were coming down!' Zeus my bouncer exclaimed when he saw me.

"You weren't supposed to. How's business?" I asked as I slapped hands with him.

"No doubt, no doubt. Business is booming as always. You do as much during the lunch rush as you do during the dinner rush." He said.

"Good to hear. Of all my restaurants, this is the one that gives me the least trouble. You're doing a helluva' job man." I said.

"Why thank you sir. It's a good job and I love it." He replied

"That's what I like to hear. You'll see a considerable raise starting on your next check." I said.

"Thanks, boss!" He said very grateful.

"No, thank you." I replied.

"Excuse me Mr. Rich." I heard Greg say from behind.

"Greg." I said.

"Your guests have arrived, and they're waiting in the sitting area." He said.

"*Who's* here?" I asked.

"Sorry about that. Craig, head of the hustlers, Pete from the hustlers, and Jay, Pete's friend." Greg said.

"Thank you." I replied as I pressed the elevator to head up to my office.

"Mr. Richards, I am so sorry, I didn't mean for things to get out of hand like this. It was never my intent.." Pete started as soon as I stepped off the elevator

"Quiet." Craig silenced him.

Pete sank back in his chair and fell quiet, while his friend Jay looked around confused.

I walked out into the sitting area and the three men stood to their feet.

"Craig." I said extending my hand to him.

"Mr. Richards, how was your flight?" Craig asked as he shook my hand.

"It was a flight, what can I say. Step into my office gentlemen." I said as I used the key to unlock the door.

"Nigga the fuck you got me into?" I heard Jay's voice ask.

"You did this bama ass shit nigga, you just better hope... Never mind, because if they don't get you, *I will*." Pete said.

I walked over to my desk and took a seat in my chair to log into my computer. Craig and Pete stood in front of their chairs while Jay plopped his ass down.

151

Pete grabbed him by his arm and pulled him back up to his feet.

"What man?" Jay exclaimed.

"You an ignorant son of bitch ain't you?" Craig asked him.

"Nigga what?" Jay bucked.

"What?" Craig asked walking up on Jay.

I looked up at Jay and cocked my head to the side.

"You *are*, aren't you." I asked.

"Man, I don't know what y'all think *this* is, but it ain't about to be *that*." Jay said defiantly.

"Have a seat fellas." I said as I sat back in my chair.

"Mr. Richards, may I speak?" Pete asked.

"*May you speak*?" Jay mumbled as he frowned his face up.

"No, I think I much rather hear from Jay. What's up Jay, what's good wit'cha?" I asked folding my hands.

"Shit tryn' figure out why I'm here, and why this nigga on his knees." Jay said pointing towards Pete

"You feel like because he has respect, he's on his knees?" I asked.

"What is he respecting? He' a man just like you' a man. But fuck all that, why am *I* here?" He asked.

"You're here, because you fucked up." I replied as I sat sup.

"Yeah, that's what I do best, what else is new?" He asked.

"Jay, I don't have one doubt in my mind that you're a fuck up, but this time, you *fucked up*. You see, apparently you got it floating all over town that my wife is no some hustler girl shit.

152

You felt the need to come back down here, and make her the topic of discussion." I said.

"Angel, is *your* wife?" He asked shocked.

"Angel is *my* wife." I confirmed.

"That's hard to believe, Angel was a hoodrat. Nigga's used to pay her to fight bitches for them. She used to smoke weed all day long, she smoked weed and she sold it. And she's your wife? Dog, you shoulda' done your research on that chick." Jay said with a chuckle.

I looked on at Jay and smiled before speaking.

"You mean like, Janice Spiral who lives over on Stanton road Southeast with her boyfriend Keith and her daughter Layla. Or Kesha Dancer who lives on R street, Northwest with her two year old son lil Jay, and an elderly grandmother. You mean research like that?" I asked calmly.

"Why are you coming for my family?" Jay asked with less arrogance in his voice.

"*I'm* not coin for your family. *You* came for your family, when you put your mouth on *my* family." I said pointing at him.

"Can I save them?" He asked somberly realizing for the first time

"I have no intentions on harming your family, not unless you make it necessary of course. No, my point is, you're basking in sheer ignorance right now, and I needed to shut that shit off. It's clear to me that you don't know who I am, and what I represent, and that's cool. There is no reason for you to give a fuck about me, and quite frankly I don't give a fuck about you. But, it seems that you've caused some issues for my wife, and in that event it would've been wise for you to do your own research. That night at the Karaoke Bar, after you saw your man apologize profusely for trying to irritate my wife. It should've dawned on you then, that she is no longer the woman you once knew, and thusly understood that she did bare a keen significance that

153

demanded respect. But instead of you putting two and two together, you opened your mouth and tried to blast her." I explained.

"Hey, look, all I did was ask around. I didn't say she was rocking with a hustler, I just asked if she was. I may have mentioned one or twice that she got inside of a Mercedes Limo with a chauffeur. I mean, what was I to think, we don't see people like you and all that other stuff in the city all day. I was just asking." Jay tried to explain.

"Yet, the shit spread like wildfire, because it got back to her, and she was very upset." I said as I stood up to sit on the front side of my desk.

"Mr. Richards, in his defense he didn't know, he doesn't know about The Big Boys." Pete said speaking up.

"But *you* did, and this is your man." I said.

"Yes sir." Pete replied lowering his head.

"And yet you failed to school him. So technically, this is *your* fault." I said.

"It is." Pete agreed.

"Nah, nah, I take my own beef. He can't control me, he could'a told me whatever, but I'm a man, I'm gonna do what I'm gonna do." Jay said looking from Pete to me.

"Well, here's what you're gonna do, you're going to be recorded making a public apology." I said waving in my muscle Lester and Randal.

"Nah, I'll apologize to shawty, but I ain't fuckin wit' being recorded." He said shaking his head.

"Oh, my bad slim. You were under the impression that you had a choice. Excuse me for that, I tend to be pretty bad with words. Words are a conundrum for me." I replied as the two men lift Jay up out of his seat.

"What the fuck is this? What's going on? Pete, what is this man?" Jay shouted as he was being dragged from the room.

"Shut him the fuck up. I want him eating soup" I demanded.

"Yes sir." Lester said before shoving his elbow into Jays face breaking his nose.

"Now, as for you." I said looking down at Pete who looked nervous.

"Yes sir." He replied after swallowing hard.

"For not teaching your boy better. You are hereby stripped of your hustler privileges. give Craig your ring. You are not to attend or receive any benefits of your old position. You will serve the niggas you once ate with. You will shop for the niggas you once shopped with, and you will work the corners." I said.

"Yes sir." Pete replied as he took off his ring and passed it to Craig.

"Now, get the fuck out of my office." I said as I walked back around to my seat.

"Yes sir." Pete said as he stood to his feet and rushed out.

"You went easy on him." Craig said as he stood to his feet.

"So it would seem." I replied with a smile.

"Later Boss." Craig said with a chuckle before leaving my office as well.

******

CHAPTER 12

ANGEL

"Girl, you going all out for this lil picnic with your husband." Brad said looking around at all of the bags of things I purchased. We were on the way back to the house after a long afternoon of shopping for me and Deytwon's night time picnic. The idea excited me so much because It was new to me and I would've never thought of it in a millions years.

"I just want to make sure this night is perfect." I said with a chuckled looking over the bags myself. Maybe I did go a little overboard.

"Chile please, show up in a teddy, it'll be a night you'll never forget!" Brad said with a finger snap.

"Not outside, that's crazy!' I laughed.

"Hmmm, honey you' crazy if you put a limit on sexcapades with your own husband. When it comes to that man you're supposed to be down for whateva' wheneva' howeva' foreva'!" He said.

"Believe me hunty, I know what I'm doin' and he loves every bit of it!" I said.

"Okay, I see you!" Brad exclaimed giving me a high five.

When we got to the house Brad and the chauffeur carried everything into the house, then I had a car take him home.

I looked at everything and all of a sudden felt too tired to put it all away. I purchased everything from a tent, a large blanket, tiki posts, bug repellant, and of course clothes and shoes for me.

I eventually shook my head and grabbed my purse to head to the television room where we had a 70 inch TV mounted against the wall. A few seconds after I got comfortable my phone rang.

"What's up girl?" I asked answering the phone seeing that It was Salisha

"What are you doing?" She asked with a sense of urgency.

"Chillin, why, what's up?" I asked.

"Are you with Deytwon right now?" She asked.

"No why, what's wrong?" I asked as I started getting worried.

"Did you tell Deytwon what I told you about Jay?" She asked.

"Yeah, why, will you get to the point please??" I yelled anxiously.

"Look, go to yube videos and type in DC Apology." She said.

"*What*? Why?" I asked feeling annoyed that she hadn't gotten to the point yet.

"Please, just do it." She exclaimed.

"Aright, fine." I said walking into my office. I sat at my computer and logged in.

"What are you doing? Are you doing it?" Salisha fussed.

"Chill man, I'm pulling it up now." I said. I typed in Yube Video, and when the page came up I typed in DC Apology into the search. Seconds later a video came up of a guy standing in an empty room ass naked.

"What the fuck you got me lookin at?!" I yelled thinking it was some kind of sick porn. The man's face looked badly beaten.

"Calm down and look Angel! Look at his face! Doesn't he look familiar?!' Salisha exclaimed.

I looked at his face and noticed that he did look a little familiar, but I couldn't place him.

"He looks familiar, but I can't place him." I said.

"Then listen to what he's saying." She said. That's when I realized I had the sound on mute. I restarted the video and turned the sound up.

"My name is Jason Branch, known around the way as Jay. I want to apologize for running my mouth about things I know nothing about. I now know to keep people name out my mouth. This is what happens to sucka ass niggas like me. I'm sorry I lied." He said through swollen puffy lips.

"Do you get it now?" Salisha asked.

"Oh my gawd.. Oh my gawd! I panicked when I realized the guy in the video was the guy who had been spreading rumors about me after seeing Salisha and I at the Karaoke bar.

"Girl, who the fuck is your husband?! How did he get Jay to make this video? What did he do?" She shouted.

"I think I'm gonna be sick!" I said as I dropped the phone. I belted over holding my stomach as I ran towards the bathroom where I spilled my guts in the toilet. After cleaning myself up I crawled back to the phone not trusting my legs to carry me.

"Salisha, I can't watch the rest of the video. Is he dead?" I asked as tears burned their way to my eyes.

"I don't know, the video gives no indication either way. But look at this shit, it has only been posted for two hours and it already got two thousand views, with no tags. This is some crazy shit!" Salisha said.

"This is too much." I said shaking my head.

"Angel, I always thought Deytwon was too fuckin' serious to be so young. I think he's a dangerous man. I think he's into some mafia style shit!" Salisha exclaimed.

I thought back to when I kept trying to get Trish to tell me more about them and how hesitant she was. She eventually told me that The Big Boys were above the law, and they don't get penalties for the things they do. My heart tweaked at the thought of Trish, I still couldn't help but feel guilty, because I knew that I was the reason she was dead. Now this fool Jay may be dead, again, because of me. I began to feel overwhelmed and light headed. This was all too much.

"ANGEL!" Salisha called out to me.

"Lish, I got to go. I need to process this shit, this is too much." I said.

"Angel, are you in danger? Tell me are you scared of him?" She asked.

"No, he would never hurt me, this I'd bet my life on." I said meaning every word.

"But he would hurt someone because of you. That makes you just as responsible as he is." Salisha said.

"First off all, you have no proof that it was him. You don't see him in that video, and hell he doesn't even mention me, so this may not have anything to do with him running his mouth. You really need to chill out speculating about shit you know nothing about!" I exclaimed not so much mad at her as I was that my emotions felt like they were in complete disarray.

"Angel, I am trying to help you. You don't need to..." She started.

"Salisha, I have to go, keep this shit to yourself until I tell you otherwise." I said.

"What, who you think you talkin to slim?" She asked.

"Don't do that." I said.

"You know what, you get your lil self together and I will talk to you later, 'cause you got me fucked up right now. I'm tryn' make sure you're good and you goin' go on me? Yeah, aright." She said

"The world is bigger than you and what you think is big Salisha!" I said.

159

"You talkin' to me? No, the world is bigger than you Angel, but you wouldn't know that because it's been all about you since your ass stepped foot in my house. From you getting left by a nigga who ran off to join the *minor* leagues, to you getting fired from the library, to you running behind a married man who dogged the *shit* out of you, to you now being married to a psychotic ass man! No Angel, the world is bigger than *you*!" Salisha shouted.

I nearly lost my breath gasping so hard at her audacity to try to throw salt on me and my life. Not my girl, not my sister, not my ride or die. No the fuck she wasn't coming for me.

"Angel, she's sorry baby, she didn't mean any of that. She'll call you later. Take care." I heard Anthony say after wrestling the phone out of her hand then he ended the call.

I dropped the phone onto the floor and stomped it until it broke. It didn't help anything but it did relieve some of the stress that I was feeling.

I looked back up at the computer screen and caught my reflection. For the first time I saw the woman I used to be. The angry bitter woman who was always ready to fuck something up or get fucked up. My eyes were red, my hair was all over my head and my lips were curled into a snarl. I couldn't believe how easy it was for me to become her again. I didn't want to be her, I didn't want to live in anger and resentment. I didn't want to be quick to fight and hate. I wanted to be loved, and to be loving. I wanted to be free and happy.

A few seconds later I felt my babies sliding across my belly. I looked down and gently rubbed my stomach as tears fell from my eyes.

"I'm sorry guys, your mommy tends to get crazy every now and then. But I swear I'm gonna do better. I promise." I said looking down at my stomach.

I looked back up to see the video and tried to exit out of it, but it disappeared. I typed it back into the search but it didn't come up. It had been deleted.

MARCUS

"Son, what a surprise." My father said as he appeared on the screen. I had been thinking a lot about my great-grandfather saying that he had Alzheimer disease and wanted to know what the plan was and why my father and grandfather had yet to contact me about it.

"Yeah, so tell me what's going on with great granddad." I said skipping passed the pleasantries. I wasn't as close to my family as Deytwon was to his. We didn't call one another to be social, it was always about business.

"That's a pretty broad question, you want to be more specific?" He asked.

"Is it really that much *I* don't know?" I questioned.

"You called, you must want to know something." He said after taking a puff from his cigar.

I smiled and nodded my head.

"You know, we play these games far too often. Then one day I realized, it's not just you and I, me and granddad, or you and granddad playing games. It's all of us. You know some things that I don't know, and I know things that you each don't know. So I tell you what, let's keep playing, and I'll just see you all at the finish line." I said.

"Why son, whatever do you mean?" He asked.

"Mean, about what exactly?" I asked playing stupid.

"Son, just kill the woman, that's your primary concern. It's all we need, after that, we'll be living freely. Big Boy money will cover you and Deytwon for generations to come. You never have to work, or worry about anything ever. Just give back by taking care of this one thing." He said.

My father had never really been one to speak on Angel, but now he was pressing the issue as though we've had these conversations before.

161

"Indeed. Good evening, *adviser*." I said before ending the call.

I decided to call Henry, the man whom I appointed to be my grandfather's doctor. I met Henry on a business trip I took to Belize. He had gotten tired of the hype of living and working in LA, so I sold him on the idea of becoming a private doctor for my great-grandfather. He even moved to Mexico to live near him.

"Mr. Jones, how may I help you?" Dr. Henry said after his face appeared on the screen.

"Just calling for my six month update on my great-grandfather. How is he?" I asked.

"He's as strong as a horse. His vitals are all good. Good healthy heart. Very strong for a man of his age. If he gets rid of the salt in his diet, he'll be perfect. You know your great-grandpa loves his salt." Dr. Henry said.

"Yes he does, so no colds no viruses, no diseases. He's physically and *mentally* in shape?" I asked.

"Put it this way, he keeps it up, he will outlive me, and I'm his doctor!" Dr. Henry said with a chuckle.

"Mmhmm. Well, that's wonderful news. I thank you so much for your time Dr. I'll be sure to take care of you for the update." I said.

"Not a problem, thank you Mr. Jones." He said just before I ended the call.

"What are you up to old man." I said to myself just as my cell started ringing.

I looked down at my phone and saw the number Anthony had called me from earlier. I started to ignore it, but something told me to answer.

"Yo." I said answering the phone with the irritated voice.

"*Why* do I have *your* number?" A woman's voice asked.

"You tell me. Who *are* you" I replied.

"This is Salisha, Marcus! Why do I have your number in my phone?" She asked.

"I have a better question, if it were a problem, why are you calling?" I asked.

"I, you.. Is this the creepy shit that got Angel stuck on your ass, because I can assure you I'm not going for it." She said sounding as though she may have been rocking her neck.

'Yeah, you're curious, bitch' I thought to myself as I let out a slight chuckled.

"What's funny?" She asked with an attitude.

"You are." I replied.

"Explain that!" She demanded.

"I'll do you one better. I'll be in DC tonight, let's meet up." I suggested.

"And why would I do that? I'm a married woman, and you're slime!" She said.

"When he strokes you, does it drive you crazy, or do you have to fantasize your way to a nut?" I asked.

"That's none of your damn business!" She shouted.

"When he banging you from the back, does he give you that feel good pain, or that pitty pat hip to ass slap?" I asked.

"Fuck you!" She exclaimed, though with less anger.

"Do you ever say that to him?" I asked.

"No, I love him, he's a good man!" She declared.

"He ain't hitting it right. I bet he hasn't even found your spot yet. I bet he don't stroke nowhere near it." I said.

"My man sexes me real good!" She exclaimed.

"That's the problem, he's sexing a woman that needs to be fucked." I said.

"What the hell does that mean?" She asked.

163

"Meet me at the W tonight around 11, Pentouse1, and I'll show you." I said.

"Yeah fuckin right." She said still trying to hold on to an anger towards me that I had already defused.

"Tell me something Salisha, and be honest with me." I said.

"What?!" She asked.

"Are you wet right now?" I asked.

"Nigga what?" She asked.

"I tell you what, if you're *not* wet, you're not my type of freak anyway, so I'll leave you alone altogether. If you are wet, meet me tonight." I said.

"Why me?" She asked

I smiled to myself thinking '*this dumb bitch here.*'

"The question ain't why you, it's why Marcus, and if you cum tonight I'll show you. I'm not asking for your hand in marriage, I just want to fuck you, and I can tell that you need it, or we wouldn't still be on the phone." I said.

"You are so fuckin arrogant! I hate you!" She exclaimed.

"*Do* you?" I asked.

"Yes!" She shouted.

"Good, bring it with you tonight. I holla." I said ending the call before she could protest. There was a fifty-fifty chance that she would actually come, but I had a feeling that the odds were in my favor.

~~~~~

Big Boys -The Legacy   By Nikida Bellezza

ANGEL

I sat on the couch closest to the balcony and stared up into the sky. The sun was beginning to set giving the once blue sky had a sapphire tint. I breathed in deeply as the warm breeze flushed in through the balcony doors. This was my calm before the storm.

Twenty minutes later after I had unintentionally drifted off to sleep I heard Deytwon's voice over my light roars. Since I've gained weight I took to snoring.

"Baby, you good?" I heard him ask, stirring me awake. I sat up and rubbed my eyes to bring him into focus.

"Why are you sleeping out here, and with the balcony open. That air is no good to be washing over you while your asleep." He said closing the doors.

"Did you kill him?" I asked ignoring everything else he was saying. I just had to know.

"*What*?" He asked with a slight laugh.

"You heard me. Did you kill him?" I asked again as I tried to stand to my feet. Deytwon took my hands to help me stand up.

"Kill *who*?" He asked confused.

"*Jay*! Did *you* kill Jay!" I exclaimed out of frustration.

"Babygirl, I .."

"I saw the video. DC Apology. I saw it before it got deleted. Now that's a hell of a coincidence that he apologize the same day I told you what he did. But I don't really think it's a coincidence at all." I snapped, interrupting him.

"Well if you think you know that I did it, why are you asking me?" He asked.

"Because I don't know for sure, and I don't want to believe it. I also don't want to believe that you would ever lie to me." I said as tears made their way to my eyes.

165

He stared down into my eyes and wiped the tears from them.

"Did you kill him, Dey?" I asked.

"No, I didn't." He replied softly.

"But he is dead, isn't he?" I asked.

"Yes, he is." Deytwon admitted.

"You didn't kill him, but you're responsible." I said.

"How am I responsible for another man's actions?" He asked.

"Because those actions were influenced by you!" I said before walking away.

"So I guess we're not having our picnic now?" He called behind me.

I looked back at him and continued out of the room. I walked out to the elevator and pushed the button to go downstairs.

"Angel, where are you going?" He asked following me.

"Away from you." I said as the doors to the elevator opened.

"You are really *mad* at me." He said as though he couldn't believe it.

"Yes!' I shouted as I stepped inside and pushed the button for the doors to close.

"Why?" He asked stopping the doors from closing.

"Because I didn't know that the man I love the most in this world was capable of doing some grimy shit like that. Not you, this isn't who you are, or at least this isn't who you showed me you were." I said folding my arms.

"There's a lot you don't know." He said.

"Oh, no bullshit?" I asked sarcastically.

"Angel, just come back so that we can talk. Come on before we break this elevator, because I'm not letting the doors close until you get off." He said.

By Nikida Bellezza

"Deytwon, I just need to be away from you, please." I said.

He looked at me for a few seconds before nodding his head.

"Okay baby. I'll be here waiting for you. I love you." He finally said before letting the doors to the elevator close.

When the elevator got to the first floor I stepped off and looked around the house. If I were in DC, I'd be heading to Salisha's house. I would've probably still headed there now, only we had that big fight and I didn't think I'd be welcome.

Finally I shook my head and went into my office and locked the door behind myself. I sat on my bed and tried to process everything that had happened. I never thought Deytwon was capable of murder. I always thought he was a gentle spirit person. Sure he was always very frank about his business and the way that he wanted things done. But to kill, that was going way too far to me. I don't believe that Jay deserved to die, just because he spread lies about me, if anything talk to him and let him know that he was doing too much.

Truthfully, I would admit that I was probably more upset than I should be, but that was mostly because I felt guilty. Had I never told Deytwon what had happened, Jay would still be alive today.

Now that Deytwon was a murderer, and Marcus is a murderer, was I supposed to be next? Is this Big Boy protocol? Deytwon said that there was a lot that I didn't know, what did he mean by that? I thought to myself. That's when I remember the chest that Tabitha gave me.

I looked over at the closet for a few seconds, then I stood and walked over to get the chest. Once I had it I brought it back over to the bed and dumped everything out onto the bed. There were a lot of old documents, letters and a key.

Big Boys -The Legacy   By Nikida Bellezza

"I picked up the key and looked at it. It was an old looking metal key, something that I've only seen in the movies. I sat it down and grabbed one of the letters. It seemed to be a Will left by my great-great grandfather which read:

This is the Will and Testament of Cecil Powers Sr   *May 4th 1922*

'I Cecil Powers leave all of my worldly possessions to my son Cecil Powers Jr, but only if he continues to share with all leaders of The Big Boy Brotherhood. If he decides to leave the Brotherhood he may only take 40% of my wealth with him. The rest must be left to the two remaining leaders. If it is determined that he has been murdered, no money is to go to the remaining leaders. If it is determined that he was killed because of, or by a Big Boy leader, that leader is to be removed from the Big Boy leadership and hanged by the neck until dead....'

"Wow, it was like he knew something was wrong." I tossed the Will to the side and took up another letter that was handwritten. This one was written by Tabitha herself, which read..

'This letter is to inform the reader, hopefully someone of the Powers Bloodline, the truth about what has happened. The night my husband Cecil, the son of Cecil Jr was killed, my husband told me that he was being killed by the Big Boys. They used our nanny, Elizabeth to poison my him. Elizabeth informed me that my husband fathered a child by her daughter, Linda, a child whom she named Ricardo. I was asked by my husband to take baby Ricardo and our two girls, and flee from South Carolina. It broke my heart to know that my husband had a newborn baby, but on his deathbed he begged me to watch over this child, and so I did. I never informed Ricardo that I was not his mother. Before I left my home for the last time, I got in a fight with Elizabeth, and I shot her in the heart. Cecil's last words to me were to give him the gun and to get out. I do not feel guilty for killing the woman who took my husband from me. I do feel guilty that my husband's last words to me were not, I love you, but to get out. I raised Ricardo as my son, he grew up to marry a woman

168

named Elaine, who died during childbirth. She bore a son whom Ricardo named Rico. Ricardo later died from what we believed to be tuberculosis, though I have my suspicions. And so I raised Rico. At the age of fifteen, Rico got a young girl by the name of Ashley pregnant. Shortly thereafter Rico was murdered. This spooked Ashley's grandmother, my good friend Marilyn who then moved Ashley to Washington DC. I have not heard from them since...'

"Ashley and Marilyn?" I said to myself. Those were my mother and my grandmother's names. This is about me, that means...

"Tabitha is my grandmother." I said dropping the paper on the bed. The whole thing was so surreal to me. I had barely even heard my family history before, let alone read it.

I looked through and read everything until I fell asleep across the bed. When I woke up the next morning I made up my mind that I was going to The Big Boy museum. There was way more to this Big Boy shit than I initially thought. It seemed that they've been picking off my family since my great-great-great-grandfather's death. And that all they laid claim to, really belonged to him, which is probably why they were trying to kill us off.

When I opened the door to my office I saw Deytwon asleep against the wall next to the door. I locked my door because I wasn't ready to let him know what I had discovered, not until I knew more than the Big Boys could cover up.

I looked down at him and smiled. I watched his chest rise and fall, as his head rested against the wall. He was holding a bouquet of roses and a big brown teddy bear that had gotten away from him.

I bent down to pick up the bear and found it to be so soft and fuzzy. I knelt down next to him and placed my hand on the side of his face and kissed his lips which woke him up.

"Mhh, babygirl." He mumbled in his groggy morning voice.

"Yes, baby?" I asked.

"I never meant to hurt you, I only wanted to protect you." He said as his eyes opened wider.

"I know baby. Let's not talk about that right now." I said as I stood to my feet.

He stood to his feet then looked in his hand like he was confused before his eyes grew wide.

"For you" He said handing me the flowers.

"Thank you, they're beautiful." I said as I smelled them.

"Well, they were last night when I bought them." He said with a bashful shrug.

"I love my teddy." I said squeezing the bear.

"I love its new owner." He replied looking down at me.

"She loves you too." I said taking his hand.

"We have a lot to talk about." He said seriously.

"Yes, we do." I agreed.

"But let's go eat first." He said as he led me down the hall.

"Okay." I replied.

~~~~~

Big Boys -The Legacy   By Nikida Bellezza

DEYTWON

I had to keep reminding myself that while Angel was a full-fledged Big Boy, she still
didn't truly know our way of life and how we handled things. What seemed necessary and
common place to Marcus and I, were harsh realities for Angel. She didn't have the breading that
Marcus and I had, she was still on civilian time. I loved her innocence, but at the same time it was
more of a hindrance than a benefit. The bottom line was that I had to tell her what we were
about, what we were capable of, and how we got things done. That what may seem wrong in the
civilian world was actually necessary in our world. It was just how things were. My father saw his
father order deaths, I've seen my father do it, and my kids will see me do it.

"So how long were you outside my door?" Angel asked after our breakfast was served.

"Since about ten. When you didn't come out of the room around nine I ordered the roses
and teddy bear. Then I brought them to your room after they arrived." I said.

"So why didn't you knock?" she asked.

"I did, but then I remembered that your office is soundproof. So I waited, when you still
hadn't come out, I sat on the floor, and ended up falling asleep." I said.

"I was shocked to see you there when I came out. You looked so damn cute, I couldn't even
stay mad at you." She said with a smile.

"It's hard to sleep without you." I admitted.

She smiled and used the fork to play with the food on her plate.

"Baby I…"

"Baby we…" We both started to talk at the same time.

"Go 'head baby." I said encouraging her to speak first.

"Well, I want to go to The Big Boy museum." She said. I wasn't expecting that at all.

171

"Okay, we can do that." I said.

"I mean, come to the island with me, but I feel like I should go to the museum on my own." She said.

"Really?" I asked confused.

"Yes, I feel like I want to spend the day exploring my past, and since that's where most of my family information is. I want to learn as much as I can." She explained.

"On your *own*." I added.

"Right, does that bother you?" She asked.

"Nah, not at all. I mean, you have a right to roam this earth however you please. You're not just my wife, you're a Queen." I said.

"Okay, so, you have some free time next week?" She asked.

"For you, I will cancel every plan I have for the rest of my life, if you asked me to." I said.

"You would, wouldn't you?" She asked with a smile.

I nodded my head yes. She smiled then she got up from her seat and walked over to me and sat on my lap,

"Good thing, I would never ask you to." She said before kissing me.

"Whenever you're ready to go, just say when. But for now, we need to go have some make up sex." I said as I stood with her legs wrapped around me.

"Wow, you can still lift me with all this belly?" She asked with a laugh before throwing her arms around my neck.

"Never talk about yourself like that. You are the most gorgeous woman in the world to me." I said.

"You flatter me." She said.

Big Boys -The Legacy   By Nikida Bellezza

"Call it what you want, as long as you never doubt it." I said as I pressed the button to call the elevator.

She looked at me with her big brown eyes mesmerizing me the way she always did. I loved her more than life. She was my missing piece. All that crazy living I was doing, thinking that I reached the epitome of everything I ever wanted in life. I had no idea that this was waiting for me. I was glad none of my death wishes came true. I was glad I didn't die on my bike, or jumping out of the plane into the ocean to see how long it would take me to swim to shore or any of the other dumb shit I used to do to get an adrenalin rush.

Angel gave me that complete feeling that I spent my life looking for. As educated as I was I didn't have the words to express how she was my weakness, and I'm her soldier on standby, ready to kill anybody that tried to take her happiness away.

We went up to the room and made love in the shower, then we made love a couple more times in the bed. Afterwards I watched her fall asleep in my arms. Life didn't get any better than this. I kissed her stomach and closed my eyes to take a nap.

******

CHAPTER 12

MARCUS

I sat in the recliner in front of the fireplace and puffed on a cigar as I watched lightning contract the sky from dark to light just before the sound of thunder roared to life. The sound of the hotel phone ringing was nearly drowned out by the sound of the thunder, but I was able to catch it on the last ring.

"Jones." I said answering the phone.

"Yes Mr. Jones, I apologize for disturbing you, but there is a woman here by the name of Salisha she said that you are expecting her." The desk agent said.

"She is correct, you may send her up." I replied.

"Right away sir, thank you for staying at the W." He said.

"No problem." I replied before hanging up the phone.

Even though I knew that she would come, she lost points with me for not putting up more of a fight, especially after all that '*I love my husband*' bullshit she tried to feed me. But I was far from shocked because for most people loyalty wasn't shit but an English word.

When I heard the taps on my door, I stood and walked over to the foyer area to let her in.

"Damn, this room is bigger than my entire apartment." She said as she stepped in and sat her umbrella against the wall.

I silently watched her take off her coat and fold it over her arm as she fiddled with her hair.

"What's up?" She asked with a shrug.

"Take off your clothes." I demanded.

"What?" She asked with a frown.

174

"Take off, your fuckin clothes." I said again.

"Who are you talking to like that?" She asked cocking her head.

I snatched her by her collar and pulled her close to me.

"Take off your fuckin clothes or I will rip them from your body." I ordered.

She looked at me and smiled as she let her coat fall to the floor. Then slowly she reached for the buttons on her shirt and eased them out of their slots.

I dropped my robe and reached in my boxers to pull out my dick while retrieving a condom from my pocket. She slipped her arms from her shirt as she watched me slip the condom on.

I couldn't tell if she were trying to be seductive my moving slowly, but I was starting to get bored watching her pull at her belt to take off her skirt, so I snatched her around and bent her over the couch.

"Damn!" She said as her legs swung up nearly kicking me. I raised her skirt and ripped her panties off. Then I positioned myself behind her. I let my dick find her opening and without warning I drove it up in her until I couldn't push any further.

"Oh *SHIT!*" She shouted after the first charge. She was wet but she wasn't ready.

I grabbed hold of her shoulders and continued to ram her with all the force I could muster. I wanted to gut the fuck out of her, for all the shit she talked while I was fuckin Angel, for all the looks when she came around even after Angel was with Deytwon, and because I knew it was what she wanted.

I wanted to get her to be hooked like crack, so that she could be my branch to Angel. She was going to tell me everything I wanted to know, and unwittingly lure Angel into my trap.

I banged her into three orgasms, and then finally I got tired and backed off of her. She fell forward on the couch cushions breathing as though she had just ran a marathon. I pulled the condom off and dropped it into the trash, before walking over to grab a blunt and a lighter from the coffee table.

Salisha lay flat across my couch with one leg up hanging over the back of the couch, still breathing like oxygen was no longer plentiful.

"Watch out slim." I said before sitting down. She moved her leg off the couch and was no spread eagle.

"One things for sure, I see why that bitch kept coming back." Salisha panted as she rubbed herself.

"What bitch?" I asked lighting my blunt, pretending not to know that she meant Angel.

"Angel, how would I know who else you were fuckin'?" She asked.

I looked over at her blowing smoke from my mouth. I really didn't care why she was referring to her as a bitch now, when they proclaimed to be as close as sisters. What I did care about was the fact that it could mean they were no longer cool, which is something that I needed them to be for my plan to work.

"Bitch huh?" I asked.

She shrugged her shoulders before sitting upright on the couch.

"I ain't know you were so fickle. First you hate me, now you fuckin' me, and now you hate your girl" I taunted as I handed her the blunt.

"I'm not *fickle,* and I still got love for her, we just had a fight. And I still hate you, I just needed some dick" She replied taking the blunt.

"Sure ya right." I replied as I started beating my dick, which is something I wasn't used to, but she was making me lose my erection, and I still wanted her to suck it.

"All that fuckin and you ain't cum yet?" She asked looking down at my dick.

I glanced at her and shook my head while stroking my dick.

"You must beat it a lot to not be able to cum off straight fuckin." She said.

"It ain't that, you just talk too much. " I said taking my blunt back.

"Nigga, fuck you!" She exclaimed rolling her eyes at me.

"Suck my dick." I said after taking a pull from the blunt.

"Suck my ass!" She retorted.

I grabbed her by the back of her neck and yanked her face down towards my dick.

"Suck my dick." I said again but this time slower and more forceful.

"Whatever, only because you ain't get your nut yet." She said before lowering her head into my lap. She took me into her mouth and smoothed her lips down my shaft until she reached the base, then she smoothed them back up, flickering her tongue along the way. She repeated the deep throat move a couple times before releasing my dick for air. Soon this became her repetition, but what she didn't know was, I didn't have all night to fuck around with her.

I gripped the back of her head and forced her to take as much of my dick into her mouth until I heard her gag, then I pulled her up by her hair and pushed her back down. I did this until I bussed cream into the back of her throat, then I let her go.

"Muthafucka!" She yelled wiping her mouth.

"Yeah, yeah, get the fuck out." I said standing to my feet. I walked to the bathroom to take a shower.

When I came back out Salisha was gone but there was a note written on a napkin sitting on the coffee table that simply read *'FUCK YOU!'*

"You'll be back." I chuckled to myself as I tossed the note into the trash. If she didn't already know It, she learned tonight that she like that shit rough.

~~~~~

Big Boys -The Legacy   By Nikida Bellezza

ANGEL

It had been about a week since Salisha and I had our fight and we still haven't spoken to one another since. It felt really odd to not talk to her almost every day, because we've never really gone this long without speaking, with the exception of the time that I moved into Marcus' condo in Georgetown. I missed her and had so much that I wanted to tell her, but I allowed my stubbornness to get the best of me. I knew that she wasn't one to hold a grudges for long, but I also knew that when she felt like she was right, there was no changing her mind.

I loved living in New York, in this big beautiful house with Deytwon, but I missed DC because it was full of people that I knew. Even if I were mad at Salisha, I still had people I could talk to and chill with, like my homie Steve whom I hadn't seen in a couple of years, but I knew that he'd still be there for me if I needed him to. Here, I knew no one, and while it was safer for me this way, given my status, the isolation was killing me.

It got so bad sometimes, I even thought of becoming friends with Marcus' wife Tiffani, but that would've been way to awkward given that I used to fuck his brains out.

I had to shake my head at my stupidity on that thought. What the hell was I thinking going all in with him like that. The sex was good as shit, and he was fine as hell with a swag that could never be duplicated, but he was poison, and I was just as bad going along with what he was doing. Then to discover that he was doing the shit to keep me from Deytwon.

"Damn that shit was crazy." I said to myself.

"Hey baby, you ready to go, I got a surprise for you." Deytwon said as he walked out onto the balcony where I had been sitting.

"Ready and waiting." I said with a smile as I held my hands out for him to help me up.

"Cool, let's be out." He said helping me up,

179

We went down and got into the waiting limo where the chauffeur opened the door for us.

"So can I get a hint about what this surprise is?" I asked kicking my shoes off to allow my feet to breathe.

"You want a hint huh, let me see, it's a very big deal." He said as he pat the seat for me to hand him my feet.

I twisted my body around until I was able to kick my feet up on his lap. He laughed at me as he started gently massaging them.

"First of all, that's not funny it takes a lot for me to get around this belly! *Second*, that's not a hint, *everything* you do is a big deal!" I said.

"Fair enough." He replied laying his head back on the seat.

"Sooooo?" I asked.

"Soooo, what?" He asked back.

"Baby, what's my hint?" I asked.

"I gave you a hint." He said.

"That wasn't a good hint." I said folding my arms.

"It was the best I have." He said with a chuckle.

"You suck." I pouted, as his phone rang.

"Hold that thought." He said before answering his phone.

"Richards... yeah, we're on the way now, you have it ready?... Bet, that works... Aright, be there in about twenty minutes... Cool, later." Deytwon said.

"That was about the surprise?" I asked.

"We be eavesdropping now?" He asked.

"Fine, whatever, don't tell me." I said waving my hand at him and turning my attention towards the window.

"You mad at me?" He asked.

I ignored him and kept staring out of the window. That's when he moved down to where I was and put his arms around me. He looked at me for a few seconds before letting out a slight chuckle.

"Don't be mad baby. You're gonna love it." He said. I looked down at him and smiled.

"I already do." I said giving into him with a kiss. He laid his head on my chest and I stroked the top of his head the way I always did when he came home after a hard day. I didn't need another thing.

Thirty minutes later we arrived at an airplane hangar with several planes that were either being serviced or cleaned

"Baby, we're here." I said waking him up.

"Okay." He said as he sat up and grabbed my shoes. He put them on my feet and helped me up in time for the chauffeur to open the door for us.

"What are we doing here?" I asked confused. Whenever we took a plan or a jet anywhere it was from our own property.

"Let's go find out." He said as he took my hand and led me to the entrance of the hanger.

"Mr. Rich, welcome." Said a man who walked out to greet us. He shook hands with Deytwon then turned to look at me.

"Ed, good to see you, and this is my wife, Angel." Deytwon said introducing me.

"Hello Mrs. Richards, you are looking exquisitely lovely this fine afternoon." Ed said.

"Thank you, nice to meet you." I replied.

"So let's see it." Deytwon said with a pat to the mans back.

"Of course, right this way. Jenny bring the design please." The man said leading us in the opposite direction.

"Yes sir." Jenny replied going back into the hanger.

We walked around to the side of the building and stopped when we came to a large private plane.

"Here we are." Ed said stretching his arms out.

"So what you think?" Deytwon asked nodding his head towards the plane.

"What do you mean?" I asked looking at the beautiful plane.

"This is yours." He said.

"What? Oh my gawd, are you serious?!" I asked shocked and surprised.

"Yeah as a queen, you need your own means of transportation. You don't always have to wait for me to go or do anything. You want to visit your girl in DC, you want to go shopping in Cali, or Milan, whatever, this is yours to do just that." He said.

"Oh my gawd Deytwon! It's beautiful! I don't know what to say, I never expected this!" I said covering my mouth.

"Here you are Ed." Jenny said handing Ed a large sign.

"Mr. Rich." Ed said handing Deytwon the sign.

Deytwon looked at it for a few seconds then nodded his head in approval.

"What's that?" I asked.

"Remember that day, when it was raining and we were bullshittin around the house. You drew a picture and said if you ever have a business, this is how your logo would look." Deytwon said.

"Yes." I asked ready to scream again.

Deytwon smiled and turned the picture around for me to see. It was the exact replica of what I drew, down to a T, only it was much larger.

"Oh my gawd, its beautiful!" I shouted.

"This is going on the side of your plane, that is, if you want it up there." Deytwon said.

"I do baby, I do!" I said jumping up and down.

"Whoa babygirl, don't shake up the babies." He said rubbing my stomach.

I shook my head and threw my arms around his neck.

"I love you, so much!" I said to him as tears formed in my eyes.

"I love you more." He replied.

"Okay, so we will get to working on the logo. The plane will be ready by this time next week. We'll get started today." Ed said.

"I appreciate that." Deytwon said as she shook Ed's hand.

"Thank you." I said wiping my eyes.

"My pleasure ma'am." Ed replied as he tossed Deytwon the keys.

"Shall we go in?" Deytwon asked dangling the keys.

"Yes!" I replied.

We walked up the steps and entered the plane. It was a spacious six seater with pink interior. Each seat was made to look like a recliner and had built in snack tables next to them. The plane had a restroom, a bar and even a small open area that I couldn't figure out the purpose of, but I loved it all the same.

"Baby, this is amazing." I said as I sat in one of the chairs. It was so soft and cozy I just knew it would put me to sleep.

By Nikida Bellezza

"Well baby, it's really time for you to start coming into your own. You're not a housewife and while everything that's mine is yours, you do have your own. It's time for you to branch out and set your own tone." He said as he sat in the seat across from mine.

"You mean, like start my own businesses and stuff?" I asked.

"Anything you want, you want to take over a franchise, you want to start one, you want to open up a string of daycares across the country, or even write a poetry book, it's all up to you." He said.

"You know, It's funny, I haven't written anything since we moved out here." I said after really thinking about it.

"I've noticed." He said.

"Oddly enough, I write a lot less when I'm happy." I said with a shrug.

"What's odd is that you've been so unhappy that you can measure it by the amount of time you spend writing. But don't stress it, when it's time for you to start writing again, you will." he said.

"I know." I agreed.

After we left the airplane place we went to grab something to eat and spent the rest of the day joy riding in the limo. It was the perfect day.

The next morning while Deytwon was away on business I decided to call Salisha, it had been long enough and I really missed my friend. Besides, I needed someone to talk to about the letters I found in my great great grandfathers old chest.

"Hello?" She asked answering the phone.

"What's up, you busy?" I asked.

"Nah, just at work, but you know I ain't doing shit. How you been?" She asked.

"Pretty good, and you?" I asked.

"I been cool, but I gotta tell you something, you're going to think I'm crazy in the head girl." She said.

"I already do, but look, I got to tell you something too, and I've been dying to tell you because I can't tell anybody else, well, not right now anyway." I said in a hushed tone as I headed outside.

"You go first, what's going on?" She asked anxiously.

"So about a month or so ago, I'm out shopping for baby stuff right, and I go into this store, the sales lady started treating me like I was some shit and couldn't afford anything in the store, right." I began.

"Little did *that* bitch know." Salisha said with a chuckle.

"Right, so anyway, her grandmother comes from the back and shuts her down, then she says, you're the Big Boy Queen. I'm like, how you know that? She's like because of the ring. So anyway, she starts telling me all this stuff about my great great grandfather and showing me all these documents…"

"What the fuck?!" Salisha asked interrupting me.

"RIGHT!, So she starts telling me that my great great grandfather didn't step down, he was killed, and his wife ran off with the children. Girl, whole time I'm not buying anything she saying, but when she showed me the papers, I don't know, it was like she had proof." I said.

"This is crazy as hell Angel, I mean, what are you going to do?" Salisha asked.

"I don't know, because all Deytwon ever told me was that my great great grandfather stepped down. That's the same story Trish told me too." I said.

"Who is Trish?" She asked.

"Oh, this chick that used to dress me when I was going to different events with Marcus. But anyway, I wasn't paying what the lady was saying no mind, until at the Announcement ceremony Marcus' great grandfather said that Cecil, my great great grandfather stepped down, sixty-four years ago." I said.

"Yeah, I heard him say that, but what about it?" She asked.

"According to legend, Cecil stepped down fifty years ago. Remember them saying that at my coronation." I said.

"Right, oh my gawd, that does sound like a cover up somewhere. What are you going to do?" Salisha asked.

"Well, there's a Big Boy museum on Big Boy Island, it has all of the history of the Big Boys and apparently my great great great great grandfather has a secret compartment there. So I'm going to go there and try to find it. I have to know what's going on." I said.

"I don't know Angel that sounds dangerous. If they've been covering this shit up for sixty-four years, it's for a reason. Do you think Deytwon is in on it too?" Salisha asked.

"I really don't know. I think the cover up was before his and Marcus' time and for that reason they may have been kept out of it." I reasoned.

"It still sounds pretty dangerous. I don't know." Salisha said.

"I mean, I could live my life in the dark, but it just feels like I'm cheating myself of vital family information if I do. Salisha besides you and my grandmother, I have no family, I have no family history. Maybe now I can find out that I do and what it is." I said.

"I understand, you gotta do what you gotta do. Just be careful girl." Salisha said.

"Always, so what did you have to tell me?" I asked.

"Oh, uh,, what was I going to tell you? Oh yeah, Anthony's party, are you gonna be able to make it, its next Friday." Salisha said stammering over her words for a second.

"Of course I wouldn't miss it. Just tell me where and I'm there." I said.

Salisha and I talked for a couple hours before she really had to start doing some work. Her stammering over her choice of words about what she wanted to tell me did stay in the back of my mind during our conversation though. But at the moment it didn't really matter to me, I was just happy to have my best friend back. Whatever it was that she *really* had to tell me would come out eventually, it always does.

******

CHAPTER 13

DEYTWON

Now that Angel had her own personal plane she was one step closer to independence. It was easy for me to allow her to live as a housewife, because I could protect her better, but the fact of the matter is, she's a leader, and needed to branch out to start her own endeavor. Of course anything that was mine is hers, but she's going to have to gain experience, because if there's ever a meeting that Marcus and I couldn't attend for whatever reason, she would need to be present, and she'll need to show authority.

I had an important business meeting coming up and I wanted her to attend to see how one should conduct business. I wanted her to understand the type of authority she would need to show, and the respect she should be expected to receive.

But first, I needed to explain to her the harsh reality of how we get things done, and how we got the respect that we received. I put together a presentation for her of who The Big Boys were, our assets, our affiliates, our ties, our enemies and how we handled those who stepped out of line.

The meeting that I wanted her to attend was being held on some property that I owned in Texas. A small time contractor wanted to build on my land. Normally I wouldn't attend such a meeting, but It was a good opportunity to get Angel some experience. Before the meeting I set up a little training session for Angel in one of my smaller more private board rooms in the same building.

"Okay, so you're saying I need to always be in control of the meeting, even if others are taking, they should feel as though they are being allowed to talk versus being free to talk?" Angel asked.

"Exactly, you don't have to say very much, just so long as what you say is exact, authoritative and unyielding. If there is something you don't want, don't like or will not tolerate, do not leave room for doubt. Don't keep reciting that something is on or off the table. If you say no, remain unwavering and firm. If they become insistent, end the meeting. Because if they are not taking no, or yes for an answer, they are showing lack of respect for your authority." I explained.

"So what happens when I have a problem like, Jay?" She asked a bit hesitant.

"We handle it accordingly. See, the thing I need you to understand the most is that we aren't citizens governed by a judicial system. Our authority runs deeper than the laws of the land, and it must remain unquestioned. Now, I know that you look at Jay and you feel that he was too small scaled to be made an example out of, but the truth is, we have small scale affiliates as well. We don't need them to become low level problems when we have large scale problems that require the most of our attention. When we can nip something in the bud, that's just what we do." I said.

"We, as in me too?" She asked.

"Especially you, because you are a woman. While there are some women in power, there aren't many.

"Yeah, but I don't know if I can..." She started.

"You, can do anything that you believe you can do." I said interrupting her.

"I was going to say that I can't be the one who chooses to take another person's life." She said.

"It's all a part of the job Angel. There has to be order and balance." I said.

"Then you know what, I don't want it." She said surrendering with her hands up.

189

"I'm afraid that's not your call babygirl. This is your birthright, and you have a mandate to make this shit work, and survive. This Is how." I explained.

"Is this the secret to why Marcus always acts invincible, and why you always seem so serene? Because at any given moment you can snap your fingers and make things happen, including death?" She asked.

"With great power comes great responsibility." I said.

"Yes, and absolute power corrupts, absolutely." She argued.

"Well, who knows Angel, maybe you'll bring a sense of compassion to the table. Just don't let it get out of control. Think of us as the government over a country, we need to have order, control, and discipline. I said.

"We're really that big?" She asked.

"Bigger than that. A lot of decisions that we make along with a few other factions, effects the world. We are a part of a powerful syndicate called The Rule. The Rule is made up of five of the most powerful brotherhoods in the world. We meet twice a year to discuss world business, unless something pressing comes up, then we'd have an emergency meeting. The headquarters is in Rome. All members are members for life and are branded when they reach maturity in their own brotherhood. When the Big Boy torch was passed on to Marcus and I, we were taken to Rome to be branded by our fathers and grandfathers." I said.

"Branded, you mean like they do cows?" She asked.

"Exactly, but the iron isn't as big." I said as I took off my suit jacket. I unbuttoned my shirt at the wrist to raised it up above my branding symbol on my forearm. It was a crown with the letter R rising through it.

"Oh this, I thought that was some Big Boy tattoo, I saw that Marcus has one too." She said

190

running a finger across it.

"Yeah, we were branded at the same time." I said lowering my sleeve and buttoning it again.

"I know that had to hurt." She said shaking her head.

"It does, but it's a necessary evil. It's recognized amongst power entities all over the world." I said.

"So, I have to get one?" She asked.

"Yes, but after the babies are born. As a leader of the Big Boys it's important that you too are branded with the symbol as a sign of respect and conformity." I said.

"There's way more to this than I thought." She said,

"There is, but you're not alone. All I need you to do is start thinking about things on a larger scale. Sky is not the limit, space is not the limit, and this galaxy is not the limit.

"Okay baby, I will do my best." she replied.

After our discussion we went to the meeting where I had Angel take notes and pay attention to every person there, from their body language to their responses. When we got back home we went over her notes and discussed things in more depth. She was still a bit skeptical about her role, but she was beginning to understand the causes and effects of Big Boy behavior.

~~~~~

Big Boys -The Legacy   By Nikida Bellezza

MARCUS

It had been about two weeks since I fucked Salisha's brains out. Since then she's been texting the shit out of me. I mostly ignored her as a way to keep her ass baited. For some reason, the more you ignore a chick after giving her good dick, the harder she'd come after you. That was some funny shit, but it was even funnier in Salisha's case because nearly two years ago I was the scum of the Earth to her while I was fuckin' Angel.

After all the *'I wanna see what that dick do again'*, and *'Cum punish me.'* messages she's sent, I decided to see how badly she wanted it. In one of her texts she mentioned that tonight was the night of her husband's birthday party, so I decided to make a trip to DC and make her choose.

"Hello?" Salisha ask in a hush tone. Her husband must've been close.

"What's up, I'm in DC, you coming through?" I asked

"I can't, I'm at my husband's birthday party." She mumbled into the phone.

"True, aright." I said

"*WAIT!*" She yelled out before I could hang up.

"Waiting is a game that I don't play, shawty. " I said.

"Where you staying, I'll meet you now." She said.

~~~~~

ANGEL

Tonight was the night of Anthony's birthday party. Deytwon said that he couldn't make it so I brought Brad with me. Deytwon insisted that I take security with me as well, so I agreed to take one guard with me.

We flew to DC in my private plane. I was so excited because it was my first flight. Once we landed I arranged to have a limo drive us to the banquette hall where Salisha was hosting the party. It was my first time back in DC in years and I missed it, from the smell, to the sounds, to the accents. There was no place like home.

"Hey girl, glad you could make it, Anthony, look who's here!" Salisha said calling Anthony over as we walked in.

"Hey lady, how are you and the little one?" Anthony said as he reached for my stomach but Roland my security stepped in and grabbed his arm.

"Whoa, my bad dog." Anthony said taking his arm back.

"Sorry about that, but I'm good. This is my assistant Brad, Brad you remember Salisha, and this is her husband, Anthony." I said.

"Yeah, I remember you, how you doin?" Brad asked Salisha.

"I'm good." She replied.

"Nice to meet you Anthony, Happy Birthday, from the Richards." Brad said handing Anthony the gift Deytwon and I had picked out, which was an expensive diamond watch.

"Thank you, I appreciate that. Well come on in. Angel you probably know some of these folks, just get on in there and mingle." Anthony said.

"Thanks Ant." I said as Salisha linked arms with me and walked me away.

"So." She said as though she were waiting for me to tell her something.

"So what?" I asked.

"No one's heard from Jay since the video." She said.

"You ain't even about to bring that up are you?" I asked annoyed.

"I was just wondering." She said.

"Well wonder about something else." I replied.

"Fine, fine… so anyway Steve is here." She said

"Really?" I asked surprised. I hadn't seen Steve since I moved into Marcus' condo. I missed him dearly, he was one of the few guys I knew that kept it one hundred.

"Yup, right over there, talking to Linda, his new woman." Salisha said nodding her head towards Steve who was leaning against the wall listening to whatever Linda was telling him. She had her arms around his neck while his hands were stuffed in his pockets.

"How long they been messing?" I asked.

"For a few months now. She told me they talkin about moving in together and everything. But you know her crazy ass baby father Gary ain't having it." Salisha said.

"Steve ain't worried about him." I chuckled remembering how good Steve's hands were.

"Nah, but I can't imagine the shit is worth it. But anyway, you want to go say hi?" She asked as we stopped in the middle of the floor.

"Nah, not while he all boo'd up. I'll catch him before I leave." I said wishing that I could go over and speak. I really missed his friendship.

"Well, that's fine, let me see who else is here. Oh, and I ran into Leslie earlier today over by the Shrimp Boat. She just got in one of them town homes over there she said." Salisha said.

"Oh yeah, I ain't talked to her in a minute, how she doing?" I asked remembering that I forgot to check up on her after I got out of jail.

194

By Nikida Bellezza

"She good, she said she ain't seen you since y'all both was locked up? " She said looking at me quizzically.

"Oh, yeah." I replied forgetting that I never told Salisha that I had been arrested back when I was dealing with Marcus.

"So what you get arrested for?" She asked folding her arms.

"This was a long minute ago, back when I was dealing with Marcus. I had got in a fight with some chick and I got arrested." I said shaking my head as I thought about how stupid I was back then.

"So why you ain't call me to come get you out?" She asked.

"Lish, it's a long story, Deytwon ended up coming to get me out. I called the first person that I thought of which was Marcus, but somehow Deytwon found out and came and got me." I said.

"Uh huh, so how is the situation between you and Marcus now?" She asked.

"Nonexistent, we barely see each other, and when we do, we don't acknowledge one another." I replied.

"Oh well, Le-le she said she might come through tonight if she can get her grandmother to babysit for her." Salisha said.

"That's what's up. Look, I need to get off my feet." I said as I sat down at the closes table. My feet and ankles were swollen something terrible.

"Okay, well you want me to bring you something?" She asked.

"I'll get it, you ladies go on and continue with your girl chat." Brad said before walking away.

"Well, I guess he really does come in handy." Salisha said.

195

"I guess." I replied as I looked around the room for more familiar people. I missed the shit out of DC, I felt like I was at a high school reunion or something, and really, I hadn't been gone that long.

"Sup stranger?" I heard Steve's voice ask as I felt someone tap my shoulder.

"Hey you! What's up?" I asked excited as I tried to stand to give him a hug holding up a hand to keep my security back.

"Whoa slim, what's this?" He asked pointing at my stomach.

"What it look like?" I asked as he helped me up.

"Looks like you 'bout to be somebody's mama." he chuckled as we hugged.

"Yup, in about five months." I said once we let go.

"That's what's up, go on and sit down before your water break or some shit." He said.

"Too early for that, so what's going on. I heard you mess with Linda now." I said.

"Right. So what's good, last time I saw you, you were loading a uhaul heading to Georgetown." He said dismissing my comment about him and Linda.

"Oh my gawd, so much has happened since then." I said with a laugh.

"Yeah, I heard you're married now." He said.

"Yup, I am, to the perfect guy." I replied.

"Judging by that rock, you sayin' the right thing. Long as it ain't that nigga Marcus you was gone on." He said.

"Nah, it's not Marcus, its someone else. He has no prior wives, no extra girlfriends and he loves me more than even I think I deserve." I said.

"Well I can say this, you glow when you talk about him, and that's something you never did when you spoke on Marcus." He said.

196

"Because for the first time in my life ever, I'm happy." I said.

"That's all I want to hear." He said as Linda walked over.

"Hey Angel, long time no see." She said as she sat on Steve's lap.

"Likewise. I hope you're taking care of my best friend, he's good people." I said looking at Steve.

"Oh, I'm on my job, so how many months are you?" She asked.

"About four" I said rubbing my stomach.

"Oh, girl I thought you was about to say you due next month, look at that belly." Linda said with a chuckle.

"Not cool slim, why don't you go play for a lil while." Steve said.

"It was a joke baby, lighten up." Linda insisted before kissing him on the cheek.

"Here you are Mrs. Richards." Brad said handing me a cup of punch.

"Thanks Brad, must've been a hell of a line huh?" I asked sitting the punch on the table.

"No, actually you see that gentlemen over there in the gray vest and ripped jeans? His name is Willie, and we had gotten caught up in a very interesting conversation." Brad said smiling and licking his lips.

"Uh huh, so, we'll probably be here for a couple hours. If you want to go back and chat, that's cool, just check in." I said.

"Ohh, that's why I love you honey!" Brad said with a kiss to my cheek before sashaying back to the guy.

"Who is Brad, and why is he calling you Mrs. Richards?" Steve asked.

"Not important." I said before sipping my juice.

"Look who fell out the muthafuckin woodwork!" Karen shouted as she approached us.

Big Boys -The Legacy   By Nikida Bellezza

"What's up Karen?" I asked laughing happy to see her.

"Shit, what's good with you, hold up slim, you pregnant in these streets?" She asked leaning in to give me a hug.

"Oh, you know that was on the way." I joked as we let go.

"True true, so what's been up? Ain't seen you since you pulled up to the shop in that Benz a couple years ago. What you been doing?" She asked.

"Shit, living, doin' me, what you been up to?" I asked knowing what she really wanted to know. It was interesting how Salisha said everybody was hawking her to confirm or deny Jay's gossip on me, but none of them seemed to want to ask me themselves.

"Coolin, oh, you know I got another shop now, it's on Rhode Island ave, by the station, you know them new lil strip of stores they put over there?" She asked.

"Yeah, okay, that's what's up. Congratulations." I said.

"Thank you! Yup yup, life is gooder' than a muthafucka!" She said.

"It can be." I replied.

"Yeah, I heard if anybody know it, it's you." She said.

"Everybody get a turn sometime, right?" I asked.

"No bullshit." Steve said giving up a little chuckle.

"True, ahhh shit, they playin the electric slide. Come on out here pregnant mama, shake that ass like you did to get pregnant!" Karen said as she started dancing.

"Girl I don't understand why black folks won't let that damn song die!" Linda said.

"Because, just like the songs '*Before I Let go*' and '*Living for the love of you*' the '*Electric Slide*' is a traditional party songs. Now bring your boogie ass on to this dance floor!" Karen said as she pulled Linda's hand.

198

"Aright, I'm in." I said thinking I'd better have some fun while I can.

"Yeah man, that's what I'm talking about! Come on pregnant ma!" Karen said as she danced her way towards the line that was forming.

"You coming?" I asked looking over at Steve.

"Yeah, soon as she throw on some 'RE' or 'JY'!" Steve said with a laugh.

"You know Salisha ain't into them, but you might get some *'Back'* though." I said as I stood to my feet.

"Don't hurt yourself." He said.

"True, let me take off these shoes." I said as my Security walked over to me.

"Ma'am." He said when he approached me. I almost forgot that he was there, he was posted against the wall behind me.

"Hold my shoes for me please." I said.

"Yes ma'am." He said taking my shoes.

Steve frowned up his face as he pointing towards the security.

"Long story." I said then I walked out to the dance floor to join the line.

"Oh my gawd, how y'all get my girl to come out here!" Salisha shouted when she saw me standing in the line dancing.

"That's a grown ass woman right there!" Karen shouted.

"Come on girl, let's do this like we used to do back in the day!" Salisha said moving in next to me.

"Yeah, but I can't touch the floor!" I laughed.

"Aww true, but still, we can do everything else." She replied.

We danced through three line dancing songs before we sang Happy Birthday and watched

Anthony open his gifts.

"This has been a really fun party. It's been so good seeing everyone." I said to Salisha after everything settled down.

"Yeah, like old times, huh?" She asked.

"Definitely." I replied as her cell started ringing.

"Oh shit." She said looking down at the number.

"What's wrong, who is it?" I asked.

"Uh, my mother girl, you know how she be. I'll be right back it's too loud in here. I'm going to take it in the hall." She said leaving before I could say another word.

"Mrs. Richards, this party is way live. I didn't know y'all got down like this in DC." Brad said as he danced up next to me.

"I swear I keep forgetting that you're here." I said with a chuckle.

"My bad, I guess I just got a little comfortable and forgot that I'm working. I promise I won't be out of your sight for the rest of the night." Brad said putting his hands up.

"Nah, I ain't trippin, it's been a really good night. But when we get back to New York I'm going to need you back on track." I said.

"Yes, ma'am. Oooh girl, they about to do the 'cha cha slide' up in here. Please tell me you know how to do it, because if I can't join the line I'ma have to do it right here next to you!" Brad said exclaimed as he started dancing.

"I do, but I'm a little worn out. You can go on." I said as Salisha walked back towards me. She had a worried look on her face.

"Oh thank you lady!" He said giving me a slight hug before jogging over to the dance floor.

"Girl, they about to do the cha cha slide, you better get over there, your man is doin it!" I laughed after Salisha approached me.

"Angel, I got to make a run, I need you to cover for me." Salisha said completely ignoring my statement as she slipped her cell into her hand bag.

"Is everything okay, you look stressed?" I asked studying the perplexed expression splattered across her face.

"Nah, I'm cool. I just need to go check up on his surprise. They said it might not be ready and I've been on them for weeks about how important this night is." She said.

"Well, do you want me to go with you?" I offered.

"You and your entourage, no thanks" she replied with a sarcastic giggle.

"I have one security guard, and one assistant with me, and they're only here for my protection." I said feeling a little offended. Pregnancy hormones are a bitch.

"I'm sorry girl, like you said I'm just a lil stressed. I wanted this night to be perfect for him, and now it may not be." She said changing her tone.

"Lish..." I started but she cut me off.

"Angel, just cover for me. I'll be right back." She demanded before walking away. I watched her push past people until she reached the door and walked out.

"Where is she going in such a hurry?" I heard Anthony's voice ask from behind, startling me.

"Oh, you scared me. What was that?" I asked holding my chest after turning around to face him.

"My bad 'mommy to be'. By the way you're simply glowing." Anthony said.

"Thank you, Anthony." I replied.

"No need for that. I can't wait for the day Salisha and I will be as blessed." He said.

"Soon enough, don't you worry." I assured him.

"Speaking of my wife, where did she go?" He asked. I looked back over towards the door before returning my attention towards Anthony.

"Well, I probably shouldn't tell you this, but she said she had to run out to get your surprise." I said with a shrug.

"Yeah? She got me more gifts? That's what's up!" Anthony exclaimed beaming from ear to ear.

"Excuse me, Mrs. Richards, it has reached 11pm." My security leaned in to say.

"So it has. Well, Anthony, I apologize, I won't be able to wait for Salisha to get back. I must be going now. Tell her that I'll give her a call sometime this week." I said giving him a slight hug.

"Oh, okay, and will do. Have a safe flight back." He said.

"Most certainly." I replied signaling for Brad to come along.

When we stepped outside I noticed a Cadillac limo parked in the alley between the banquette hall and the shop next to it. I walked towards it thinking that It were mine but couldn't quite figure out why it was in the alley.

"Mrs. Richards?" Security called behind me.

"Yes, why is he parked there?" I asked.

"I'm sorry madam, but you're limo is here." He said holding his arm out to the limo pulling up in front of the banquette hall.

"Oh." I said glancing back at the limo in the alley one last time. That's when I caught the tag that read *'Power'* which automatically made me think of Marcus, but it couldn't be him, why

202

would he be in DC.

I climbed into my limo and rode to where my plane awaited us while listening to Brad yap about how much fun he had, and how he couldn't wait to call the guy he met at the party.

When I finally got home a couple of hours later, I stripped naked and went straight to sleep.

******

CHAPTER 14

DEYTWON

"So baby, have you been thinking about what kind of business you'd like to start, or take over?" I asked after Ms. Rosa served us our lunch on the back lower patio that over looked the water.

"Baby, it's only been a couple of weeks since you first started trying to teach me. Can I marinate in the lessons? Why I do I have to jump out there?" She asked.

"You don't, but I don't want you to settle for just being a wife. You're a wealthy woman with or without me. Being a leader of the Big Boys makes the world your platform." I said.

"So I'm just supposed to go out there and start throwing money around?" She asked shaking her head.

"Yes! Boomerang that muthafucka!" I said with a chuckle.

"Okay baby, well, let me contemplate a need that I can fulfill, and that will be my business idea." She said after laughing at me.

"That's a good start." I said feeling better that she was starting to get on board with the idea. Sometimes I felt that I cheated her by making her my wife before allowing her to get a feel for being a Big Boy leader first. So from time to time I'd push her into discovering her own path outside of me. If it were up to me she'd never have to do or worry about shit, but because she was a Queen, It was only right that she understood her position and her rights. I had no right to deny her of that just to satisfy my own comfort level.

After lunch Angel went off to enjoy a spa day while I went into my office to conduct a few meetings through video conference.

"Hello Mr. Richards, how are you today?" Asked Tony, my underworld contact in Miami.

By Nikida Bellezza

"That depends on what you have to tell me." I replied.

"Yes sir, Gumpy's debt has been paid off, but he has been killed." Tony said.

"I care that he's dead?" I asked wanting to know why he was telling me this.

"Well, I'm not sure. He called himself telling his connect on you. He was going to make a deal for your head, but he didn't know his connect was an affiliate of the Big Boys. The affiliate killed him and his family, shutdown his entire operation down and turned over all money to you." Tony said.

"Who is this affiliate?" I asked curious.

"Dougie Mann, but as a connect he's only known as Beast." Tony said.

"Yeah, Dougie Mann." I said recalling the name. Dougie and I hadn't spoken in years, and while I appreciated his show of loyalty to me, he really didn't have a choice. He was one of the leaders of The Fellas, a powerful group of men who took orders from The Big Boys.

"He didn't brick my money did he?" I asked.

"No sir, it's all green, waiting in a safe at the Miami restaurant Sides." Tony assured me.

"Very good, anything else?" I asked.

"No sir, everything is well and running smoothly." He said.

"Perfect. Thank you Tony, I appreciate you being on top of my shit out there." I said.

"My pleasure." He said.

"It will be, when you see your next paycheck. I holla." I said ending the call.

I noted to give Tony a raise before tuning in to my next conference.

"Mr. Richards, how are you today?" Priscilla asked

"I'm good, what's going on?" I asked

"Well, you outbid everyone but Vandt Co. So the property is going to him." She said sounding disappointed.

"Really?" I asked.

"Yes sir." She replied.

"Okay, anything else?" I asked.

"No sir, well, there's still the property Upstate, you're in a bidding war with him over." She said. I suppose trying to offer me a glimmer of hope.

"Keep an eye on it for me." I said.

"Yes sir." She replied.

"That's all for me." I said.

"Okay sir, I will let you know if anything new happens or changes." She assured me.

"I appreciate that. Goodbye." I said before ending the call.

I made a call to Scotty, my stock broker to buy up ten more shares of Michael Vandt Co. Now he didn't outbid me, I outbid myself, using his money. I was certain I'd be hearing from him soon and I couldn't wait for the day.

After the call to Scotty I decided to relax, so I spend the rest of the day chillin. A little time in the jacuzzi, the rest reading until Angel got home.

~~~~~

ANGEL

"Who in the fuck is this calling my wife this time of night?" I heard Deytwon shout waking me up out of my sleep.

"What?" I asked as I sat up in bed. Deytwon had my cell to his ear listening to the explanation he demanded.

"Dog, I can sympathize with you, but it's three in the morning. You don't call another man's wife at three in the morning. That's disrespectful as shit, to me and to my wife... Yeah, yeah, I hear you, let this be the last time, feel me?" Deytwon said.

I moved in closer to Deytwon trying to see if I could catch the voice. I had absolutely no idea who it could be.

"Look man, you don't need to keep apologizing, I can dig your stress, so long as I'm understood. Bet, Angel is awake now, hold on..." Deytwon said before handing me my phone.

"Who is this?" I asked looking from my phone to Deytwon.

"Salisha's husband, he can't find her. Let your girl know I don't appreciate her husband hitting you up off the late night." Deytwon said before lying back down.

"Oh my gawd, hello, Anthony?" I exclaimed into the phone more worried about Salisha than Deytwon being annoyed.

"Angel, please tell your husband that I am sorry. I haven't talked to Salisha since this afternoon after she arrived in New York. When you picked her up from greyhound, did you take her straight to the hotel?" He asked sounding like he was near tears.

'Oh my gawd, no this bitch didn't lie and drag me into the shit!' I thought to myself.

"Uh, yeah, I took her to the hotel, then we hung out for a little while. Her phone died while we were on our way back to her hotel. Maybe two hours ago now. I'm sure she's sleeping, just

207

relax and hit her first thing in the morning, okay?" I said lying.

"Okay, you're probably right. Thank you so much Angel, you two have a good night, and please tell him again I'm sorry, no disrespect intended " Anthony said sounding relieved.

"He knows Anthony, now get some sleep. Good night." I said.

"Okay, Good night." He replied.

I quickly ended the call with Anthony to immediately call Salisha.

"Who you calling now?" Deytwon asked annoyed.

"My trickass best friend to find out why she got me lying for her." I said as the phone started ringing.

"Uh uh, don't put no stress on my baby." Deytwon said as he sat up again.

"Hello?" Salisha asked in a groggy tone as I waved Deytwon quiet.

"Don't hello me trick. Why you got me lying to your husband for you? And why you ain't tell me you were coming to New York?" I asked.

"Anthony called you?" She asked snapping out of her groggy mood.

"Yes, I just got off the phone with him. You got him worried sick! Salisha what's going on?" I asked.

"Girl you wouldn't understand, but thanks for covering for me." She said.

"I wouldn't understand what, I'm your best friend! Where are you staying anyway?" I asked as Deytwon tugged at my night gown.

"A motel in Brooklyn." She said

"BROOKLYN?! You ain't nowhere near me! What the fuck is going on Lish?" I asked worried about my friend.

"That's it, hello, look it's late and my wife won't come back to bed until she knows you're

208

straight. So give me the address to where you are, I'll send a car to come get you and drop you off at a hotel out here, cool? Bet, baby hand me that pen over there." Deytwon said. I reached into my nightstand and grabbed a pen and a pad.

"So you're where? Cool, got it. Get dressed." Deytwon said before handing me the phone. He got out of bed and walked over to the computer on the other side of the room.

"Hello?" I asked.

"Yeah girl, you guys really don't have to do this." Salisha said.

"Salisha, what are you doing here? What's going on?" I asked ignoring her statement.

~~~~~

MARCUS

I shook my head as I stepped into my jeans. This bitch is too sloppy. I told her to call and text her bitchass husband every few hours to let him know she was good. But nah, she had it under control.

"Angel, it's okay, I'll talk to you about everything tomorrow, I promise. Let me get my things together. Okay. Okay, bye bye." Salisha said hanging up the phone.

"Sorry, I didn't think Anthony would call Angel to check up on me." Salisha said as she watched me buckle my belt.

"Yeah, 'cause why would cuz worry about his wife who traveled to another state and proceeded to ignore his calls for five hours straight." I asked sarcastically.

"I guess I wasn't thinking, too busy taking pipe." She giggled.

"You so full of shit slim. Your husband know that?" I asked as I stepped into my shoes

"I don't know, does your wife?" She asked back.

I walked over to her and choked her against the wall.

"Talking about my wife in any kind of way, will get your teeth knocked the fuck out. Check yourself bitch, I ain't the rest of these niggas out here." I said before letting her go.

"Damn, you act like I said something bad." She said touching her neck.

"That's the problem with you side bitches. Y'all always wanna' fuckin matter. Can't never just take shit for what it is." I said ignoring her.

"*I'm not her*!" She shouted.

"Her who?" I asked looking at her like she was crazy.

"Angel, I'm not Angel. I don't want to matter to you, I have a man that I matter to." She sassed.

"You definitely ain't Angel." I chuckled

"Hmm, that don't bother me, I don't need her problems anyway." Salisha said as she started putting her clothes on.

"Yeah, and what problems are those?" I asked.

"The problems that's got her going to Big Boy Island to try to resolve." She replied rocking her neck.

"Shawty, if you got something to say, either say that shit, or stop talkin altogether. " I said getting frustrated.

"Let's just say she ran into someone who told her somethings about the Big Boys and she wants to go see if there's any truth to what they said." She said before giving up a long sigh.

"So she chasing behind the word of some clown off the street?" I asked.

"It's some old lady, What she say the lady name was, Cynthia, Arbith...Tabitha, some lady named Tabitha. She said she knew her great great grandfather, and that she should go to the Island to learn more." Salisha said.

'Hmm, Tabitha huh? I didn't know the name, but if she knew Cecil then I'm sure my folks would recognize the name. Of course, I wasn't about to tell them shit until I figured out what the fuck they were really up to. ' I thought to myself.

"So when she supposed to be going there?" I asked.

"She said she was going Monday morning." Salisha said with a shrug.

'That's perfect, that's enough time to get a message to Cocoa to end this bitch.' I thought to myself.'

"Well look, I'm 'bout to jet, I'll holla at you." I said as I headed for the door.

"Just like that, you can't wait with me 'til the limo gets here?" She asked.

211

"Let me guess, you care about everybody you fuck, huh?" I asked.

"You are one cold ass muthafucka." She said shaking her head.

"Yet, you can't seem to keep my dick out your mouth. Go figure *that* shit out." I said before opening the door to leave.

When I stepped outside of the motel I walked over to my Cadillac and got inside. I activated my video chat screen which appeared in the windshield. Once the screen was up and ready, I pressed a button to call Cocoa, my favorite assassin,

"Yes sir?" She asked after appearing on the screen.

"I have a job for you, meet me at the warehouse Monday morning at 8am. For this hit I need you to be out of sight, got it?" I asked.

"Yes sir." She replied.

"See you Monday." I said before ending the call.

"Sorry Deytwon, but you never should've stepped in while I was talking to that detective, you would've never known about her to begin with." I said to myself as I pushed the button to start up my car and hit the gas.

******

CHAPTER 15

ANGEL

I woke up the next morning showered and threw on some sweats and a t shirt. I was brushing my hair up into a ponytail when Deytwon finally woke up.

"What time is it?" He yawned as he pushed the covers away.

"Its eight-thirty, why you up baby, I thought you were chillin' today?" I asked as I secured the ponytail.

"I am, but that don't mean I need to be in bed all day. Where you about to go?" He asked standing to his feet.

"To see Salisha and find out what she's doing here." I said as I sat on the bed to slip into my tennis shoes.

"You know why she was here, she's obviously fuckin' around with someone." Deytwon reasoned.

"We don't know that, besides, that's not even her style." I said.

"It's either that or drugs." He shrugged.

"You always automatically go to the worst case scenario, why is that?" I asked looking over at him.

"I'm being realistic, why else would she come four hours away from home and ignore her husband's calls?" Deytwon asked sitting next to me. He leaned on me and tried to kiss me.

"You do have a point, but I don't think so. I'm telling you, that's not her style." I said pushing him away.

"You mean that *wasn't* here style. Gimme a kiss!" He said trying to hold my hands down.

"No stinky morning breath! You know I hate that!" I laughed as I tried to get away from

213

him.

"Kiss me, kiss me." He taunted moving closer to me.

"Deytwon cut it out! Go brush your teeth!" I said laughing at him.

"Yeah, aright. So you giving her my day off or what?" He asked as he stood up and headed to the bathroom.

"I doubt she'll be here all day. I'm just going over to the hotel to find out what's going on, we'll probably get some lunch, and then she'll most likely be heading home." I said following him into the bathroom.

"Aright, well let's do something tonight then." He said turning on the water to splash his face.

"Like what?" I asked leaning against the doorway.

"Anything, it don't matter. Let's decide when you get back." He said as he started brushing his teeth.

"Works for me. Okay baby, I be back." I said kissing him on the cheek before leaving out.

I went down and got inside the limo which took me to the hotel where Salisha was staying.

When I got to her room I knocked on the door twice before it was answered.

"Who is it?" I heard her ask.

"Angel, girl open up." I said.

"Hey girl, you here early. Did you eat breakfast?" She asked after opening the door for me.

"No, I woke up, showered and came right over, so spill it! What the hell are you doing in New York, and please don't say you came to see me. I live nowhere near Brooklyn." I said as I took a seat in the recliner near the window. Deytwon didn't only get her a room he got her a suite

214

that overlooked the city.

"Okay, well lets order room service, I am way too tired to face the sun right now." She said grabbing the menu.

"I'll bet. Order me any breakfast with eggs and bacon." I said.

"Cool, let me order now so that they can hurry up." She said picking up the phone.

"Good, then after that, you can tell me why you're here." I said using the crank on the side to prop up my feet.

Salisha looked over at me and shook her head.

"You wouldn't believe me if I told you." She finally said.

"Try me." I replied.

~~~~~

MARCUS

While Tiffani was out shopping with a couple of her girlfriends, I decided to use this time to do a little research on this Tabitha woman who felt the need to school Angel on her heritage. I didn't have a last name on her, but I did have a hunch. I knew that no one from the Jones family could be the culprit, and I doubt the Richards would either. However, if the women knew Cecil, and encouraged Angel to visit Big Boy Island to find some truth, it stands a good chance that she could somehow be related to the Powers. So I ran the name Tabitha Powers, originating in South Carolina, through the secured search.

It took about ten seconds for the search to run every Tabitha Powers that ever lived in South Carolina. Finally the search came to a halt with one Tabitha Powers from South Carolina remaining on the screen, and every move she's ever made since.

"Get the fuck outta here!" I said aloud after reading over the results.

"Hey baby, are you in your office?" I heard Tiffani's voice ask with a tap against the door.

"Yeah babe, you back already?" I asked getting up to meet her in the hallway.

"Yeah, Christina had to go, the babysitter had a family emergency. So Krysee and I just had lunch and called it a day." She replied.

"So what's good, what you tryn' do today?" I asked really more anxious to get back to the results than I was in hanging out.

"Nothing, I'm kind of tired, I just want to go lay down for a while." She said.

"You okay?" I asked as I pulled her close by her waist.

"I'm good baby, just tired." She said with a yawn.

"Aright, so then go 'head up to the room, I'll be up in a minute and we'll take a nap together, cool?" I asked.

"Okay baby, see you in a bit." She said with a smile before walking away.

I walked back into my office and sat behind my computer once again. I studied the information that was made available about Tabitha Powers and her family and started adding up dates realizing that a lot of what I'd been told by my father and grandfathers wasn't adding up.

"The fuck are they trying to hide, and from me no less." I said shaking my head.

~~~~~~

ANGEL

"So I called Anthony this morning, he was so worried about me." Salisha said as we ate.

"That surprises you? He's your husband." I replied,

"No, it doesn't surprise me. He's always been so good to me, always making sure I'm straight." She sighed

"Uh-huh." I said encouraging her to get to her point.

"He's a good man, and I don't deserve him." She said.

"Lish, why would you say something like that? You're a good person too." I replied.

"Because I'm a tramp!" She declared dropping her fork and buried her face in her hands.

"*What*?" I asked confused.

"Angel, I've been sneaking around... with Marcus. It's the reason I left Anthony's party early. It's the reason I'm out here now." She said.

"Noooooo!" I exclaimed in shock as I covered my mouth.

"Don't you judge me! You've done dirt too! Just because you're living high off the hog don't make you exempt from being wrong!" She said pointing at me.

"Salisha, what the fuck are you thinking? All that time you spent bashing me for fucking around with him? I mean what the fuck, did you secretly want him?" I shouted.

"Chick please! It just happened, it wasn't planned. It was a mistake, but don't come for me on this. He was married when you were fuckin him too!" She said.

"Salisha, look, yes, it's bad that he's married, but Marcus isn't your average nigga. He doesn't do anything that doesn't benefit him. He has a plan and a purpose for every move he makes! He's dangerous as hell!" I shouted now wondering what it was that he was really after.

218

"You are so damn dramatic! All he wanted was some ass, just like that's all I wanted, and I gave it to him. That's it, and that's all. Don't sit here and fake like you really know him based off that phony ass relationship y'all had, because in reality, it was only real to you." She said rocking her head around in a show of pure attitude.

"Please don't tell me you believe that what you two have is real." I said with a chuckle.

"Uh, no, I'm not delusional like you! I know we are only fuck buddies, that's the difference between me and you. I know what it is, you tried to make it what it wasn't and he cold carried the fuck out of." She exclaimed.

"Salisha, you know what, you're my girl, so I'm going to ignore you right now. My advice, is to go home to your husband, and lay whatever was going on between you and Marcus to rest. Please, he is not who you think he is. Just, please, listen to me." I said calmer than I felt. In reality I wanted to fuck her ass up, but seeing how I was pregnant, that wasn't an option.

"Thank you for the advice, but being that I'm a grown ass woman, I do as I damn well please. Now, if you don't mind, I need to be taking a shower. I holla." She said as she walked over to the door.

"So you're putting me out of *my* room? Yeah, okay. Just be sure to take care of yourself, and call me if you need me." I said as I stood to my feet.

"*Need you*? Girl bye." She chuckled as I reached the door.

I shook my head and continued walking until I was out of the room.

I didn't know what was going on with Salisha, but my biggest concern was on Marcus and his pursuit of her. What did he want, what was his angle, and why was he using her to get it?

~~~~~~

DEYTWON

I sat on the balcony reading when I noticed Angel's limo driving through the property. I hadn't expected her to be back this soon, but was happy nonetheless. We hadn't had a lot of alone time lately and today was the perfect day for it.

I told Rosa to bring lunch up to the balcony so that we could start eating as soon as she came up.

"Your lunch Mr. Richards, is there anything else that you require?" Rosa asked as the maids set the table and arranged the food.

"No, thank you, Rosa." I said as Angel walked out onto the balcony.

"Hey Rosa, hey ladies." She said dully as she took a seat next to me.

"What's up baby, how'd it go?" I asked.

"Bad, I don't know what's been up with Salisha lately, but she doesn't seem like the same person, or maybe its me." She reasoned.

"It could very well be you. You're not the woman you were, you've grown a lot." I assured her.

"Yeah, but I don't want to outgrow my friends." She said.

"You can only outgrow a person who isn't growing at all." I replied.

"True, or if they're growing in a different direction. I just get the feeling that she thinks I think I'm better than her or something." Angel said as she started picking at her food.

"Do you?" I asked.

"No, that's my girl." She said shaking her head.

"Maybe she's just having a hard time with you not needing her anymore." I said.

"Maybe. So anyway, this is depressing me I don't want to talk about it anymore." She said sitting the fork down.

"Aright, well, let's talk about tomorrow. You sure you can't wait to take that trip to Big Boy Island until Tuesday? I have an important meeting tomorrow." I said.

"Nah, I don't want to wait. I feel like I've waited long enough. Besides, I should probably be alone. You *know* your history, I'm *just* discovering mine." She said.

"I feel you, but your history is also my history, and Marcus' history as well. Our pasts intertwine." I said realizing that I didn't know much about Angel's family history at all.

"I know, but I just want to do this on my own first. Whatever I discover, we can talk about it." She said.

"Fair enough. So what you want to do today?" I asked changing the subject.

"Cuddle." She said smiling.

"I'm wit' that, let's go." I said putting all the food I wanted to take with me on a plate. Then I grabbed my drink and followed her into the house.

******

CHAPTER 16

MARCUS

'I'm at the Waldorf in case you want to get it in one last time before I head back to DC.' Read a text from Salisha. I rolled my eyes and tossed the phone into my passenger seat. That bitch was becoming a nuisance. I treated her like pure shit. I fucked her in cars and cheap motels. Even when we were in expensive hotels I never let her touch the bed, and she was still coming back for more. Where these bitches be getting their self-worth from is beyond me.

When I arrived at the warehouse I saw Cocoa's black Aston Martin One-77 parked in back. When she saw me drive up she stepped out of her car dressed in a black leather body suit that covered everything but her face. She wore black shades that covered from her cheek bones to above her eyebrows. She wore her infrared rifle scope roped around her shoulder and was ready to make it burn

. She was a badd bitch, the only badd bitch I knew personally that I never fucked. I wanted things to always be about business between her and me so I always kept it professional.

"Welcome." I said as I walked towards the warehouse and unlocked the door.

She followed me inside and over to the room where I conducted such business. Once inside I put on a pair of protective gloves and picked up a container of poison.

"Put these on, take out your bullets and drop them in here. Let them soak for fifteen minutes, then load up. These are what you will use in the strike." I said tossing her a pair of protective gloves.

"Yes sir." She replied as she did what she was told.

~~~~~

DEYTWON

"So you're not even taking Brad with you?" I asked as I walked Angel over to her plane.

"No baby, I told you, I'm just going alone." She said as she slipped her bag on her shoulder.

"Okay baby, I'ma stop giving you a hard time. Just, call me when you get there okay?" I asked.

"Okay baby, now, you said a limo will meet me when I land and carry me over to the museum?" She asked.

"Right, your driver's name will be Henry. He will take you to the museum. When you get there, you'll meet Gunther, he's the curator of the museum. If you have any questions about anything, he'll answer them for you. If you decide you want a tour, he'll lead you. Also, if you're still there when it gets dark, just have the driver take you to the mansion, and stay there for the night. The servants will attend to your every wish." I said.

"Baby, baby, breathe, it's okay." She said jokingly as she pat my chest.

"I just want to make sure you're good baby, that's all." I said.

"I know, but I have a question. Do people actually live on Big Boy Island?" She asked.

"People who serve us do, but it's not populated by regular citizens, because we're not there to govern it. None of us live there." I explained.

"Why is that?" I asked.

"I really don't know, that's just the way it's always been." I answered never really thinking about it.

"Okay, well, let me go, I want to get back before it gets late." She said.

"Bet, I love you lady." I said leaning down to kiss her.

"I love you too." She replied when we pulled away.

After one long hug I helped her board her plane. I nodded my head at the pilot and stepped back off.

Angel looked out the window and waved her hand and blew kisses at me. I waved and did the same. I hated not being able to go with her, but on the other hand, I was happy that she was gaining a sense of independence, and the least I could do was encourage It.

I stepped back as the plane ran down the runway and eventually took off. I hoped that she would find what she was looking for, and that it would complete the missing pieces of the puzzle in her life. Meanwhile, I had a meeting to get ready for, so I went into the house to get dressed.

~~~~~

ANGEL

When I arrived on Big Boy Island sure enough there was a limo waiting to take me to the museum.

"Welcome home, madam Powers-Richards." The chauffeur said with a bow.

"Thank you Henry. Its more beautiful than I remembered." I said taking in paradise. The skies were a deep comforting blue, the grass was a rich green and the water was sparkling blue. Flowers were of all colors were all over the place. It was gorgeous.

"Shall we?" He asked as he opened the door for me to enter the limo.

"Yes." I replied as I stepped inside.

The ride to the museum was smooth and perfect and the scenery along the way looked like something you'd see on a postcard. I loved it.

When we arrived at the museum I couldn't get over how much it did look like a volcano. Henry opened the door for me and I stepped out and looked around.

"Madam, I will be right here until you come back out, please take all the time you need to enjoy yourself." Henry said as he bowed again.

"Thank you, kindly." I said as a man stepped out of the museum and approached me.

"Mrs. Powers-Richards, I presume! Welcome home and to your museum. I am Gunther, your curator, here to provide you with anything you may need." Gunther said with a slight bow.

"Thank you Gunther, if it's all the same to you, I'd much rather just walk around and see it for myself." I said as he escorted me into the building.

"Of course Mrs. Powers-Richards, whatever you require shall be obliged to you eagerly." He said.

I looked at him and smiled as I barely understood what he was saying.

225

Big Boys -The Legacy   By Nikida Bellezza

"Here is a map of the museum, and there are phones every fifteen feet just in case you are in need of anything at any time." Gunther said handing me the map.

"Thank you much. Let me get started, I'll phone if I need you." I said.

"Please do madam." He replied with a smile.

Speaking of phone, I forgot to call Deytwon to let him know that I was there. So I took out my cell and dialed his number.

"Hey baby, so you made it there alright?" He asked sounding happy to hear from me.

"I did." I replied.

"Cool, so how they treating you?" He asked.

"Like royalty." I replied as I started walking.

"As they should, well, okay baby, I'll be heading over to the conference center in a few. Call if you need me. I love you." He said.

"I love you too." I replied ending the call.

I looked down at the map and Saw the section called Powers Hall and walked in that direction. When I got there I saw bust statues and wall paintings of what I guess was my great-great- great grandfather Cecil Sr.

I stared up at my grandfather's picture hanging from the wall. He looked very distinguished with the low brow, tight lipped and scouring look he wore. I touched the painting, running my fingers along the surface over his face down to his chin.

I didn't see myself in his face, but his eyes did seem oddly familiar, like I've seen them before. The painting gave me mixed feelings. On the one hand it felt good to know that I do have a family. I belonged to people who shared the blood in my veins. On the other hand, I was all that's left of them. This made it so important for me to have these babies. Even though Deytwon

226

was the bloodline, the child will also carry Powers blood in it too.

"My little Princes, you will be born into a good life." I said as I rubbed my stomach. I leaned back on my grandfather's picture and admired my baby bump when suddenly the wall opened and I fell through into what I could only imagine was a concrete slab.

"Ahhhh!" I screamed from the startling fall.

When I was finally able to scramble back to my feet, I looked around the tiny space trying to figure out where I was. It looked like some sort of entry room. I searched the map but didn't see anything that even resembled a room like this on it.

"Where the hell am I?" I asked scanning the little room again, and I saw a wooden door with a lock on it. It was then that I remembered the key in Tabitha's box. I moved the bag on my shoulder around to the front and felt around inside for the box, which I pulled open and felt around until I found the key.

I made nervous steps towards the door feeling a bit eerie about the possibility that this key may very well open this door. I slipped the key into the lock, took a deep breath and then gently turned it to the right and heard the lock snap back.

"Oh my gawd." I gasped.

~~~~~

Big Boys -The Legacy   By Nikida Bellezza

MARCUS

Once I finished giving Cocoa her instructions I decided to go pay 'ol Tabitha a visit. I took off my ring and slipped it into my pocket before entering the store where the research I had done said she would be.

"Hello sir, and welcome, how may I help you today?" Asked a young woman who approached me.

I looked down at her and noticed that she was smiling hard in my face. So I smiled back.

"How you doin' lady? I'm looking for a woman named Ms. Tabitha, is she here today?" I asked politely.

"Oh, that's my grandma, yes, she's here, I'll get her for you!" She replied cheerfully.

"Beautiful and helpful. Your man is the luckiest." I said flirting.

"Well, I don't have a man right now, but I sure know how to make a man feel lucky." She giggled.

"Shit, I feel lucky right now, maybe after I speak with Ms. Tabitha we can talk about some things." I said reminding her of what I came for.

"Oh, okay, yes, I'll get her now. Just wait here, don't leave." She giggling as she moved towards the back of the store.

I nodded my head for fear that if I opened my mouth I would laugh at her goofy ass. Flirting was in my blood, I couldn't help it, especially when there was something I wanted from a woman.

"Hello, do I know you?" I heard a woman's voice ask. I turned around to see a very old woman standing down at the end of the aisle with a walker.

"I think you might…" I replied with a smile.

228

"Oh, oh oh my gawd, Art!" She exclaimed covering her mouth.

"Excuse me?" I asked as I moved closer to her. I could've sworn she said my grandfather's name.

"Oh, I am so sorry, you're the spitting image of a man I knew a very long time ago." She said moving her hand down to her chest. She looked very nervous to see me, so I knew that I had the right woman.

"I wouldn't doubt it, Tabitha." I replied.

"Grandma, who is this?" The young woman asked noticing her grandmother's expressions.

"Lady, why don't you give me and your grandmother a few seconds, I'll catch you before I leave." I said winking at the young woman.

"Okay." She replied blushing again.

"Ellen, head on home honey. We're going to close up early today." Tabitha said staring at me.

"Not on my account, of course." I said innocently.

"Of course not, sir." The woman who's name I now knew was Ellen said.

"Goodbye Ellen." Tabitha said again.

"Okay grandma, I'm going! Sheesh." She said as she gathered her things and headed for the door.

"I trust that my grandmother knows how to get in contact with you?" Ellen said before she walked over to the door.

"No, but if necessary, I know how to get in contact with you." I said with a wink.

She smiled before leaving out of the store.

"So, why have you come here?" Tabitha asked as she took a seat in a chair against the wall.

"First of all, do you know who I am?" I asked.

"Yes, you're Art's great great grandson. I know exactly who you are." She said.

"So then you already know why I'm here." I said.

"I know exactly why you're here. In fact, I've been expecting you, ever since my conversation with Angel." She said.

"And what exactly was it that you disclosed with Angel?" I asked.

"I told her who she was. I gave her all of the information that I could and told her to go seek more." Tabitha said.

"Which is why she's on her way to Big Boy Island?" I said.

"Exactly. Don't you think a person has a right to know about their own heritage? Isn't there a point where the manipulation has gone too far?" Tabitha asked.

"Tabitha, I have a heart for 3 things, myself, my money and my wife. Your attempt to reach a compassionate place inside of me is futile." I informed her.

"And Deytwon?" She asked.

"What about him?" I asked back.

"He has no place in your heart?" She asked.

"Is that a threat?" I asked.

"I have no power to threaten you. I am only pointing out that without Angel, his heart will turn black, and cold." She said.

"No one knows him better than me lady. But enough with the mystery, who are you *really*?" I asked.

DEYTWON

"*Go to hell Richards*! I will *never* work for you!" Michael Vandt screamed at the top of his lungs as he tossed the contract I gave him into the air.

"Well, technically Vandt, you already do. I'm just trying to sweeten the deal for you. The fact of the matter is, I own fifty-eight shares of Michael Vandt co, and I certainly don't need you to operate it, the brand name alone is all I really need." I replied calmly.

"You may have my business, but you will never have my name! I take that with me!" He said.

"That's fine too, Richards is a more reputable name anyway. I'm not a bully, no one is afraid to go into business with me." I replied with a shrug.

"You cocky mutherfucker! I will see you in court! You think you're slick, you think you're going to run a monopoly in America unnoticed! HA! If they caught Bill G, surely they'll catch your smug ass!" Michael shouted.

I smiled and nodded my head at him as I sat back in my seat to get comfortable.

~~~~~

Big Boys -The Legacy   By Nikida Bellezza

ANGEL

I turned the knob and pulled the door open which drew a lot of dust from the edges of the door. I coughed waving the dust away before entering the room. The room was very dusty and full of heavy spider webs which creeped me out, but not enough to curve my curiosity. The sunlight shined in every crevices of the room as it did all over the museum. There was no way to build a dome over the volcano that it was built in. Instead they built a tiny netted screen over the opening to keep the rain out. The screen covered this secret room as well.

There were about a dozen dusty boxes lined around an old wooden table and a chair. On the table was an old fashion feather pen sitting next to a sheet of paper. I gently grabbed the pen and attempted to scribble on the paper but all it did was make an imprint on the rough paper. So I sat the pen down and walked over to the boxes.

I took a paper towel out of my bag and tried to wipe the heave dust away, but only the top layer of dust moved, the rest seemed to be one with the box. I pulled the top off and let it fall to the floor. Inside the box I found wooden figurines that looked hand carved. There were small statues of people, wooden bowls, spoons and other things that I didn't recognize. The two other boxes underneath had the same type of things inside. So I moved to the next stack of boxes

I removed the lid to see a stack of papers inside. I carefully pulled them from the box and shook slightly to remove the excess dust. The words on this paper looked as though they had been typed with a typewriter, and on top was my great-great-great-grandfathers name.

"*Cecil Powers Philips Confessions... Powers Philips?*" I said reading the heading of the paper. There were a set of papers in Tabitha's box where Cecil refereed to himself as Powers-Phillips too. I knew that the slave Masters' last name was Phillips. I suppose he took on his master's last name also, but at what point was Phillips dropped? I wondered as I continued to

232

Big Boys -The Legacy   By Nikida Bellezza

read through the document...

Before my last day on this earth, I want to tell the truth so that the future families will know what really happened, who they are and where they came from.

Starting from the beginning. I was born a slave in 1845 to Earl and Pauline. My father Earl was traded when I was still a young boy. My father always taught me to do the right thing and to help others. My mother told me that it would be an honor to my father's memory if I did all I could to make sure others were well.

When the elder master died his son Norris Phillips took over as master. He was a young man, who liked books. He once told me that he didn't want slaves, but he took them as a promise to his father. Norris was a very kind man, not at all like his father or the surrounding masters.

When I became a man, myself and two good friends of mine, Thomas Jones, and Curtis Richards, came together and started a brotherhood that we called the Warriors. We met every day and talked about what needed to be done and who needed help. Word of our helping ways spread and other masters would come to Norris to complain about us. But Norris would not listen to them. He liked us and would sometimes call us his Big Boys.

One day Norris asked The Warriors to come with him to trade the cotton. We traveled late into the night and camped in the woods. We were attacked by men wearing bed sheets, but we beat them to their death. Norris was so happy that we saved his life, that he was much nicer to us than he was to all the other slaves.

Thomas' brother, Cornelius didn't like the nicer treatment that we were receiving, and started hating Thomas. One afternoon he asked Thomas to take a walk to the river with him, but Thomas never came back.

Cornelius said they were attacked by more men in bed sheets like we were before, and they

233

killed Thomas. So Cornelius, took Thomas's place as a Warrior, and became Thomas' sons Edward's father.

Even though we had been the Warriors for a long time, Cornelius wanted to change the name to The Big Boys. He like this name because when the master would refer to his male slaves as big boys in a good way, it gave them pride. He didn't realize that calling us big boys, was the masters way of not calling us men.

I tried to explain this to Cornelius, but he wouldn't hear of it and eventually gained the support of the rest of the men to change the name to The Big Boys. Cornelius and I never saw eye to eye after this. Instead of seeing me as a brother the way his brother Thomas did, he saw me as the one in the way.

After we began having children, me, a daughter whom I named Esther, Curtis a son whom he named William and Cornelius, a son whom he named Arthur, in honor of his grandfather, Cornelius started making plans for his son Edward, to have a seat in leadership. We explained to him that there were only to be 3 three leaders, and Thomas' son Edward would be the 3rd heir. Again Cornelius was not happy but after seeing how protective I was over Edward, Cornelius seemed to back off. By this time Cornelius had gained everyone's trust, but I knew that he could not be trust. It wasn't until Edward was a bit older when Cornelius attempted to kill him, that I confronted him, telling him that I would expose him for what he's done to Thomas if he didn't back off of Edward. Cornelius said that if I told, he would turn my daughter Esther over to the master claiming that she was a thief. Theives were tortured and hanged for their crimes. I knew that he could do as he said, he was very manipulative, and easily gained the support of everyone in his path. Therefore, I kept quiet until now because I could not take that chance of him killing my daughter...'

"Oh my gawd, so Marcus' family aren't even the rightful heirs." I said aloud looking up

Big Boys -The Legacy   By Nikida Bellezza

from the document.

CHAPTER 17

MARCUS

"I am the wife of Cecil." Tabitha stated.

"Really, Cecil Jr? Wouldn't that make you over a hundred years old?" I asked with a disbelieving chuckle.

"No, Cecil junior had two sons. Angelo, and Cecil. I am the wife of Cecil, who was killed in 1950." She explained.

"So in a nutshell, you're Angel's grandmother?" I asked.

"Yes, and no. I am her step grandmother. Cecil had an affair and with that woman he birthed Angel's grandfather." She replied.

"I always wondered about that time line, so all along there was a missing son. Now that makes sense." I said.

"Yes, when I left South Carolina, I was forced to take the son of my husband's mistress with me. No one knew that he was Cecil's son, only the mistress and her mother, and later me. He was still a newborn when he was given to me." Tabitha further explained.

"And all this time you've been on the run, why?" I asked wondering what she knew.

"Because your family has been killing off the men in the Powers bloodline since the death of Cecil Sr. I was on the run to protect the Powers children, especially Ricardo, the only son Cecil had." She said.

"*My* family huh?" I asked.

"Yes, your family has a secret that it wants to keep hidden. A secret that I'm sure not even you know, but it's the source of your manipulation." She said.

"*My* manipulation." I said as though she was crazy.

"Yes, you are being manipulated by your family." She started but then her head dropped.

"The *fuck*?" I asked trying to figure out what happened.

"The fuck is right, what in the hell was taking you so long?" I heard my grandfather's voice ask as he walked out from behind Tabitha holding a gun with a silencer attached.

"Granddad?" I asked shocked to see him.

~~~~~

ANGEL

I looked through the rest of the documents and found a Will left by the slave master, a will left by Cecil Sr, and other papers and documents of significance. All of these things were crucial and now I began to understand what was really going on. Marcus's family had been trying to kill off my bloodline since slavery. They couldn't care less about killing, because they'd kill their own just to get ahead.

I wasn't quite sure what I wanted to do with the information because I knew how Deytwon felt about Marcus, but at the same time, myself and our children could be in danger, especially since I discovered the secret. I needed to get to Deytwon with this information. I knew that he'd know what to do with it.

I packed everything I could into my bag and rushed out of the little room. I closed the door and locked it back. Then I pushed against the wall where I first entered until it gave way allowing me to get out. Once I got back into the hall of the museum I rushed to the entry door and headed towards the limo. When Henry, the chauffeur saw me he hopped out of the limo and opened the door for me.

"Thank you, to the plane, I need to get there as quickly as possible!" I exclaimed.

"Yes madam!" Henry said closing the door behind me.

Henry got back into the limo and sped off like a bat out of hell. I was grateful, but also a little terrified. I had never been in a limo doing top speed.

We arrived at my plane in ten minutes flat. I tipped Henry and quickly boarded the plan, pressing the pilot to hurry.

~~~~~~

MARCUS

"Let's get out of here." He said taking me by the arm.

"Whoa, hold up, what's going on?" I asked yanking my arm away from him.

"This is Tabitha, we have been searching for her, for over sixty years." My grandfather said.

"Why?" I asked.

"Why were *you* here?" He asked back.

"To get the answers I was on the verge of getting before you killed her." I replied accusingly.

"She didn't have answers son, all she had was lies." He said with a pat to my shoulder as he continued for the door.

"Is that right?" I asked following him to the door.

"She's been trying to turn our family against one another ever since she married Cecil. That's why she's been in hiding. Come on, let's go get something to eat." My grandfather said as he held the door open for me.

"I'ma' have to take a rain check on that, I have some business to take care of. But I do have a question for you." I said.

"What's that?" He asked.

"How'd you know that I was here, or that she was here?" I asked

"Because we've been bugging her files, when you tapped into them the other day we got a signal and it lead us here." He explained.

'So really, you've been watching me.' I thought to myself.

"Gotcha." I replied.

Big Boys -The Legacy   By Nikida Bellezza

ANGEL

When the plane arrived back in New York, I had the pilot take me to Deytwon's conference center where there was an airstrip for landing. I could feel something urging me to call Deytwon but my words were curdled in my throat, so I felt it was best to just show him the information. I just couldn't believe all the secrets, lies and deceptions that have been going on for decades.

I knew that The Big Boys were larger than life, but with all of this information, they seemed larger than that. No matter the risk I had to protect myself and my babies by all means.

When the plane stopped and the steps were let down for me, I rushed off the plane holding my bag for dear life.

"Ma'am, would you like a ride?" Fernando the pilot asked.

"No, thank you. Thank you for everything!" I shouted as I walked as quickly as I could towards Deytwon's reference center which was just a couple feet in front of me.

"Almost there, almost there!" I heard myself saying as I was losing my breath.

I rushed and rushed until I felt something pierce and burn my chest.

"What, what?" I asked thinking that I had somehow overexerted myself. I felt tears fall from my eyes as the burning sensation began to spread. I didn't even realize that I hit the ground until just before I closed my eyes.

******

CHAPTER 18

DEYTWON

"Do what you must Michael, but be sure to use restraint and check your emotions before you make your move. You're not challenging your average white collar businessman, or the nigger you must think you see when you look at me. I will checkmate your whole life until the thought of suicide comforts you." I said.

"We'll see my friend. I know people in high places who live to destroy maggots like you. We'll see if you're still as arrogant when you're sucking dick just for permission to breathe." Michael threatened.

"You know those people, I *am* those people. Now, because I am a fair man, I'm going to advise you to sleep this shit off before you make a bad move, because once I make my move, I won't stop until I am the only one left on the board." I replied.

"You can't intimidate me. I *will* see you again." He said with a chuckle as he stood to leave.

"I'm looking forward to it." I replied as my phone rang I looked down to see Angel's pilot calling.

"What's going on, Fernando" I said answering the phone.

"Mr. Richards, its Mrs. Richards, she's been shot!" Fernando exclaimed.

"Whoa, what?!" I asked as my stomach tied itself in knots and my heart beat went from regular to a pounding that seemed to ripple throughout my entire body. I jumped out of my seat and headed for the door as I listened to Fernando explain.

"When we landed at the air strip at your office on Richards way, where she thought you were. She got out of the plane and started walking away, from out of nowhere she falls to the ground. When we turned her over, we saw that she had been shot. We don't know where it came

241

from, it was silent." Fernando explained.

"Where is she now?" I asked taking the stairs. When I got downstairs and out into the lobby, Vandt was just pulling off in his limo.

"Richards Medical." Fernando said. I was happy to know that she was at my hospital where she'd have a fighting chance.

I hopped into my car and sped out of the parking lot.

"Fernando, level with me, tell me the truth and not some bullshit answer. Is she, is my wife okay?" I asked. I couldn't bring myself to ask whether or not she was dead or alive.

"I don't know sir, she wasn't responding. I am so sorry sir" Fernando said. I crushed my phone in my hand as I felt tears fall. Angel was my whole life, and while she wasn't always a part of it, now that she was, she was what I lived for.

I arrived at the hospital in less than ten minutes. I stopped my car at the entrance and ran inside..

"Mr. Richards, she's in room 108!" Said the woman behind the desk.

I nodded my head and headed back to Angels room. When I got there I saw tubes going every which way between her and machines. Her eyes were closed, she looked to be sleeping.

"Oh Deytwon." I heard my mother say as her heels screech across the floor.

"Mom, dad, what are you doing here?" I asked shocked.

"We haven't been back to Italy since the ceremony, we've been traveling the country. We just got here this morning. We planned to surprise you, but then we got an alert that Angel was here" My dad said. Whenever a Big Boy leader is brought into Richards Memorial an alert is sent to all of the Big Boy leaders.

I looked back over at Angel and noticed that her breathing seemed labored, but it was enough for me that she was breathing.

"Babygirl, I am so sorry that I wasn't here to protect you." I said as I took her hand into mines.

"Mr. Richards, you're here." The doctor said as he walked into the room.

I barely heard him, I was lost in my thoughts.

"How is she?" My mother asked the doctor.

"It's not looking good. She is literally fighting for her life." He said softly as he touched my mom's arm.

"And the babies?" I asked still looking down on my wife.

"We believe she's lost one. We're going to have to perform an emergency caesarean in order to save the other." The doctor said. Right then and there I knew who was responsible. That bitchass nigga that I once called my brother.

I felt another tear escape my eye as my heart pumped with extreme heaviness. Before I realized it, I was backing out of the room when my father caught my arm.

"Deytwon, please, your wife needs you here, son." He pleaded, seemingly already knowing what I was going to do.

"I am here. I'm not the one fighting for my life." I said as more tears fell.

"Then be by her side. She can feel your presence." He said with ease.

"That's not good enough." I bucked as my heart filled with uncontrollable anger.

"Son, you are too angry, I've always taught you to organize your thoughts so that your moves can be calculated and precise. Please, I beg you not to do something that may turn into a grave mistake." My father's voice trembled when he spoke.

243

I had never heard my father speak with anything less than confidence and authority. But right now, he sounded the equivalent to a man begging for mercy. The situation at hand was serious. My choice at this moment would either promote my life, or my death. I have never disobeyed my father before, and never intended too.

 I looked over at my wife, who was struggling to meet the standards of the machines that she'd been hooked up to. My heart felt like the life was being choked from it, and my eyes bled more warm tears. I turned back to look at my father who seemed to grow smaller as my anger and hurt grew larger.

"I'm making a leadership move, step down." I spoke feeling like a man possessed.

My father stepped back and nodded his head surrendering to my authority. Without saying another word, I walked out of the room and took the freight elevator down to the lobby where I got in my car and sped off.

Like a low jack, I knew exactly where to find the bitch that did this, and I did 80mph through red lights to my destination. Even though I was chased by several officers, I didn't care because I knew that once they got close enough to see my tags, they'd fall back, which they all did.

When I arrived at the house, I grabbed my gun from the glove box, then I jumped out of the car and slammed the door closed with so much force it shattered the window.

I walked up to the door and shoot the lock off, then I kicked it open to see Marcus in a chair carelessly hitting a jay.

"Dey, my man, what's good?" He asked off his chill shit.

I walked over to him and jacked him up out of the chair.

"Bitchass nigga! I know you called the hit on Angel!" I shouted.

244

Big Boys -The Legacy   By Nikida Bellezza

"Hit? What hit my nigga?" He asked playing dumb.

I slammed him against the wall.

"I swear on your life, if she dies, you will die the same day." I growled as I felt love,

compassion and reason drain from my heart. I turned to leave ignoring everything inside me that

begged me to kill him right then and there.

"Dey, I ain't never seen you like this dog." He called behind me as I opened the door.

"All this, over a bitch though? That's who we are? That's what we've become?" He

shouted following me outside.

I walked over to my car and kicked the glass out of my way.

"We brother's nigga! Always been, since birth, and this how it's gonna end?" He asked.

I looked over at him to see that he had a gun pointed at me.

"Do it. Fuck I got to live for without my wife!" I asked ready to die, but knowing that I

wasn't about to. Marcus was a lot of things, but a killer wasn't one of them. He can plan it and

pay for it, but he wasn't built to do it.

"She *will* die, those bullets were dipped in ricin. I did that part myself. The genius part

about it, It's untraceable. So they think she dying from the shots, but really it's the poison" He

said with a chuckle.

I shook my head as I raised my gun and pulled the trigger. The gun in Marcus' hand

dropped, then he looked down at his chest and back up at me.

"You *shot* me?" He asked slowly before dropping to the ground. That's when I snapped

out of my anger and realized I shot my brother. My nigga for life.

I dropped my gun and ran over to him. The blood was pouring from his chest as his body

twitched. I lifted him into my arms and looked down at him.

"You shot me." He mumbled.

"What you expected me to do my nigga?" I asked as tears formed in my eyes.

"I wasn't, I wasn't.." He tried to talk.

"Stop talking man, let me get you some help." I said as I pulled out my business cell. I called the private hospital that we used in confidence. Even the elders didn't know about it. The ambulance arrived within five minutes.

Marcus' breathing had slowed and his eyes rolled around in his head.

The crew jumped out of the black vehicle and ran over to us, to service Marcus. They knew to do everything they could because they were paid triple if we survived. This is where I wanted to bring Angel but they had already taken her to the hospital.

"Are you coming sir?" One of the paramedics asked me.

I shook my head and backed up so that they could close the door and leave. I walked over to my car and pulled out my cell.

"Mr. Richards." The doctor said as he answered the phone.

"Treat her for ricin poison." I said.

"Ricin? But sir…" The doctor started.

"Doesn't her systems seem a little strange for her to have only been shot? Don't debate me gotdamnit, do what I say!" I shouted then I ended the call.

I got back in my car and drove back to my hospital. This time I drove slower, I needed to clear my head and think about my next move. If Angel didn't survive my heart would die with her, and our remaining child would be raised to be as cold as this world is. The only reason I knew that love existed was because of the love I felt for that Angel.

By Nikida Bellezza

"You didn't give her to me, just to take her from me, did you?" I asked aloud speaking to God. I hadn't had a conversation with God in a long time, and I figured we were about due.

People always say that God allows things to happen so that he can get our attention, well he definitely has it now.

"Please Father, don't let my wife die, please, I need her." I pleaded.

When I arrived at the hospital I parked my car and went back up. When I got to the room I saw that my parents were standing at Angel's bedside. I walked over to them to see Angel looking up at them with her eyes open.

"You were right Mr. Richards." The doctor said walking in behind me.

"Deytwon, oh Deytwon it's a miracle!" My mother exclaimed after the Dr. alert my presence.

"Dey." I heard Angel say in a weak voice as my parents backed away from her bed.

I walked over to her and took her hand into mine.

"Hey babygirl, how do you feel?" I asked leaning down.

"Sore, but so happy to see you." She said trying to muster a smile.

"Not as happy as I am to see life in your eyes." I said as I brushed her hair from her forehead.

"Uhm, let's give them some time." I heard my father say.

"That's fine, Mr. Richards we'll be ready for her in the OR in fifteen minutes." The Doctor said to me. I nodded my head at him then turned my attention back to Angel.

"In the OR for what?" She asked.

I looked away from her and shook my head.

"They want to do an emergency cesarean on you." I replied, not really ready to tell her that we lost one of the babies.

"Why, am I hurt that badly?" She asked.

"Pretty badly, you lost one of the babies, and they want to get the other out so that he can be treated." I said.

"I, I lost one of our babies?" She asked softly.

"The impact of the fall, and the poison." I said.

"I don't believe this, our baby is gone?" She said shaking her head.

"Yes." I replied for a lack of anything else to say.

"I'm so sorry Dey, if I had just not gone to Big Boy Island, if I had just waited for you like you asked me to. I killed our baby!" She said crying.

"No ma'am. You did nothing of the sort. You did not do this, nor did you call this on yourself. This is not your fault." I said turning her face towards mine trying to suppress my own tears to be strong for her.

"My bad choices always get me in trouble, they always get me fucked up. I can't seem to do shit right!" she cried.

"Angel this is not your fault. It's my fault, I should have been there to protect you, instead of going to a meeting that I knew would be pointless. I like to flex too much, and that's what I was doing instead of being by your side. No baby, this is my fault." I said.

She cried harder and harder, I didn't know how to comfort her, so I simply held her in my arms.

Fifteen minutes later they came and gave her something to calm her down some. Then five minutes after that they wheeled her off to the OR.

I lay back on her bed and stared up at the ceiling while my parents went down to the cafeteria.

A few minutes later I heard a knock against the door. I looked over to see Fernando holding Angel's bag.

"Mr. Richards, sorry to disturb you. This is Angel's, it fell from her hand when she was hit." Fernando said as he walked into the room.

I sat up in the bed and moved around to stand to my feet.

"Thank you Fernando. So tell me again what happened?" I asked taking the bag from him.

"Well, once we landed, Mrs. Richards stepped off the plane and started jogging towards your office. She did not wait for an escort. Then the next thing I knew, she fell to the ground. She didn't answer to her name, but when I turned her over, I saw that she had been shot." Fernando recounted.

"Did she say why she was so anxious to speak with me?" I asked.

"No sir, but it seemed like whatever she wanted to tell you, has something to do with this bag. It was tucked under her arm." Fernando said.

"Thank you Fernando, you may go." I said pulling some money from a clip and handing it to him.

"Thank you Mr. Richards, my prayers are with you and your wife." He said.

I nodded my head before turning around to head over to a desk next to Angel's bed. I opened the bag and pulled out what looked to be old documents, some handwritten and some typed.

"*Cecil's True Testament..*" I read the heading of the typed document before continuing on.

"Hold, what the fuck?!" I exclaimed as I read the truth behind The Big Boys.

******

CHAPTER 19

MARCUS

"Mr. Jones, we were able to remove the bullet, but you lost a lot of blood so we just want to get you stable before you head home." The doctor said as the nurse checked my vitals.

"Bet." I said in a grumbling voice that didn't sound like mine.

"You may be hoarse for a few days, but that will subside." The doctor assured me.

I nodded my head just as Deytwon appeared in the doorway.

"Okay, do you have any questions for me Mr. Jones?" The doctor asked.

"No, just, have the nurse close the door on y'all way out now." I said noticing that Deytwon had some papers in his hand.

"Yes sir, come nurse Michelle." The doctor said.

"See you soon." The nurse said as she slid a finger up my arm before leaving the room.

"Mr. Richards." The doctor said acknowledging Deytwon.

"Doctor." Deytwon said as he walked past the doctor.

"Came back for more?" I asked Deytwon after the doctor closed the door.

"Cool it out, we got bigger problems." Deytwon said tossing the stack of papers onto my lap.

"What's all this?" I asked taking up the papers to skim through them.

"Apparently Cecil didn't step down, he was killed." Deytwon said.

"Welcome to the inside circle." I replied.

"Knew that did you?" He asked.

I shrugged my shoulders and continued skimming through the papers.

"But do you know why?" He asked as he pulled a chair from the desk sitting by the

251

window.

"I have a theory, but I'd much rather hear what you know." I said looking up at him.

"Apparently the legend is, The Powers had more shares of the riches, that's what you know, right?" Deytwon asked.

"That's what I've always been told, So what do you know?" I asked.

He stood to his feet and fished through the papers he'd given me and pulled the one he was looking for from my hands.

"According to this, that bullshit you've been taught, that hatred you've been trained to have for Angel and her bloodline comes from this." He said handing me the paper.

"*Cecil's Confession, I swear before the almighty, all powerful God that these statements are true...*' Oh, he swearing to God, this *must* be true." I replied sarcastically.

"Just read it man, what you got to lose?" Deytwon asked.

"Fuck it." I said giving in. I started reading it just to get through it, but the more I read, the more things started making sense.

"So hold up, my great-great-great-great grandfather was killed by his brother Cornelius, who then usurped his position as a Big Boy and took my great-great-great grandfather and raised him like a son, but then booted him out of position and put his own son in?" I asked confused.

"Basically." Deytwon answered. I shook my head as I continued to read on through the document.

"Ok, so this is saying that, the Big Boys were originally known as The Warriors. My grandfather was killed and my uncle took over as head of the family. The money was left to Cecil, and in Cecil Sr's will, Cecil Jr was to take over The Big Boys upon his death." I said trying to see if I understood everything.

252

"In a nutshell." Deytwon replied.

"So I'm my grandfather's descendent and not my uncles?" I asked a little confused.

"Well, your grandfather had one son, and then your uncle had a son, and tried to take control from your grandfather's son. Cecil discovered this and threatened to tell, but didn't because your grandfather threatened to kill Cecil's daughter. Now, the Jones' have been killing' off the Powers bloodline anyway, every time they discovered one just in case Cecil had told someone. The fact of the matter is, Cecil shared his riches with all the men equally. I figured, the only reason to kill him, would be because he knew the truth about your uncle." Deytwon explained.

"So basically, I should trace back to see if I'm of my uncle's bloodline?" I asked curious as to where his head was in all of this.

"It doesn't really matter, it's the same blood, the problem is how your uncle came into power? But, on the other hand, your uncle has no parts to this empire, *if* he murdered the original leader." Deytwon said.

"What does that mean to me? I was born into this shit." I said.

"Well, we can do a trace to see what really happened, if what Cecil is saying is true about the Jones' elders." Deytwon suggested.

"If it's all true, then what?" I asked already knowing.

"Come on man, you know what." Deytwon replied.

"This is our option?" I asked.

"You see another one? We are the leaders now, the men we called our fathers and grandfathers have been and still are deceiving us. You were a pawn and I was the fuckin board they played on. There's no way we can leave this shit as it is. Shit, if *we* can figure it out, *anyone* can, and what would that say about us? They gotta' know that we ain't accepting bullshit from inside or outside this brotherhood." Deytwon said upset.

"What your folks do?" I asked noticing that he said "our"

"You can't tell me my great to the 4th ain't know shit. They were on the same fuckin plantation, why would Arthur want to kill Cecil and not Curtis, unless he was cool with the shit?" He reasoned.

"How can you prove that? Your grandfather never even met Curtis." I said.

"That's the part I haven't been able to figure out. Unless, the tale has been passed down from father to son." Deytwon said.

"*And*?" He asked.

"And when I ask my folks, if they don't seem surprised." Deytwon said but stopped.

"What if they don't seem surprised?" I asked.

Deytwon shook his head before answering.

"I shot *you*, didn't I?" He asked.

"So what's the plan?" I asked.

"We call a meeting between us, and the elders. One month from today on Big Boy Island." Deytwon suggested.

"And if we hear some shit that we don't want to hear?" I asked.

"We leave them there. But here's the thing, I need to know that you're on board. No more secrets, no lies. We are nothing like them, our foundation has to be solid." Deytwon said.

"You're the only one I've ever known that I could trust, and now I know that for a fact. They've been playing me, and fuckin' over everybody else." I said sincerely.

"And Angel, because she's not just my wife, she's a leader too. You gotta' let all that old

254

Powers-Jones rivalry die with them." Deytwon said.

"Now that I know the truth." I said as I extended my hand for Deytwon to shake.

"What the world gonna' say when they see we no longer have elders?" He asked shaking my hand.

"Whatever the fuck we tell them too. They'll see then that we're not to be fucked with." I replied.

"No doubt." He replied.

******

CHAPTER 20

ONE MONTH LATER

ANGEL

I sat on the throne next to Deytwon and Marcus wearing my Big Boy crown. We quietly awaited the elders arrival. With all of the information I got from Tabitha and the Big Boy museum we pieced together that the problem between us wasn't us, but them. They were cancerous to the survival of the Big Boys and they had to be stopped. If not, the battle would always go on, and we would eventually lose the essence of who we were meant to be.

As the elders slowly began to arrive, they came in all smiles. First there were The Richards, Deytwon's father and grandfather. In the tradition of the Big Boys, they lowered their heads in a bow before us before taking their seats.

Then finally entered the Jones', Marcus' Father, Grandfather and Great-grandfather. They nodded their heads before taking seats across from the Richards.

Once everyone was settled, Deytwon spoke calling the meeting to order.

"Welcome gentlemen. Thank you for coming to this hearing." He said.

"Hearing, what's going on?" Marcus' great-grandfather asked.

"It has come to our attention that some things that have happened in the Big Boy past is affecting its leadership today. If it's affecting the leadership that means it's more powerful than the leadership." Deytwon continued.

"And there is *nothing* more powerful than the leadership." Marcus spoke up.

"Son, I think you should explain." Deytwon's father said.

Deytwon looked over at me and nodded for me to speak.

"There have been crimes committed against the Powers Bloodlines, and those crimes have gone unpunished for over 7 decades. I call for justice today." I said.

"How do you propose getting justice for crimes that happened when I was a young boy?" Marcus' great-grandfather asked with a chuckle.

"Arthur Jones, did you aide, or have any knowledge of the plot against Cecil Jr, or his sons, Angelo, or Cecil, or Cecil's son and Grandson's Ricardo and Rico's deaths?" I asked.

"First of all, Angelo died from tuberculosis. Now unless you're calling me God, I had nothing to do with that. I never met Ricardo nor did I know Rico." He said sarcastically.

"And Cecil Jr?" I asked.

"I personally didn't put my hands to any of them." He said.

"But you knew?" Deytwon asked.

Arthur looked up at Deytwon and lost the defiant look that he wore across his face when speaking to me.

"What do you have to say about all of this? You weren't trained to be quiet in such situations. You're not going to defend your own bloodline?" Arthur asked Marcus.

"Defend *my* bloodline, the same bloodline that made a flunky out of me? The same bloodline that didn't trust me enough to tell me the truth about what was going on?" Marcus asked.

"What truth?! You bonded with him! Your loyalty was always with him over us! Tell you the truth? For what, so that you can go to his goody goody ass and have him thwart everything that we worked so hard for?!" Arthur shouted.

"Go ahead and condemn yourself so that I can stop hearing this bullshit." Marcus said.

257

"You gonna kill me? Is that the plan here? You three wouldn't know how to wipe your own asses if we don't tell you where to put the toilet paper! I told you they weren't ready to be in charge, look at this shit here!" Arthur said now shouting towards Deytwon's and Marcus's fathers and grandfathers.

"Yet, you haven't answered the question. Need we remind you that we are the leaders? We are in control. You will answer the question, and it will not be asked again." Deytwon said.

Arthur turned around and looked up at Deytwon as though he lost his mind. His lips curled up into an evil smile before he parted them to speak.

"Do you think that just because I stepped back from the Big Boy leadership, that I've also left other brotherhoods too? I am affiliated with ten of the most powerful brotherhoods known to man. All the power you think you have, is nothing compared to the power I do have." Arthur said.

"Should I tell him or should you?" Marcus asked Deytwon.

"This is your grandfather, you take it." Deytwon said.

"Bet, do you sit in leadership of any of these brotherhoods?" Marcus asked.

"It doesn't matter where I sit, because I am in them, and as a member, I am immune to *any* punishment." Arthur said.

"Arthur, every brotherhood that you're in membership of, I am in the leadership of. I can sit here and show you all of the branding's I have for each one, but I'll do you one better. Do you recognize the name, King Jomar?" Marcus asked.

"King Jomar? No, you can't be." Arthur said as the smile dropped from his face.

"Yes, King Jones Marcus. Ever wonder why most of my license plates say King?" Marcus asked.

"But how?" Arthur asked.

"Because like you and the blood that flows through my veins, I don't just want to be powerful, I want to be all powerful. The one thing I did learn from being a Jones is how to crave and obtain power." Marcus boasted.

Arthur dropped to his knees and so did his son and grandson as well as Deytwon's grandfather.

"What's going on?" I whispered to Deytwon.

"They recognize Marcus' Brotherhood name. Apparently they're in at least one brotherhood that he is the head of. This means he lords over them, and so they are required to bow in his presence." Deytwon explained.

"Do we get an answer now, or what?" Marcus asked.

"Yes, I have knowledge of and have orchestrated the deaths of members of the Powers-bloodline." Arthur admitted.

"As have I." Admitted Marcus's father and grandfather.

"I too have had knowledge of the Jones' plans through my own father. Who admitted to helping plot against Cecil." Deytwon's grandfather admitted.

Marcus looked on at the men and shook his head, while Deytwon looked at his grandfather with sadness in his eyes.

"And you have no knowledge at all?" Deytwon asked his father.

"I've heard rumors, but no facts." His father admitted.

"The lies and deceptions of you all were none of your faults because it started before even you were born. However, the seeds have been planted in you. You all took those same seeds and tried to plant them in us, and it nearly destroyed us. With Marcus seeking to kill Angel, and then

259

me in return seeking to kill Marcus out of revenge, there would be no leadership left. These plans

that you all attempted to carry over into this future generation would have been the end of the

Big Boys altogether. Therefore we have decided that greed can no longer be the foundation on

which we stand, but rather a united front based on a collective desire to see that The Big Boys

prosper both in unity and in honor, amongst its leadership. We have thusly taken a vow to

destroy any and everything that tries to come between us in anyway. Including you." Deytwon

said.

"Son?" Deytwon's father said.

"Guards." Deytwon called out.

Seconds later men in combat gear carrying guns walked into the room and over to where

the elders were sitting.

"Take them to the chamber." Marcus said.

"I'm sorry son." Deytwon's father said as he stood to his feet to follow the guards out of

the room.

"So am I." He replied watching the men leave the room.

"Baby this is hard." I said ready to cry.

"We don't have a choice." Deytwon said watching them until they were completely out of

the room.

"You know this means, we're on our own now." Marcus said looking at Deytwon.

"Actually, we always were." Deytwon said as he took my hand.

"What will happen to their wives" I asked.

"They will be confined to housing on the island. They will be taken care of, but they will

no longer be allowed in the mansion." Marcus explained.

MARCUS

After taking care of the elders, Angel went into the nursery with my wife of the mansion with my wife Tiffani, to care for her newborn preemie, whom they named Deytwon II. I finally introduced Tiffani and Angel after Angel had the baby, and the two women bonded like old friends.

I walked outside of the mansion and saw Deytwon sitting in a gazebo that overlooked the ocean. He seemed to be staring out over the water thinking long and hard about something. No doubt about his father and grandfather.

"What's up?" I asked joining him.

"Shit, what's good?" He asked back.

"Life. Look man, I never fully apologized for all that shit I did to you when we met Angel, and for trying to kill her several times." I said.

"You did, but you ain't mean it." He replied with a chuckle.

"Nah, I didn't. Not until now. Truth be told, I really like her for you. It was just what she represented that fucked it all up. Under different circumstances, I would've been happy for you." I said.

"And now?" He asked.

"I'm jive in my feelings right now." I said leaning on the railing.

"Why is that?" he asked.

"Because, I'm trying figure out, how the master manipulator, get manipulated?" I asked at which Deytwon broke out laughing.

"Because whole time, you had your guards up and down for the wrong people. You watched your back with me, and let them run loose." He said.

261

"True, but the funny thing is though, I never really watched my back with you. I trust you more than I trust anybody. I guess it was just the fact that I was doing you dirty that had me fucked up." I admitted.

"Yeah, I knew it was something like that. But it's cool because it's behind us now." He said.

"Way way behind us." I confirmed.

"So how's Tiff, she okay being in there with Angel and the baby?" He asked.

"Nah, yeah, she's real good. She's excited actually." I said.

"About?" He asked.

"Finding out that she's pregnant." I said letting out the smile that I had been trying to suppress.

"*Whaaat*? That's what's up! Congratulations!" Deytwon said smiling equally as hard as we slapped hands.

"Yeah man, finally. Had me worried there for a second." I said wiping fake sweat from my forehead.

"Nah, it was bound to happen eventually." He said.

"True, so now the legacy continues." I said holding my fist out for dap

"The Legacy continues." Deytwon replied giving me dap.

THE END

Epilogue

DEYTWON

"These are the coordinates of where I need you to drop this package. Drop it off at exactly this spot. Do you understand?" I asked after showing the map to the helicopter pilot.

"Yes sir." He replied taking the map and tucking the package under his arm.

"Great, once the job is done, you will be transferred the five mil." I said.

"Thank you, sir." The pilot said with a salute.

"Now get outta here." I said with a pat to his back as I walked back towards the warehouse. I got inside my waiting limo and was driven back to my home.

I went into my private office in the basement of our home I grabbed the picture I secured from the satellite shot that I took and fed it through the fax machine before punching in the number.

Seconds later I received the confirmation fax and smiled to myself.

"Now, we'll see how *you* like it." I said.

******

Big Boys -The Legacy   By Nikida Bellezza

COMING SOON

Cocoa Killa -*An Assassin's Heart* -By Nikida Bellezza

As I sipped at my cup of coffee is started mulling over the things in my life that have come to matter to me. I had no family since my dad got life and I was sure my mom was strung out somewhere, or worse, had already od'd. My grandmother whom I abandoned years prior never checked for me, and my father's wife was in hiding with my little sister.

While I learned long ago not to allow any of these things to bother me, I couldn't stop them from being thoughts in my mind on the rare occasions when business was slow. I didn't miss any of them per se, but from time to time it would've been nice to have a voice '*not begging for mercy'* to talk to.

My thoughts were abruptly interrupted by the sound of my fax machine rumbling to life. It was no doubt a job coming through and as bored as I was, I was all too eager to accept. I carried my coffee over to the machine and continued to sip as is watched the paper jerk its way out.

So far I was able to make out that it was a picture of a person with a low haircut. This could've been a man or a woman, though I rarely got jobs to off women.

When the eyes were revealed I got an eerie feeling as I stared at them. I knew those eyes. I hadn't seen them in a very long time, but looking into them made my heart flutter.

It wasn't until the entire face was revealed that I realized who the person was. My arm dropped to my side spilling the coffee onto my plush carpet. I stared into the picture wishing like a child on Christmas that this wasn't who it appeared to be. At the bottom of the picture in red letters were the words ENEMY #1

"Nuck" was all that I could manage to say. Seconds later I heard a helicopter flying

264

overhead.

I ran outside and stood on my front as is watched the black, tinted helicopter draw close. When it reached my property a package was dropped in my garden before the helicopter moved on.

I walked over to my garden to retrieve the large envelope and took it into my house where I sat on my chair a stared at Nuck's picture.

This all felt so dreamlike. I've never turned down a hit, and I got a strange feeling that in this case, turning it down wasn't an option. I knew that whoever sent me the hit had to be powerful in order to find the coordinates to my house. I lived on a very secluded side of a mountain and could count on one hand the number of people who knew that. This probably freaked me out the most.

They also marked him as enemy number one which meant he had to be killed. No bargaining, no investigation, just DOA. I've received E1's before, but they were normally big time contracts for elusive people who were untouchable. Nuck was large but he was an easy target for me. Too easy now that I thought about it.

Suddenly a light bulb went off in my mind. This hit wasn't about Nuck, it was about me. But why, why was this personal? All of my hits were clean and untraceable. Who in the hell did I piss off? I walked back over to the counter where I dumped the money from the envelope. The bills were crisp and brand new.

I closed my eyes as my mind began to scan through every hit I received. From witnesses against kingpins to threats and competition of government officials, to... The Big Boys.

Ding Ding chimed a notification alert on my computer. Whenever the amount of money in my bank account changed, I received a special notification for it.

I walked over to my computer, put in the codes and pulled up my balance. My heartbeat skipped before seemingly dropping down to one beat per second. A source had just deposited 50 million into my account. Source using the name Fox Ox, Rox, Alpha, Nalpha, Galpha, Elpha, Lalpha.

I looked at the words for a few seconds trying to understand the code. I knew that it was an acronym so I grabbed a pen and a piece of stationary and wrote down the first letters from each word. Which spelled FORANGEL.

"What is a *forangel*?" I thought aloud looking from the paper back to the computer. That's when I noticed again the Fox ox and rox had different endings than Alpha. So I wrote the letters again, this time separating the ox letters from the alpha letters. Now the words were clear and so was the unspoken message. If I didn't kill Nuck, I am sure to die. I stared down at the letters that now read *FOR ANGEL* and immediately knew that this was a vengeance hit, which ordinarily wouldn't strike so much fear in me, but this hit was from The Big Boys..

Cocoa Killa -*An Assassin's Heart* -by Nikida Bellezza COMING 2015

THANK YOU FOR TAKING THE TIME TO READ THIS BOOK, I HOPE THAT YOU WERE

ABLE TO ENJOY!!!

-Author Nikida Bellezza

QUESTIONS / COMMENTS / CONCERNS?

CONTACT THE AUTHOR VIA THESE OPTIONS:

Facebook: Nikida Bellezza
Twitter: @NikidaBellezza
Instagram: Nikida_Bellezza